Portia Racasi

Amy Scheibe is an editor at a publishing house in New
York City. She lives in the city with her husband and two
children.

What Do You Do All Day?

AMY SCHEIBE

PICADOR

ST. MARTIN'S PRESS

NEW YORK

For

B.P.F.

www.picadorusa.com

Picador® is a U.S. registered trademark and is used by St. Martin's Press under license from Pan Books Limited.

For information on Picador Reading Group Guides, as well as ordering, please contact Picador.
Phone: 646-307-5629
Fax: 212-253-9627
E-mail: readinggroupguides@picadorusa.com

Library of Congress Cataloging-in-Publication Data

Scheibe, Amy.
    What do you do all day? / Amy Scheibe.
        p. cm.
    ISBN-13: 978-0-312-42562-3
    ISBN-10: 0-312-42562-7
    1. Manhattan (New York, N.Y.)—Fiction. 2. Preschool children—Fiction.
3. Housewives—Fiction. 4. Mothers—Fiction. I. Title.

PS3619.C346W47 2005
813'.6—dc22

                                                                2005044138

First published in the United States by St. Martin's Press

10 9 8 7 6 5 4 3 2

Samantha looked around the playground in amazement. Her mother had been right. She really *was* the smartest and prettiest.

—Sloane Tanen

What Do You Do All Day?

One

WHEN THE PHONE RINGS I know it's going to be bad news. "Jennifer? Hillary. You do speak Spanish, don't you?" Hillary Jacobs asks me, her voice on the edge of a scream, no friendly hello to kick things off. "Sorry for the commotion, we're having a pool put in downstairs—don't ask me how we're ever going to pay for it—and you wouldn't believe the mess."

"Well, no I don—"

"Great, four, then? Hortensia will bring an *almuerzo*. What, Chloë? No, Mommy's got a playdate with the lawyers. Okay then, Jen, it's settled. But let's have that dinner soon, okay? Ciao ciao."

As I set down the phone, my heart sinks even further. I'd call Thom and complain about this development if he weren't on a plane to Paris, damn him. I guess I have to face up to spending an hour with Hortensia and Chloë without her mother present. Georgia hasn't made friends easily, and Chloë's the only child who has taken to my daughter in her first few weeks of school. Hillary Jacobs had approached me for this date, and now she's second-tiering me off to her nanny, with whom I cannot communicate. I spent four years studying French at Columbia University with a semester in Tunisia when I could have been learning a more useful language, for exactly how often do I use it? *Frère Jacques*, if you know what I mean.

The buzzer rings at 4, and even with an hour of pre-playdate planning I'm still not ready. Georgia has, as of 3:45, decided that she hates Chloë, and all the Christian charity pleading in the world has not swayed her from her pole position. Or should I say "pool position," as it is the small matter of Chloë's new pool that has put Georgia in her snit. It seems that she thinks we should put one in as well. In where? I ask her. In a better apartment with a garden and trees seems to be her solution. Getting my precious cargo into the very exclusive Park Street Preschool is looking more and more like the mistake I told Thom it would be.

I go to the door, homemade play-dough in my hair where Max smeared me with his greasy little hands. Two in four years seemed like a good idea at the Club Med "we entertain your child, you have sex" getaway beach in Jamaica. Now I'm not so sure. Don't get me wrong, Max is a dream, but he's a giant baby and has given me more than a little sciatica during his slow acquisition of walking skills. He also refuses to crawl when I'm around. He just lies there, or sits there, eyes scrunched, and screams when he wants "up, up, *up*." No words yet either, except the aforementioned *up* and that old standby, *no*. And if I were to tell you that he has some teeth, I would be lying.

Hortensia is a shockingly exquisite woman, which is more than I can say for her charge. Chloë is carrying what looks to be a homeless woman's full load of assorted upscale shopping bags: brown striped Bendel, silver SFA, elongated pink Pink, and every schoolgirl's favorite, the Barneys chic black-and-white rectangular tote. Chloë herself is a study in noir: tights, Tod's ballet flats—no doubt special order from Bergdorf's—corduroy skirt, turtleneck, and yes, God love her, beret. I expect she would snap her fingers if they weren't entwined in silk cords. Underneath all this decoration is an exceedingly homely child. She looks at me like I've stepped in shit. And not the good kind.

"Where'th Georgia, I need her to help with the bagth," she squeaks out of her too-small mouth. "Mira, Hortenthia, buthca la cocina y hacerme almuerzo."

I know enough restaurant Spanish to get that I'm supposed to set Hortensia up in the kitchen, so I usher the two into our "modest" three-bedroom loft. Through Chloë's eyes, I see how poor we are, with our Pottery Barn furniture and concrete floors. Note to self: kill Chloë. Make it look like an accident. Of course, through Hortensia's eyes, we are rolling in it with our Sub-Zero refrigerator and our enormous living room that my PC guilt reminds me is fueled by more wattage than the average Mexican village.

By the time I have understood through broken Franglish (Hortensia: I need a pan. Me: What kind of bread?) that all of Chloë's food must be steamed according to the South Fork Diet—swear to God, the flounder fillet and twigs of broccoli look like something you'd give a fifty-year-old man with a heart condition—Chloë and Georgia have emptied the shopping bags onto the middle of the living-room rug and are discussing the finer points of having one's hair straightened thermally or reverse-permed.

"You want it to look like Malibu Barbie, thirca 1971, not Growin' Pretty Hair Thkipper of that thame year," Chloë instructs, using the vintage dolls as her models. I could cry—I had these very dolls thirty years ago. I sink into a chair and observe the tutorial. "Though you don't want the tan, or you'll need Botoxth by the time you're twenty. If you mutht tan, you can get the thpray thtuff at the thpa, it'th much better for you."

My daughter sits with her wide-eyed expression propped up on little fists, her gorgeous tangled curls spilling down to her elbows. She's clearly given her hostility a rest. Up until this moment, her knowledge of hair and skin products was limited to No More Tears and NoAd SPF 30. She has one Barbie, because for the longest time she thought there only *was* one Barbie. Hers. I am likewise entranced, as I've never seen a child Chloë's age quite so articulate. Mind you, I'm not exaggerating the lisp. On the plus side, it makes her Spanish sound impeccable.

This is Georgia's first rub with the truly wealthy, and my stomach twists on itself when I think about the years to come. We really have tried to keep her needs modest, but I can't kid myself that she won't be saying "I really mutht have a pony" sometime very soon. I'm also not crazy about her school's solution to sorting the children. Rather than following the public-school standard of having an age and grade designation, Park Street has open classrooms, and G routinely mingles with kids both younger and older. She is verbally advanced for her age, apart from the usual verb tense mix-ups and lazy *r*, but is she really ready to hang with prepubescents like Chloë?

"Up up up" comes from Max's room, where he has finished his "power nap." He sleeps like an SAT math problem: six hours a night in two three-hour shifts, with two thirty-minute naps spaced four hours apart during the day. Is my darling thirteen-month-old sleeping through the night? Bite me. It seems that about the time he does fall into a full sleep, Georgia finishes her

nightly trek across the Arabian desert, and though she has four full sippy cups surrounding her bed, she's decided that the faucet in my bathroom, which she can't quite reach, is the only one that makes the water cold enough to extinguish her parch.

Hortensia, with some sort of baby sonar hardwired in her soul, glides through the room and lightly presses me back into the armchair from where I've been witnessing the destruction of my commercial-free daughter. She then proceeds to my son's room, in complete defiance of my "No, no, I'll get him." Must have been the whimpering, choking-back-a-strangled-sob tone in my voice.

When she returns, she says "Siesta" and points to my bedroom. I don't argue: this word I know.

The alarm rings thirty minutes later and I feel as though I've slept for days. I wouldn't have set the clock at all, but I couldn't risk having Hillary find out that I was asleep for the entire playdate. When I emerge from my room, I can't believe what I see. Chloë and Georgia have set a tea table with the fish and broccoli, and my daughter is holding her blunt knife and Pooh fork in the European manner. They are joined by more Barbies, Skippers, Kens, and Francies than I've ever seen. Max is in his high chair, spooning what must be mashed heart-attack diet food into his own mouth instead of the mouth of his good friend Teddy the Bear. All the toys are put away, and Hortensia is writing in what appears to be a journal while our usually unfriendly cat, Peeve, purrs in her lap. Tears spring to my eyes. I am a bad mother.

"Can you come again for another playdate tomorrow?" I ask Chloë, once they have packed up and are ready to leave.

"You'll have to check with Her," she says, apparently referring to her mother. "We're booked up awfully far in advanthe."

"Well, do you think that maybe Hortensia could come without you?" I say this after the door has closed, and mostly to myself.

Two

|ALWAYS WANTED CHILDREN. My therapist, years ago, back
when I made my own money and could rationalize paying him
two hundred dollars a week so I wouldn't feel "dizzy," tried to get
me to understand my baby lust as a by-product of my mother's
early death.

But I simply loved babies. Death? Schmeath. Besides, my father remarried before I could even say the word *mama* and so
Cheryl has been exactly like a mother to me. At the risk of
sounding perfectly hillbilly, I must admit right up front that
Cheryl is also my aunt. Her sister, Nancy, married my father first,
but when my birth mother wrapped her Cadillac around a tree a
mere few weeks after my arrival, Cheryl stepped in to help my father with me and one thing, as they say, led to another. Not only
is she my surrogate and adopted mother, in an odd way she's also
my closest friend. Since we never had to contemplate the mother-
daughter bond, we've always enjoyed an open and frank relationship. There isn't anything I can't tell her or anything she won't
tell me. All that said, I might be forced at gunpoint to admit that
choosing to drop all my hard-earned career advancements in or-

der to become what I had once sneered at—a "stay-at-home
mom"—may have had *something* to do with Nancy's death. I have
this strange, deep-seated instinct to lavish as much of myself on
my children as possible so that when I die young and beautiful,
they will always remember me as the most important person in
their little lives.

And so, my life is hell.

It's not that I never talk to an adult about anything adult, or
that I haven't had my hair professionally cut in four years, or that
my C-section scars—so erroneously referred to as "bikini cuts,"
as though I'll ever wear a bikini again—run like train tracks
across my abdomen, supporting a hideous shelf of fat and muscle
that no amount of Pilates will ever rectify. No, it's not that sex to
me is an infrequently visited foreign land, or that the forty-two
minutes a day I spend alone with my husband—when he's in the
country—are devoted to discussing what the children have eaten,
not eaten, and extruded all day.

It's basically that no matter how many organic vegetables I
buy, how many teepees I build, that I take my kids twenty blocks
out of my way to play on an arsenic-free wooden jungle gym, my
determination to keep my home Disney tie-in free, that I wear a
negligee at least once a week and balance the home budget . . .
when I stop to measure myself against the expectations around
me, I find I am left chasing my own perfectionist tail. I run after
the kids all day, exhausting myself beyond belief, then collapse
here in bed only to find I can't sleep for all the thoughts pouring
through my brain.

My ticking clock didn't stop to think about the responsibilities
that come with babies. Keeping them alive, for instance.
Babyproofing is harder than it looks, and danger really does lurk

around every corner. This is why I ultimately found it easier to keep my dumplings home with me, snuggled up safe and warm, rarely venturing out, and then only as a group. I threw myself into intensive mothering, following the guides on how to make children thrive. I neglected to think about the day when they would have to leave the nest with their carefully clipped wings.

Oh, I was perfect all right. A perfect failure.

I am currently trying to address this wrong. Georgia was recently diagnosed by a specialist as having "too-close-to-mommy" syndrome. The therapist told me that Geege needs more friends her own age. It seems that my desire to keep her safe from the world has had unforeseen consequences. It is possible that I over-reacted a little after 9/11, but Thom was away—of course—and we were all understandably a little freaked out. Maybe I should have taken her to a Gymboree or two, instead of huddling in our bunker-built apartment, reading books and creating elaborate fantasy lands with paper and glue. I've fulfilled her every need and in so doing have brought her to the brink of panic attacks. She became terrified of leaving me alone, not because she didn't want to be apart from me but because she was afraid that I didn't exist when she wasn't with me. School has helped, but to keep her from becoming a classic agoraphobe I need to socialize my pet rock, overcoming my own extroverted shyness and occasionally leaving this place we affectionately call Elba.

It's not that I don't know what's out there. I've been living in Manhattan for most of my adult life and have benefited from its endless entertainment. Some may even say I've breathed rarified air with my pseudoglamorous entanglements and unusual career path. But one of the best parts of having kids was the ability to say no to invitations, to snuggle up with the babies instead of bel-

lying up to a bar. I don't miss the nightclubs or the movie pre-
mieres; I've seen celebrity up close, and in the end it's just not all
that impressive. Unfortunately, though, I'm not terribly interested in other parents—they scare me, to be honest, and I don't
think it's very healthy for me to hang out with them and compare
my kids to theirs. I do that enough in my head the way it is.
Worst of all is encountering the working mom and measuring my
lack of accomplishment against her speedy-quick successes as all
my work suits have sagged on their hangers. I refuse to regret my
decision, even if it turns out to have been the wrong one.

Three

THOM'S HOME FROM a trip to Spain, where he went to acquire a relic of Saint Peter for one of the clients of his art and antiquities dealership, and we have actually hired a real babysitter who isn't related to either of us to be paid money to stay with our children while we enjoy an evening out together. This hasn't happened since February 2002, not that I marked it on the calendar or anything, and it may not happen again until Mars comes back close to the earth, so I spent the afternoon shaving, plucking, filing, and buffing, while the kids watched *Baby Shakespeare* six times, my guilt increasing with each "Hi, I'm Julie Clark." I'm looking about as good as I can at this point, and I'm just hoping the restaurant's candlelight will do the rest, or that our view of the city draped across the river will distract Thom enough to keep him from noticing how the fine lines around my eyes have built up a resistance to spackle.

"You are absolutely gorgeous," he says, looking right at me. I attempt to suck my cheekbones up through my sinuses.

"Well, as gorgeous as I can get, I guess."

"Honey, take the compliment. I love your hair up like that.

You're glowing," he tries again. Meanwhile, he's the one who looks gorgeous, early craggy crow's-feet blooming at the corners of his translucent hazel eyes, the barest hints of gray flecking his rich brown waves.

"Oh, that. That's the candlelight." I look up at the Brooklyn Bridge just outside the window, change the subject as I take in the view of lower Manhattan. "I really miss them, you know?"

"The kids? I'd think you'd enjoy a night away from them." He laughs, but it's a kind, soft sound.

"No, the towers," I say, sniffling a little from the champagne. "It just looks so flat down there now. I hope they manage to put up something respectful."

"You worry too much. It'll be fine." He pours more bubbly. We've finished our tuna tartare and our monkfish medallions and are now waiting the twenty minutes it takes for the chocolate soufflé to be baked. It's been a two-bottle affair this evening, and I'm feeling tipsy, tired, and emotional. I was feeling sexy about a bottle ago, but now I just want to cuddle up and drift into a dreamless sleep.

"Hey, Jen," Thom says, turning my chin back with his finger. I catch a whiff of his cologne, the same one he's always worn, that I've never smelled on any other man. "I want to thank you." He puts a long, slim blue box on the table. You know the one.

"What's this for?" I know it's not my birthday. It is never my birthday.

"Open it."

I untie the white ribbon and open the box to find a blue suede-covered box inside. I tip it out and slowly open it. I've never seen so many diamonds on one bracelet.

"What? Why? Um, it's beautiful." I strain to think where I'll ever wear this thing.

"It's a tennis bracelet; here, let me put it on you." He takes my wrist and latches a Broadway marquee to it. I hold it as far away from me as I can and, to gain perspective, try to pretend it's on someone else's arm. Now I really do glow, but a bit too much like Chernobyl.

"It's not very practical, I don't really play tennis," is all I can manage to say.

"You deserve impractical things. You work so hard. The kids are so great. I couldn't do any of this without you and want you to know how much I appreciate you. Every day." He has a point. He couldn't do any of this without me. He raises his glass. "Here's to you."

"Here's to us," I reply. I sit back in my chair, full of self-satisfaction, admire my view of the city, of Thom, of my tennis bracelet. Everything sparkles.

"Honey, I need to talk to you about something."

I smile at him, nod for him to continue.

"Well, Universal Imports is opening a satellite office in Singapore, and Bjorn has asked me to run it."

I blink like Bambi, right after he's lost his mother.

"Don't worry, I told him there's no way I can uproot my family, move you to another country."

I relax again, proud of my hunter, my gatherer.

"As a compromise, they're sending me over for three months to get things up and running."

"Three months?" I try not to yell. "So you've anesthetized me in order to tell me that you're leaving me and the kids? Go on." I'm not lying, I am pretty numb. In fact, I can't feel my feet, am not even sure I have any. And my right hand has gone cold from the price-of-admission down. "No, wait. Has it not occurred to you that Georgia is going through a pretty precarious time right now? And that Max could use a male role model, preferably one who knows how to crawl?"

"Honey, I am crawling. I haven't said yes yet, I wanted to discuss it with you first."

"I'm really not as druck as I look, Thom." But clearly as drunk as I sound. I try harder to enunciate. "*Drunk.* You only a moment ago said that you compromised, so it's pretty crystal clear that you've already packed your mental bags." I cross my arms, making sure his little bribe is in full view.

"Okay, right, I did say I'd seriously consider it, but that I'd have to tell Bjorn on Monday. If you don't want me to go, then I'll tell him no." He looks out the window, back at me, leans in. "It's just that this is the kind of thing that can pop us up to the next level. Everyone knows that you have to travel in order to get points, and there's a lot of pressure on me at the office to make this happen. It's the only way to get anywhere."

"What are we, in a movie? You sound like a movie guy. Like Nic Cage or something. Besides, you travel all the time. Don't be a jerk. You're condescending to me and being a jerk. The Thom I know isn't a jerk. Bjorn, now *there's* a jerk." With each "jerk" I give my spangle a little jerk of its own. I'd take it off and throw it in his face, but it's really pretty, and I think I can wear it with my sweats. People who play tennis sweat.

"Okay, you're right, I'm being a jerk. Let me try this another way." He looks out the window, takes a sip, and straightens his tie. "It's only three months; I'll be back before you know it. I really want to do this, it'll be great for us, and you'll see it will be good for you, too. Give you the time you need to figure out the 'what's next.' Meanwhile I'll be able to leverage this experience into a higher position—"

"It'll be good for you."

"—maybe a larger commission—what?"

"It'll be good for you. Just say it, Thom: 'It'll be good for Thom.'" I've got him, and he knows it. He sighs through his nose.

"It'll be good for me. But what's good for me is good for us, right? We're in this together, aren't we?" He reaches for my hand, and I let him. It's time for me to leverage this my own way.

"Of course we are. But what's good for me? What's good for Jennifer?" Good god, I wish I'd had some kind of warning that this was going to happen. I hate being unprepared. Drunk and unprepared. "I mean, I've been on the sidelines for five years while Universal Imports runs you all over the world, while Bjorn gets rich off your ambition and my sacrifice. Do you really think my career is just waiting for me to finish being a mommy? Five years, Thom. Will a quick trip to Singapore pop *me* up a level?"

"Give it a little longer, Jen. Please? Bjorn's talking about making me a full partner if this is successful. I need your support."

"And I need *your* support."

"But you've said yourself that you don't know what you want to do when the kids are in school. How am I supposed to support something that isn't even tangible yet? You know I'll completely support whatever you decide." He pours more champagne into his glass and knocks it back like a frat boy. I have him on the ropes. Or do I?

"I want to go back to work now. Not next year, now." This isn't the least bit true, but the idea of taking care of the kids without him for the next three months is unbearable—anything would be easier.

"Come on, Jen, you know that's not realistic. Max isn't even out of diapers yet. The nanny alone would eat up your entire salary.

We've been through this a hundred times, haven't we?" I study his voice for a whiff of condescension. This time it isn't there.

"I know, I know, my salary would be a drop in the bucket of our expenses and working would just add to our financial burden," I recite. "But maybe I can go back at a higher salary?"

"Be real, Jen, that just doesn't happen in this world, the market has left you behind and you're going to have to start back where you left off—and you don't even get adjusted for inflation these days."

"You're being a jerk again." It's the only defense I have, because even though he is being a jerk, he's one hundred percent right. I'd have to start back at my old salary, and though it wasn't embarrassing, once you take away the taxes it would just barely pay for a two-kid nanny. Add to that the wardrobe, the hair, and the shoes—the cost of going back to work instantly pushes my expenses up over my take-home pay. There's no getting around it: the math sucks.

"Okay, you're right," he says. "I'm a jerk. A jerk who's out there every day, providing for his family. Wow, I do sound like a movie guy. Listen, I won't go to Singapore. I'm sorry I didn't get a chance to discuss it with you, but it just happened yesterday afternoon and it was between me and Frank O'Neill. He doesn't have kids; he would have done it in a second. But Bjorn wants me, honey—don't you see what that means? He trusts me with his top-secret plans now and seems to be grooming me for something really big. In another five years I could be running the whole company and we'd be set for life. I really, really don't want to be away, but it's going to mean so much for us as a family. Just hang in there a little while longer, and then we'll do whatever it takes to make you happy."

"This had better not be another one of Bjorn's get-richer schemes, and he'd better not be using you to try untested waters." Bjorn, ruggedly handsome and a good foot taller than Thom, has the kind of hypnotic sway over my husband that, if it weren't benefiting my family, I would have put an end to long ago. But sometimes you have to let the men be the men, don't you?

"Honey, give me a little credit, I know a good thing when I see it." He takes my hand and squeezes. "Asia is a real growth market, with new billionaires in China buying up all kinds of art left and right."

"So go."

"Not if you don't want me to."

"You know I want you to. I just don't want you to want to without including me in the decision. Go. Discussion over." I look down at my bracelet. Is it worth it?

"Okay. I don't leave for a few weeks, so we can figure out how this is going to work. I'll get my mother to come in and help as often as you'd like. You'll see, the time will fly by." I give him a nod of the head. My impulse is to take a notepad out of my pocketbook and start making a list, but I just can't think about it anymore tonight. And if we start talking about his mother, we'll be eating brunch under the Brooklyn Bridge come morning.

Our soufflé arrives, a tiny caved-in and weeping molten chocolate mound. There's a single candle stuck in the middle. The waiter places it in front of me.

"What's this?" Now that the conflict is behind me, I can't help but feel like this little brown cake. I weep along with it.

"I first saw you ten years ago this very night." Shit. It's October fifteenth. I completely forgot. Again. *Now* who's the jerk? "It was the defining moment of my life. I love you, Jennifer Bradley, and can't live without you. You are my very life." He brushes my cheek with the back of his hand and I lean into it, softening, re-membering our language.

"I say, Lawrence, you are a clown," I tell him, quoting from our favorite movie.

"We can't all be lion tamers," he replies, taking my hand and leaning his head toward mine over the table. "Here now, make a wish."

I close my eyes and wish for a way to go back those ten years so that I can tell Jennifer Probstfeld to be very careful about what she wishes for.

Four

THOM SAW ME FIRST. I was in Egypt, taking the weekend away from a dig in Carthage during my semester abroad, shopping for amulet replicas at the Cairo market to take home as souvenirs. I had run all the way to North Africa to escape a rapidly imploding relationship with my adult child-actor boyfriend, after trying fruitlessly to "make things work." At first glance, Thom was everything that Heath wasn't, starting with right next to me. Thom was only a hair taller than me, and when he gazed into my eyes there was a directness that had always been missing with the much taller Heath. It was innocent enough, I guess, but quickly became quite deliciously illicit and romantic—a short fling in a long sweaty fall, an entire ocean away from our significant others. That December, Thom went back to his girlfriend, and I went home to find out what was left of my rocky relationship.

A few months earlier, Heath and I had been talking about the future. After six years of living together we were adrift, and I demanded to know where this thing was going. I guess it was the ultimatum question, though it didn't occur to me in advance to plan an exit strategy. In one of his ridiculously candid moods, Heath let these words slip: "I know I want to get married someday, I'm just not sure you're the person I want to marry." *Okay, asshole*, I thought at the time, *I quit*. I packed my belongings the next week and moved into a tiny studio apartment way uptown. He begged me to come back, said that he couldn't sleep without me. I told him I needed time to figure out what I wanted. To ease the sting, I enrolled in archeology camp at Columbia, and off to Tunis I went.

When the semester was over, I called Heath with my flight information; he promised to meet me at the airport, champagne and roses in tow. Even though I thought that Thom was perfect for me, he was going back to Gina, so I wanted to make sure the attraction wasn't just a get-even-quick reflex. In any event, Heath didn't show. I caught a cab to his apartment, let myself in the door, found him in bed. Well, you know, not exactly alone. Seems he was sleeping just fine without me.

After I spent too many nights feeling sorry for myself, my friend Portia dragged me off the couch and to an art opening. This time I saw Thom first. And he was with *her*. Gina was gorgeous, the type of woman who throws her head back to laugh—but Thom wasn't amused by whatever had caught her fancy. The physical distance between them was enough to leave room for me to slip into. And I did, and now I'm here.

There was a time—a recent time, it seems—that Thom and I could finish each other's thoughts, that we would stay up and pillow talk long after the children were asleep and get into nonsensical heated arguments about nothing, regardless of how exhausted we were. One week we had a five-part discussion about genetically modified corn. We both actually read up during the day so we could reengage each night. This odd camaraderie didn't change when we had one kid and then two. We've always been that couple other people envy—holding hands at parties, whispering at dinners, sharing with each other the littlest stories of our ordinary days and still finding great joy in the smallest details.

But lately there's been a seismic shift, and so it terrifies me to think of Thom widening that gap with a continent and an ocean. During the past few months the travel has increased, and the Thom I love is ever less present. Though he's been away on business plenty in the past, he's never missed a holiday or birthday or forgotten a date like October fifteenth even when it has slipped *my* mind entirely. Bjorn can get into his head, make him rejigger his priorities with the promise of making one more deal, landing one more big client, the pressure of which seems to be consuming Thom in a way I don't like. It's almost as though he's trying harder to please Bjorn, and it's starting to feel like a competition, like Bjorn is the other woman. But I need him more— he keeps me sane, keeps me from smothering myself in this web of mothering I've spun, engages with me and the kids every minute he spends with us. Until recently. Last month he missed Max's first birthday due to a trip to South Africa for a rare coin auction. He was no happier about it than I was, but since then we've felt unhinged. For the first time in a very long time, I honestly do not know where we go from here. Or where "here" even is.

Five

GEORGIA IS SLICKING THE LAST of her baby curls to the side of her head with shampoo, standing up in the tub to get a better look in the mirror at how she'll appear after her $800 Japanese thermal treatment at Fekkai.

"Jen-fur," she calls me, having decided, according to Chloë's unofficial handbook for almost-five-year-old behavior, that *Mommy* is over and *Mom* too middle-class. I've been told that Chloë is actually younger than G by a whole month, but until I see her birth certificate I will remain unconvinced. "Do it work for you if I stop taking baths with the baby?" She's also decided that Max is now "the baby."

"No, that *doesn't* work for me." Preschool once taught kids how to read; now it seems to teach a high-priced version of the street.

"I'm not down with this, Jen." Now she's starting to push it. "Look, he has a *penis*. . . ."

"Really. Is that so?" It hadn't occurred to me, considering that Max has such a grip on said penis that I can't get my ducky-washcloth-covered hand into the stinky little folds of flesh around it at the moment.

"And I have a *vagina*," she says, leaning between Max and me to look me in the eye, trying to impress on me that this is in some way a questionable state of behavior.

"You got me there, G, but until you prove you can bathe yourself, I really don't have time to wash you separately." I gently move her out of the way as I try to stop her brother from drinking the bathwater.

"Chloë has a shower just for her. She says only little kids take baths, and I'm almost *five*." I should have killed Chloë when I had the chance.

"How about we ask your father?" This is a classic push-off. I'm being lazy, tired of saying no and having to explain why not. Within days of promising me that we'll "work out the details" of Singapore, Thom is in Seattle sorting through a container full of possible Ming dynasty treasures. It will be days before Georgia asks him, and maybe by then I can guilt him into giving all the baths before he leaves. Let them figure it out.

"But Daddy's working and I want a shower *now!*"

Before I can even think, I have Max out of the tub, the curtain pulled, and the shower on full. I don't even check the temperature of the water, but it's always lukewarm when it comes on, so don't call child services. To my surprise, Georgia doesn't scream, but she does stamp her feet so hard in the tub I'm afraid she'll slip, so I set Max on the floor and rattle open the curtain.

"Cut it out or you'll never see Chloë alive again!"

That stops her. She looks at me, trying to figure out if what I said is what I mean and why I would throw an "alive" into a sentence she's heard countless times. Always one to weigh her odds, Georgia does a quick eye-sweep of the room and sees her way out.

"Look, Mommy, Max is *crawling!*"

In the instant I spin in his direction, he manages to flop over onto his back. But his progress toward Peeve's litter box confirms that he has indeed moved. And the small Tootsie Roll shape in his penis-free hand is not candy.

"Oh, Christ," I say, and my Georgia peach says, *"Mommy!"*

It costs me twenty thousand dollars a year for my daughter to learn how to speak in *italics*.

Today's playdate was for Max's benefit. I'd read on the Internet that if babies see other babies do things they are capable of, they will start to do them too. A monkey-see monkey-do approach to behavioral programming. I needed someone to bounce this theory off of, so I called my friend Penny. We first met during my days working the door at the Limelight nightclub—she was a coke whore, and I knew the likeliest suspects for her to hit up. She supposedly needed the coke to keep her place in the Joffrey Ballet corps, and after her friends had to intervene she ate herself right into modern dance. Like me, Penny is an SAHM, but she still manages to choreograph and perform a show at the Joyce Theater every year. After we got caught up—sometimes it takes me six months to call a friend—she suggested bringing her son Mikhail over so he could set a good example. He's a month younger than Max and already walking.

When Max was born he was nine pounds, ten ounces, and an astonishing twenty-four inches long. That's two feet. He was curled like a snail in my tummy and had put his hand over his head in solidarity with the downtrodden and in protest of my contractions, keeping me from dilating. So much for my hard-sought VBAC. At least it didn't take the twenty hours that Georgia needed to shit herself into a C-section. But I digress. Every well-baby tune-up thus far has charted Max in the 97th percentile for height, 95th for weight. We were secretly thrilled at first, boasting to anyone who would listen. Then, as other babies started to crawl past him, we smiled through our worries. That was when Thom's mom decided to sneak Max to a specialist, who told her he would crawl in his own time. Or perhaps he would just get up and walk one day. He was fine. I think he's just a little faker. Somehow, I'm sure, it must be my fault.

Mikhail started cruising at eight months and will no doubt do a double pirouette on his second birthday, but Penny doesn't rub it in. He's a big-headed baby with teeth that already protrude, so I find great comfort in that.

When Penny came over this afternoon, we put Max and Mikhail in the playpen—I'm a big fan of what we like to call "baby cage matches"—threw in about twenty assorted plush balls, and let them go at it. We'd only barely settled on the floor with our lattes when Penny opened the can of worms I've spent almost five years soldering shut.

"Don't worry, Jen," Penny said, her yoga-enhanced posture ramrod straight. Her hair has gone through every imaginable shade since I've known her, but now she's let it go, as she says, *au nature*—an Annie Lennox super-short white. "Not only will Max walk, he'll probably be one of those babies who go straight to running. What I want to talk about is you."

I didn't want to jump to the defensive. It could have been something good about me, such as "I really like what you're doing with your hair; would you mind cutting mine for me?" So I just stayed still and let her continue, putting out of my mind the residual effects of her old habit: a nasty, frequent snort/grunt and the inability to keep from sticking her reconstructed nose into my business.

"I mean, you need to get out more, treat yourself better. When was your last manicure?" I resist sneaking a look at my nails, knowing how chewed to the quick they are. "Why don't you hire a part-time babysitter? Thom makes enough money, and besides, he does whatever he pleases. It's time to get back to what interests *you*. It's like I was saying to my friend Madeline the other day— you seem so adrift, never seeing your friends or talking about going back to work. You only have a couple more years before Max is in school, you know. What about that book you were going to write—wasn't it about pirates or something?"

"Hannibal. It was about Hannibal. A biography. I wrote six chapters and went dry," I said, buffering myself for my favorite question.

"What do you do all day?" Yep, that one.

"What do you mean?" Of course, I knew what she meant, but I wasn't going to let the little dancer off easy. Sure, she works hard at her dance, but her husband is an artist whose crap sculptures of realistic-looking landfills in miniature sell for tens of thousands of dollars. Even up, I guess he makes the same as Thom, but he works at home and takes Mikhail everywhere he goes. And it's not like Penny has an almost-five-year-old with burgeoning appearance-hypochondria to put through Sarah Lawrence someday. I may have told Thom I wanted to go back to work, but there was no way I'd give Penny the satisfaction of being right.

"Do you ever look at Max and just want to shove your tongue down his throat?" Penny asked out of nowhere. I wasn't surprised, though, as she has no sense whatsoever of the inappropriate. "I mean, look at the lips on my baby. Ugh, I could just chew them right off."

"They're nice lips." Considering they don't meet over his teeth. It would be like French-kissing Gerald Ford, and not necessarily the Gerald Ford of 1974, either.

"Well, Jen, I don't know how to put this delicately, but some of us have been talking and we just can't figure out why you're not doing something with yourself. I mean, shouldn't you be working on the 'what's next'?"

If only she knew how frequently I lock myself in the bathroom. If only I had the time.

"Well, Pen"—I stifled a sob—"it seems as though I have two children with very specific needs to manage all day. Shopping to do, a house to keep clean, endless laundry, and oh, occasionally servicing my husband—who, you may have noticed, travels much of the week. Maybe you and your friend Madeline should find something else to talk about." A funny thing happens when I get mad. Instead of yelling or reacting in some sort of contained way, I start to cry. Penny knows this, she saw the tears welling. She went too far, and now she has to backpedal. This is also how I keep some of my friends in check.

"Sorry, sorry—I didn't mean to say you don't do anything. Of course you do." She perched on her knees and embraced me. I cried onto her shoulder. "You do a lot. And you know I fully support your choice of staying at home; heck, I do it myself, we're in this together. You're great. You're doing a great job, just look how happy Max is. . . ."

And with that, my son rode a silent scream into a heartbreaking, babbling sob. You may have wondered why I've not interjected updates on what the boys were doing while we had our little tête-à-tête. Well, it's because I don't know. I wasn't watching. There were no objects small enough for either of them to choke on, no sharp edges to poke out an eye, both babies are good-natured and play well with others. I can't even tell you now why Max wailed. It's just like that sometimes. Babies cry. I'd like to think it was because Penny made me cry, and Max was tuned in to my hurt. In any case, I picked him up up up and sweetly suggested the playdate should end end end.

"Please don't take offense," Penny said, her revenge intervention thwarted for today.

"No, I won't," I lied.

"I love you, you know."

"Of course." But did she? Had she ever? Max and I cried for a while after she left, which made me wonder why I'd ever called her in the first place. And then I had to wonder why we were friends, and then I had to question my ability to choose friends, and then, and then.

And then I had to take Max uptown and pick Georgia up from school. Twice a day I schlep there on the subway, hefting Max in his ultralightweight stroller up and down the stairs. I must talk to Thom about hiring a car once G is okay with leaving home every day. And then I become a person I don't recognize—the one who sends her four-year-old to private school in a chauffeur-driven Town Car. What kind of mother am I really? If only I knew.

Six

LOVE MEANS NEVER HAVING to say you're sorry. I was watching VH1 the other night while Thom was in Atlanta to appraise a private collector's Civil War memorabilia, and this fantastic show, *I Love the 70s*, kept me up until Max's bedtime. Celebrities were commenting on the tagline from *Love Story* and what a load of horseshit it is. I have to concur. I've never seen the movie (a) because I didn't go to Harvard, and (b) because I, unlike a whole subset of women in my generation, was not named after the ballsy, frail, gorgeous character played by Ali MacGraw. Which is just as well, since I am none of those things. No, I was named after a character on a soap opera—Dr. Jennifer Hardy. At least she was a professional.

When I quit my job at Christie's auction house, it wasn't just to stay at home with Georgia. It was also because I was tired of working in a corporate art environment. Being pregnant somehow took the edge off my ability to figure out the politics and make my own way in a job that required more gamesmanship than I was willing to play and higher heels than I ever felt comfortable in. Thom's career with Universal Imports was starting to take off, and he needed to focus on making his name in the international art scene, so it felt like a natural time to step out and support his dream. Due to my once exquisite taste and photographic memory, I was a prized possession, and my boss, the aptly named Christy Bloomington, tried hard to keep me—suggesting I work four days a week, giving me an office so I could pump in private, even offering me a raise and promotion if I stayed. She's a childless single woman of a certain age, the last person you would expect to extend such a generous hand.

I didn't go into maternity leave knowing I wouldn't come back. In fact I did go back—for exactly one week, before I realized I couldn't "have it all." The lure of the baby seduced me. My hard, repulsive labor aside, Georgia really was a peach, her fuzzy newborn head as round as a ripe and tender fruit. She was what people call a trick baby. She slept well, ate well, smiled well, all of it. She only cried when she met Dr. Ferber at six months. And who can blame her? Once broken, my girl would sleep from eight until eight. We were in love. We still are in many ways, but each day from day one she has moved a little bit further away from me, try though I may to stop her. But that's okay, I found a way to make peace with her eventual leaving: I had another baby. And from the looks of it he's never going anywhere.

As for frail, at my five-foot-nine, 165 pounds—well, you can do the math, especially if you're a woman. Oh, that weight will fly right off! Breastfeeding just *melts* the pounds away! Chasing after kids is the best way for a woman to get her shape back! Myths. Between the two cherubs, I must have breast-fed for three years, on and off, and any time I dropped below 160 the milk would go away and AF would return. If you've never spent precious read-to-your-newborn time in a breast-feeding chat room, you don't know that "AF" is chat-code for "a friend," which is more modern than "Aunt Flo" and decidedly more annoying and immature than "period." Women in these rooms will go to any lengths to keep AF from re-rearing its ugly head. They visit their child in kindergarten for a quick lunchtime feeding session to stave off that vile, insidious creature. They will mechanically pump milk out of their boobs six times a day, wear nursing pads, and wash countless bottles and pump horns, all to keep from seeing a little blood once a month. The most amazing thing about the chat boards, though, is when you stumble across one that's all about sex—for a bunch of girls who are afraid of their periods, these women are beyond obsessed.

I was once beautiful, and many say I still am—most important, Thom—but by the time the kids are in high school, my MYLF card will be revoked to make room for the AARP. It's truly my one regret of not having them earlier. I'll never be anyone's Mrs. Robinson, except for Thom, who is a soul-reassuring six years my junior. He wasn't even born when *The Graduate* came out. Or *Love Story*, for that matter. I comfort myself thinking he'll never leave me for a younger woman, since it's clear that he prefers them older. And besides, I've got Max now, so who needs him?

My therapist once told me that if I were to have kids I would experience true unconditional love. That children, like puppies, give love until it breaks your heart. I'm not sure I believe it. Some days love is never having to say you're sorry, but then other days a trapped feeling wells up in me so hard and fast that I have to walk into the other room for fear it will blind me to those creatures I've enslaved with their own need. And when I come back in, without thinking, the words tumble out of my mouth.

"I'm sorry."

Seven

N OW THAT GEORGIA IS IN SCHOOL for the better part of the day, I have fully devoted myself to educating Max and getting him out of the house before I ruin him too. This way I can kill two birds with one scheduling stone and avoid thinking about the "what next" while I teach my child a life-saving skill. And to be honest, I forgot how dreadfully boring being home with a pretoddler can be. For example, we read *Brown Bear, Brown Bear*—a book with no more than fifty words—twenty times this morning.

We are in the pool at the McBurney Y at ten o'clock Tuesday morning. I am the only mother. That's not to say it's me and a bunch of babies: no, it's me, Max, a bunch of babies, and a bunch of nannies. Black nannies. White babies. Me. Max. The instructor is a gay boy with abs of steel. The rest of us have billowy bodies and dimpled legs. One of the babies looks like a sumo wrestler, his copious folds of fat keeping him so afloat I doubt he'll catch on to the crawl, much less ever have a reason to. His nanny is the only skinny chick in the crowd. Her name is Soledad and she is very tall. I position myself next to her, not because she makes me look thinner but because her baby does.

Max is in the intro class, surrounded by eight-month-old babies who all seem to have teeth. One of them has close-set eyes, another is bald as a cue ball and will most likely always be except for about eighteen years in the middle of his life. One of the little girls has a pink ribbon glued to her swim cap, and I swear to god she's the dykiest baby on earth. But hey, Rosie O'Donnell convinced millions of uptight people she was straight, so this kid's still got a shot at her own talk show. The other babies don't hold a candle to my guy, and I'm quite pleased with myself that he's the sleekest, most gorgeous one in the pack. And yes, it does occur to me how pathetic I am.

"Good morning, my little shrimps, my little kippers. My name is Sven, are we ready to swim?" As mentioned, Sven has abs of steel. He also has blue-black hair that swirls into a Superman curl in the middle of his forehead. He is a god.

As we chorus a yes, Sven encourages us to take turns introducing ourselves, our shrimps and kippers, and to tell each other what we hope to get out of this class. He has got to be kidding. We hope to teach our babies to swim, Sven. And maybe tire them out enough to take a nap. Oh, and to feel at one with the universe, of course.

Soledad emits a little runway-model snort, then introduces sumo-baby. I do not care what his name is, he will always be sumo-baby to me. Or perhaps lard boy. One of the benefits of being a grown-up is that we don't have to make the rest of the playground laugh at the fat kid; we can keep it in our own heads and get one of those deeply pleasant internal laughs. I'm sure in his own way he's laughing right back at my girth.

We are all in the pool, and I must have misread the brochure because we are not teaching our babies to swim. It seems my romantic notion of babies being natural swimmers is a load of what-to-expect bunk. Sven tells us that babies can indeed swim from birth but that they unlearn this handy life-saving instinct soon after. It's really only good for waterbirths, it seems, but it's clearly a tad too late for that. No, we are simply conditioning our children to not be afraid of water. I should have put my $180 toward installing a Jacuzzi.

"Okay, ladies, let's bob our babies up and down to 'Ring around the Rosy,' and when we get to 'all fall down,' fall up instead!" This is clearly a man who has not been up since five a.m. Max pissed himself awake an hour early this morning and wouldn't go back to sleep. On the plus side, he said "Mama" like he meant it, saving his little rabbit skin from becoming a bunting. When Thom is home, he's usually very good at the early rise, but now he's already changing his time-clock upside down to prepare for his new life without us in a foreign land and spending those wee hours in the office making arrangements.

A muddle of words and accents stumble through five rounds of ring-around-the-rosy, and I'm about to haul my large white ass out of the pool, nonreimbursable fee be damned, when Max, on the cue of "up," decides to go down. Under the water. I grab for him, certain for sure that my bad attitude really has killed him this time, when he resurfaces into Sven's arms, all shits and giggles. Sven, in a cool, impersonal voice, asks me to get out of the pool. My slippery little guppy stays with Sven, where he's clearly much safer, until the class ends, when the nannies shoot me you're-not-fit-to-be-a-nanny looks as their clearly better-adjusted, well-behaved babies coo in swaddled towels.

"You can come back in the pool now," Sven says once they're gone. "Are you okay? That must have been quite a fright for you." He doesn't slap me on the wrist or lecture me on the finer points of keeping your child alive. He's actually worried about *me*. I want him to be my new best friend.

"Oh god, Sven." Please like me please like me. "I really did have a good grip on Max. Oh shit, I'm sorry, let me take him from you." While trying to prove what a good mother I am, I've completely forgotten about my child.

"Jennifer, calm down; it's okay, it happens in every class." Did I mention this man is a god? "I'm really impressed by Max, he's the best swimmer I've ever seen."

My child is the best swimmer Sven has ever seen. I don't know how long Sven's been teaching and I don't care. Max is the best swimmer. He may not crawl, he may not chew, but he can out-swim any baby out there.

"Thanks, that means a lot." I don't want to leave the pool, but I notice that Max's fingers and lips are bluing up, and another class is starting to assemble in the lanes to our right. "I guess maybe I'll see you next week?"

"I'd like that." He'd like that. "But why don't we have a private lesson?"

"Should I bring the baby?" I'm only half kidding. "I can't re-ally swim. I mean, I can swim, but I can't dive or put my head under water without plugging my nose. I need help too." Max splashes me in the face; I hold him closer.

"Okay, we can put Max in the daycare while I give you a lesson and then we can give him a lesson after. How does that sound?" It sounds like my heart leaping through my chest.

"Great. Just great." Sven gives me a plastic card with his cell-phone number on it, and I slip it into my swimsuit, next to my heart.

"Okay, it's a date then? I've got my next class." I wait for him to turn so he won't see how my thighs rub together as I make a run for the showers.

Eight

MOTHERFUCKER.

Before I had kids, this was my favorite word. Not since childhood have I had to watch what I say so carefully. When I was in sixth grade, a boy in my class got his hair shaved into a buzz cut, and one of the other boys called him "prick." I thought this was hilarious and not a bit dirty. When I recounted this incident in the car with my parents and younger brother, Andy, they went silent and he started snickering. "What?" I said, knowing that something odd had happened. It came on me like a heat wave that I'd sworn, and in my abject embarrassment I felt a surge of verbal power.

It was the morning I went to retrieve Georgia from her crib and she said "mamafucka" that I knew I had to cauterize my speech. Thom had warned me that this day would arrive. And I could practically hear Thom's mom up in Old Greenwich slapping her hands together in "I told you so." When I had said repeatedly to my enormous belly in the ten days past my due date, "Come out, you little fucker, come out now," Vera had cautioned, "You know, you can't talk like that when there's a child in this house."

I didn't read until I was six. This was not unusual—on the

contrary, if your kid started school knowing how to read it defeated the entire purpose of first grade. Besides, Cheryl was too busy putting food on the table to bother. When applying to get into the Park Street School, Georgia not only had to read a paragraph from a junior edition of *Ulysses,* she had to pose as a statue of her favorite character. Don't ask me which character she chose, I've never read the book. Let's just say Molly and leave it there.

It was all Vera's idea. We—Thom and I—were staunch defenders of the public-school system, determined to find a good one in our district, which isn't all that hard, really, considering our district doglegs from Tribeca across Chelsea and up the East Side to the Bronx. I had also researched and applied for preschool at the local Y as a starter plan. Little did I know that Vera had put in Georgia's application to Park Street before my daughter was even born. Mount Mother-in-Law is a stubborn hill to climb, landscaped in the kind of cockleburs that stick to your socks and continue to irritate you long after they're gone. Or, to extend this already tired metaphor, she's poison ivy, scaling the trellis of your love for her son, only to use it against you. "Thom wants this, he just doesn't know how to tell you."

Fuck that, I know when I'm beat, and I also know which battles to pick. But Georgia's already having difficulty with the lack of structure in her new school. Miss Cartwright lets the children eat their snacks and lunches whenever they are hungry, a concept that brings my daughter to tears on a bi-nightly basis. It seems that she's the only one who waits until ten o'clock for her carrot sticks and noon for her sandwich, at which point the other kids have finished all their food and are starving again, looking at her with moony are-you-going-to-eat-that eyes. Nothing like beggars cosseted in Nautica to make a girl sad. She's started packing oyster crackers just to keep them at bay.

It would be so much simpler if Georgia could just tell them to fuck off. I mean it. Why do we deny our children this simple pleasure? Eventually—and very early, I might add—they learn all these words and use them when we're not within earshot. As we use them when they're not around. Think about it—if we were to stick a collective pin in the power of the swear word, wouldn't it sting a lot less when the day arrives that our kids tell us we're full of shit?

Nine

I'M READING A BOOK. There are no pictures, only words. The type is smaller than I'm used to, and from what I can tell there will be no moral to this story, just a repressed housewife looking to have some hot sex. I'm curled up on the couch, the rain is sheeting down outside, and Thom is in the kitchen feeding the kids breakfast. Even though he's not leaving for a couple more weeks, I'm taking full advantage of his desire to make it up to me. Okay, I'm not really reading, I'm eavesdropping.

"So, GG, what are you learning at school?" Thom asks.

"Mhmph, mhmph," Max barks at his cereal bowl, which is shaped like a dog.

"Nothing," Georgia mutters between crunches. I strain to hear her.

"Aw, come on, you must be learning something. What's your favorite part of school?" He rephrases, the novice's approach to getting a child to open up.

"Um, coloring."

"We could color after breakfast—would that be fun?" he asks. Though I can't see her, I know she just sat back against her chair, as I hear the little scrape it makes on the floor from the force of her body weight. "Or not."

"*Abasef, abasef!*" Max yells. We have no idea what he's saying, but it usually helps to give him a spoon at this point of the daily drama he enacts with breakfast.

"Give him a spoon," I yell. Flip my book over, read the back: "Wifey is tired of chicken on Wednesdays and sex on Saturdays." Indeed.

"Or we could go to the children's zoo, pet some animals?"

"*Abasef, abasef!*"

"Daddy, it's *raining.*" Her bare heels knock against the chair. This is a sign that she's intrigued by the offer of the zoo, is weighing what it is that she really wants to do against how many things she has to turn down to make her father think he's come up with exactly the right thing.

"A spoon, Thom, give the kid a spoon." I will not go in there. I will not go in. . . .

"ABASEF!"

I get up, walk into the kitchen, retrieve a spoon from the drainer, give it to Max—who says "taka" with the smallest amount of exasperation a fourteen-month-old can manage—and return to my book. There's a naked guy in a motorcycle helmet doing something very nasty on the housewife's lawn.

"Geege, help me out here. What would you like to do today?"

"Ferris wheel."

"*Adah! Bok!*"

"Maxie boy, finish your Cheerios, good guy, big *Max!*" I imagine Thom and Max throwing their hands into the air together. "*Big Max! Maxamillion, Maxabillion, Maxatrillion!*"

"Daddy, Ferris wheel," Georgia whines his attention back to her.

"Bug, there's no Ferris wheel in the city. . . ."

"Toys 'R' Us," Georgia and I say in unison. Meanwhile, the mad ejaculator has remounted his bike. Wifey calls her husband at "the plant."

"Since when is there a Ferris wheel at Toys 'R' Us?" He's got to be teasing her, he can't be this out of the loop, so to speak.

"Since I was little! Can we go, can we can we can we?"

"*Da da up!*"

The phone rings. I make a grab for it, but Georgia's already there. She is Pavlov's dog.

"Hello? Bradley residents?"

"Give me the phone, sweetie," I say, reaching out my hand.

"Hello." She smiles. "Yeah. Un-huh. Sorta. It's okay. He's good. Yep." She hands me the phone. "It's Honey Granma." I put my hand over the receiver, tell her to help her dad get Max ready for their outing. The rain has stopped, and it looks like it's going to be a nice, childfree day.

"Hey you," I say into the phone. Georgia leans against me for a moment, then loses interest and goes back into the kitchen. "How are you?"

"Just peachy, how's everyone there?"

"Good, good, can't complain. Dad?" My question is as perfunctory as it sounds; I really don't want to talk to anyone today. As much as I love Cheryl, she has the uncanny ability to call when I'm not in the mood for chitchat.

"Oh, you know your father, up with the birds. He's been out blowing leaves since dawn."

"It's not raining up there?"

"Heavens no, should it be?"

"No, I guess not." I fold a corner and close the book for now, no way I'm getting off the phone quickly.

"When's Thom leave?" I hear her knitting needles clicking in the background. She's never once finished a project she's started. Mostly the sweaters, scarves, and hats end up living out their time on earth as odd-shaped potholders.

"Next week. We're telling G tonight." Georgia runs back into the room.

"Tell me what, Mommy?" She climbs up onto my lap. Thom follows her into the room, drops Max on the couch next to me—his face smeared with streaks of dried yogurt and a Cheerio stuck to his cheek—and returns to the kitchen.

"Bring me a wipey?" I yell after Thom, who is making kitchen-cleaning sounds. "You know what, Cheryl, I'm going to need to call you back—"

"Tell what? Tell what?" Georgia pulls on my arm.

"ADAH! BOK! BOK!" Max hands me *Brown Bear, Brown Bear*, then rips the cover off my book. Georgia climbs up onto the back of the couch and, in the process, pushes her brother with her feet, making him pitch a glass-shattering shriek.

"Yes, dear, it sounds that way. But let me ask you a quick question."

"Hang on a minute. Georgia, get down. Thom, can you maybe corral them for a second?" The room goes silent. There's a tone in my voice that no one likes. Thom comes in, his hands dripping with suds, shoots me a look, and picks up Max. Georgia follows them, whispering, "Tell what, Daddy?"

"Okay, what is it?" I say to Cheryl, feeling cranky and doomed.

"I want to invite you for Christmas. All the other kids will be there." Ever since Thom and I were married, there's been a silent war between Cheryl and Vera over who gets us when during the holidays. My vote is always that we skip it altogether and go to the Bahamas. Thom won't give up Christmas Day at his family. Each year Cheryl tries to winkle us free for both days. Nobody wins.

"Great, we'll see you Christmas Eve," I say. "Happy belated Columbus Day."

"Just this once, that's all I'm asking, just this once I'd like to have my whole family together for two days in a row. Why do you always have to run off? Ask Thom. Come here for both days, and then next year I don't care what you do."

"C'mon, Cheryl, you know the drill. I'd change it if I could."

"Do I really ask so much?"

"No, no you don't at all. Let me see what I can do." We have this conversation every year, with the same results.

"That's all I ask. So it's raining there?" A crash, then a wail, come from the nursery.

"Hey, it sounds like someone was murdered on my end—can I talk to you later?"

"Of course, dear. You know, it's only a few months now until you're for— Never mind. Ask Thom, remember?" I tell her I will even as I ignore her passive hinting about my looming milestone and we hang up. I meet Thom at the door of Max's room.

"He sort of jumped off the changing table." Max is blubbering in Thom's arms; my baby boy reaches out for me.

"That's okay, Sweet pea," I say to Max, rubbing his back. "Did you step away?" I ask Thom.

"Only for a second to get his pacifier," he says, shrugging his shoulders as though we haven't had the don't-step-away conversation a hundred million times.

"Daddy, *Ferris wheel.*" Georgia tugs his hand. I suspect she's had a role in this event, but without proof she gets to walk.

"Why don't you take G to the wheel? Max can stay home with me." I keep my voice neutral.

"Okay. Are you ready, Rudolph?" Thom rubs his hands together, washing them of me and Max.

"Ready, Santa!" She leaps into her daddy's arms, giving me a triumphant look.

After they go, I sit on the couch with Max, who falls asleep within minutes. Nothing like a good blow to the head to tire a baby out. I pick up *Wifey*, but I'm too distracted, so I sit and watch the light outside the windows darken. Thom's cell phone rings on the coffee table. I let it. The land line rings.

"Hello," I say, half expecting it to be Cheryl again, thinking "later" means ten minutes later.

"Jennifer, my one true love. It's been a long time."

"So it has, Bjorn." Thom's boss is high on my list of shit, with great potential to rank number one by the time Thom gets back from Singapore. When Thom first met him, Bjorn was fresh off the boat from Edina, Minnesota, and the two of them were trying to buy a statuary head through a local dealer—an Egyptian named Pablo, if you can believe it—in Cairo with a chunk of Bjorn's trust fund. The first time I met Bjorn—well, that's a story for another day.

"How's home life treating my queen?" Even after all these years of telling him in my head to fuck off, I still get a lurch in my stomach when he speaks in that velvety voice of his.

"Better than cataloging antiquities, that's for sure," I tell him, keeping my own tone neutral and disinterested. The problem for Bjorn back then was that Pablo was fronting for the Egyptian Museum, and neither Bjorn nor Thom had the expertise to tell whether the Nefertiti was genuine—they'd heard so many stories about the museum faking antiquities that even taking the meeting was hardly worth it. But Pablo had found them priceless amulets the month before, and so Thom asked me to come to the meeting with them as an extra pair of expert eyes. Bjorn was insulted, and we've been on opposite sides of Thom ever since.

"Helloooo, Jen, you there?" He snaps me out of my reverie. "Thom there?"

"I'm afraid you just missed him, he's out with Georgia."

"Do you know where he's gone, beautiful? I need to talk to him." I picture Bjorn in his apartment, still in his robe, tanned and toned from a morning at the spa. If I hadn't watched him screw his way through at least twenty women that first summer— one of them nearly me—I'd probably fall for his shtick too.

"They didn't say where they were going, why don't you try his cell?" Thom's forgotten it again, though for once I'm glad. That night outside of Cairo they were carrying twenty thousand dollars in cash, strapped to their bodies like explosives on suicide bombers. When we got to the house on the outskirts of town, I wasn't let in because my hair was uncovered. A good thing too, because a few minutes later the local police arrived, and I was able to make enough commotion over having to produce my papers that everyone got out the back way. A year later Bjorn sold the head through a private dealer for more than a million dollars, started Universal Imports, and took Thom under his slimy wing.

"Look, Jenjy"—I hate it when he calls me that, and he knows it—"I need Thom to fly to Greece tomorrow and pick up a vase for a client in Singapore. It's really urgent. I already tried his cell. I'll try it again. You will tell him why I called?"

"What kind of vase is it?" I can't help it, my connoisseur's curiosity is sparked by the words *Greece* and *vase*.

"Why not leave this one to the professionals, okay, sweet-heart?"

"Whatever you say." I hang up before he can belittle me any more. There goes the weekend, but it must be pretty important if Bjorn won't tell me what it is. I pull Max closer as I reach over and turn Thom's cell off before escaping back into the suburban seventies landscape of my book. God bless Judy Blume.

Ten

CHILD REARING IS AN ISOLATING OCCUPATION. Yes, there are two parents most of the time, but it's rare when the bulk of the work is evenly divided. And when there is a nanny, she tends to form as close a bond as you, like it or not. This is the main reason I've stayed home with my kids. I don't want them to have "another mom." I'm a very jealous person, and it would eat me alive if I came home from pushing paper across my desk all day just to be told that Max took his first step while I was on a conference call about some Grecian vase or editing a new auction catalog. Those things are important, sure, but Max takes that first step only once. And so I've chosen a fairly solitary life. The nannies of other children consider me the enemy, and most of the other SAHMs are just too highly functional for me to bear, even though I admire their supermom abilities from a distance.

Meanwhile, there is something comforting, in a monastic way, about spending one's day with children. Much of my inner life has become deeply buried, lost in the shuffle of bottles and diapers and carrot sticks. I might think about something weighty while mopping the floor, but by the time I've rinsed out the sponge the thought will have vanished. I used to follow the news, watching CNN take us live to the frontlines of war, but it got too depressing, and so I've fallen out of touch with Paula Zahn. Lately I've made an attempt to amend this behavior, and I now get the *Times* delivered at home, but it's a rare day that I make it below the fold. I prefer not caring, and I like the deep meditation that comes with singing the alphabet countless times or the focus required to color within the lines.

Even so, I am very lonely, and I'm worried that when Thom leaves I'll become even more isolated. My baby shower for Georgia was attended by more than fifty women I have known well— friends from school, work, and happenstance and a couple of relatives. I was completely overwhelmed when they were all in the same room, and I felt blessed to have such a wealth of experience to expose Georgia to, so many role models. Now I rarely see any of them, and Georgia knows only a handful. The ones with kids have their own kid issues to contend with; the ones without want to go out just with me, but I rarely get the tires under me to hire a sitter for a girls' night out.

I wasn't the most popular girl in high school, but I've always attracted friends easily, something that still surprises me when it happens. I'm very nurturing, it seems: a shoulder to cry on, an open door. I wasn't a part of any clique but rather was what people call a "beta girl"—one who can be friends with anyone and who keeps the peace. I had two best friends, Portia and Candy, but am not sure to this day whether they considered me the same. Since then I've had a fairly constant top five friends, but this list has shifted, and I truly hate that I can't single out one person and say, "She is my best friend." Why can't I be more like Carrie

Bradshaw and use the term indiscriminately among all my girl-friends, making each one of them feel more important than the others?

Sometimes I wonder whether I would have more energy to maintain my relationships if Thom didn't travel so much. When I lived with Heath, who also traveled a lot and hated all my friends but Penny, I found that I slowly weeded out a number of acquaintances and ended up spending a lot of time alone. Then he would go on a road tour and leave me with an empty calendar and the television schedule. Pretty glamorous life we led, all right. Dr. Kreigsman called it a "transition" moment—those times in life when you are provided with the opportunity to scour your en-tanglements and start fresh. Was that time really better spent at home watching TV than seeing three-dimensional people?

I fear I'm unconsciously making deliberate choices that run me off the friendship road. My love for Georgia and Max is fre-quently so all-consuming that I simply don't have anything left to give anyone else. Including Thom. My long days of laundry fold-ing and bottle washing give me a kind of peace that is hard to ex-plain, even to myself. And yet I fear the day when the children move away and I am left to mend all the fences I've let fall. Of course, I could always get up off my ass and find some new friends. New York is full of women like me who would like me.

Is this a biological mechanism that keeps me locked to the wel-fare of my children? If I hadn't stopped working, would I be a bet-ter friend, go to more theater, weigh less? Do I choose the company of my kids so that I don't have to work so hard to care about oth-ers? The hard reality is that sometimes I just want them, and then I want them to be enough, and then they aren't and I'm left with me. And though I do like me, I'm not my own best friend either.

Eleven

GEORGIA AND I ARE ON THE F TRAIN, burrowed deep beneath the city on our way to a playdate in Brooklyn so I can reconnect with Portia, my high school best friend. Before flying to Greece tonight, Thom is treating Max to a "boys' day," which consists of Thom's taking Max to Chelsea Piers and showing him all the sports he will one day master, and sharing with him old videos of Thom's own days as a jock. It will be years before these Elmer's-glue-on scales fall from little Max's eyes and he realizes his dad never made varsity. Except for debate, that is.

"Mommy, can we go to the toy store?"

"I don't have my wallet, peanut, just some spare change and a MetroCard." Who says I can't anticipate my child an hour in advance?

"Did you forgot it?"

"Yep, I forgot it."

"We can just *look* at the toys?" Though there may seem to be no harm in looking, the residual effect of window-shopping with a child has a proven half-life of about two weeks. But I'm so happy to have Max off my hip for a couple of hours that I'll do anything for Georgia.

"Sure thing, baby, whatever you want."

"Yay yay yay yay yay!" She quotes her brother's newest phrase. She is in one of those delicious moods, taking complete possession of what was once hers only.

"Mommy, remember when I was little, that you used to carry me in a sling?" An unbleached cotton sling woven by a consortium of twentysomethings to raise money for Greenpeace, to be precise.

"I'd swaddle you in a blankie and carry you everywhere: Old Navy, Dunkin' Donuts, the Gap, Victoria's Secret . . ."

"Willamsnoma, Starbucks, Burger King . . ."

"The MoMA, ABC Carpet and Home, REM concert . . ."

"Toys 'R' Us, U Pick Strawberries, um . . . the UN . . ."

"Graceland, San Simeon, Buckingham Palace . . ."

"Neverneverland, Pooh Corner, the *Plaza*!"

She wins this game every time. There are no rules or clear definition of what exactly winning looks like, but she knows she's won when I throw up my hands and go in for a good tickle.

I always love going to Portia's house. She is an inspiration. Of all the women in my high school class, she is by far the most successful. As VP, New Stores Coordinator, for Tiffany's, she travels the country with a team of twenty, making sure that every display in every new store is exactly like the flagship's. She has special silver rulers and tape measures to guarantee that the buyer need not beware. Much like the cookie-cutter appeal of Wal-Mart, this continuity is a comfort to the customer. Just knowing that Paloma can be found in the far left corner of every store is a great aid to the woman who travels and needs to buy earrings at the last minute. My little Portia, to whom I had to slip the algebra answers during the final exam, is all grown up and running out in front of her classmates, succeeding beyond anyone's wildest dreams. The mother of reinvention, she has gone from being a scuff-kneed tomboy to dressing exclusively in Armani skirt-suits for work.

Portia is also the mother of all mothers. She made triplets, two girls and a boy. What I used to refer to as "twenty-thousand-dollar triplets," until I witnessed firsthand her heartbreak of failed conception. Now I say, Viva technology! And bring on the insurance coverage for multiple attempts for all women, regardless of income! Fertility runs in my family, a blessing more than a curse these days as so many of my friends struggle to have kids.

Rocco, Gia, and Sofia were born just before Georgia, and if we lived closer they would be inseparable. The four of them have disappeared to the upstairs playroom, where there is a scale-model kitchen that will in the near future have the Viking stove hooked up. No cooking by lightbulb in the Mariani household.

"I've decided to quit my job." Portia has only sipped at her glass of wine when she launches into the meat of the conversation. If I'd had any liquid in my mouth, it would be spraying her, I'm so unprepared for this announcement. I was going to tell her about Thom's trip, ask her if she helped him buy the bracelet, maybe even open up to someone about how I'm feeling for once, but instead I'm relieved that I don't have to.

"Have you been headhunted for a better position?" I shrink a little at the idea of Portia breaking another glass ceiling on her way to what can only be president or CEO of a Fortune 500. The career rapids seem to be flowing past me at Mach 1, and though I want the best for my friend—really, I do—I can't help wanting a little of it for me too. Not that I know what that is or how I would balance it. I don't think I can make as much money as Portia does, and though she is the kind of mother she chooses to be, and does that really well, I don't know if I could be that kind of mother. The kind who works sixty-hour weeks and sees her kids for thirty minutes a day, who travels half the month and leaves the real mothering to her spouse. The kind of parent Thom is, come to think of it.

"No, I'm quitting work altogether. They passed me over for a promotion, and I've had it with the travel and never seeing my kids." There are red splotches high on her cheeks, and I have to guess that this decision was made with the help of Xanax. I feel a sick twinge in my stomach, what must be the reverse of envy— I'm actually happy my best friend has been screwed at work. But not the kind of happy that makes you happy.

"Quitting? Just like that? Does Mark know?" Her husband has been writing the Great American Novel. Seriously. He wrote a string of cheesy mysteries in his twenties that were so wildly popular that he has spent ten years trying to kill "Pat Bruno" and her clue-sniffing corgi with a real literary novel.

"Mark's fine with it. He's going to go back to work. It's his turn." Behind the glassy-eyed stare I detect a teardrop welling. On closer inspection, I notice that her usually perfectly dyed auburn hair is showing some gray at the roots, and that her Lily Pulitzer blouse is not only stained but has a small rip on the pocket.

"You're sure this is what you want? I mean, the kids are already in school. It's not like there's much to do with them at this age. You've pretty much missed the good stuff." Shit. I'm an idiot. Did I say that out loud? Truly, I can go hours with the kids not knowing if I'm speaking or not, so there's a chance.

Portia knocks back the wine. Seems she heard me just fine. She turns to look out the window and actually bites one of her perfectly manicured nails. The hair on the back of my neck stands up.

"Sorry, of course, there's tons to do with them before and after school. Playdates, the museum, the zoo. And maybe it's a good time to have another?" Strike two. I really should just shut up. She pours more wine for both of us.

"It's okay. We want to adopt. I've got a bad case of new-baby lust, and I can't tell you how much I've envied you all these years, having a front-row seat to Georgia's every little change. And now Max. I sometimes wonder why I went to all the trouble of having kids if I'm just going to pay someone else to raise them. Do you really think I'm making a mistake by leaving my job?"

"Well, that's not really for me to say, really. Really." She's envied me? I'm the one who always wanted her super-smooth hair, her casual appeal to men, her easy way of handling any social situation, her unstoppable career drive. I have eaten my heart out over all of her boyfriends and clothes and, well, just look at this house, would you? How could she have been envying me when I've been the Jolly Green Giant all these years?

"You're the only person who can help me figure this out. I haven't quit yet, it's not too late to suck it up. Or to look for another job. Oh, Christ, look. I'm just not good at the kid thing. I've never spent more than a couple of hours alone with them, and then I get so bored I want to kill them just to liven things up a little. I mean, how many times can a person play hide and seek? But. Oh." She sighs, winding down. "It's just that I really wanted that promotion and I've worked so fucking hard and kept it all up in the air, for what? So a woman ten years younger than me can be my boss? She's related to the CEO. I never thought this sort of thing really happened. So what do you think I should do? Should I get over myself and fight back? Look for a new job? Stay home? Is it great once you get used to it? Please tell me I'm making the right choice."

"Well," I begin, taking a drag of wine to stall for time to think, "maybe you should make a list of pros and cons. You know, one list of pros and cons for working and one for parenting." I have no idea what I'm saying, but it must sound good because Portia whips out a pad of paper and a pencil from a drawer in the kitchen counter where we sit on bar stools.

"A list! Of course!" She's got a grin on her face. "Okay. Home—pro, con. Work—pro, con." She looks at me like I've got all the answers now, at least for the home pro column.

"How about getting to see your kids more?"

"Yeah, of course, that's the top of the list. Pro. And maybe I'll do a little homeschooling. Pro. And we can have craft days. Pro. Hey, Halloween is next week, I could do a big party for all the kids in the neighborhood. Pro. Though I don't really know the other kids. Con. Really decorate the place. Pro. I don't know where to shop for decorations, really. Con. Pumpkins! Pro! Oh, but the costumes, I can't sew and there's no time to learn. Con. I could bake cupcakes. Pro . . . wow. This sounds like fun! And I can get more involved in planning their activities. We'll do theme playdates. You know, plant a tree for Arbor Day, go to Harlem for Martin Luther King Day. I've got it! Why don't you and I go into kiddie party planning? We'd be so good at it!"

"Keep your job," I say, sort of terrified.

"What?" She snaps the pencil in half.

"Go in Monday like nothing ever happened and keep your

job." She looks down at the notepad, where she has unknowingly quick-sketched the Tiffany floor, boxing the words *pro* and *con* in like diamonds and lesser stones.

"Yep, yep. Keep my job. Pro." We have some more wine and a good giggle reminiscing about high school before we sneak upstairs to find all four kids tangled in sleep on Gia's bed, Mark likewise asleep in a neighboring armchair. Portia hugs me, puts one finger to my lips, and knocks her forehead against mine.

"Though I love the way this looks," she says, fully herself again, "I don't think I'd trade places with you for anything in the world." Strike three. If she really envies me, then she would want to trade places. I don't want everything she has, I just want most of it. She's the gold standard, the uber-woman to my hausfrau, always has been. Like the French at the Olympics, if I could just figure out how to go for the silver, maybe then she really would envy me a little?

Twelve

I WASN'T BORN IN this loft. I didn't have a silver spoon or a trust fund. My father sold insurance, and Cheryl substituted as a grade-school teacher and worked as many odd jobs as she could find to keep us in soap and cereal while my father drank the part of his paycheck that should have paid the mortgage. Okay, I'm being fancy by saying mortgage. It was a bank loan. For a trailer house. In a trailer park. On the edge of town. I don't hide this part of my life, but I don't exactly volunteer it either. Sometimes I use it as an ambush, like this:

My very rich coworker Tricia, who grew up in Scarsdale, and I were discussing the merits of adoption at lunch one day. I was positing the theory that a kid who was born into poverty has the same raw materials as a kid born wealthy. She was arguing that a mother's bad nutrition, an abusive environment, impoverished role models, etc., could affect a baby's intelligence before he was even born. I said I disagreed, having been raised at poverty level myself. She knew I was a poor kid, just not how poor. So she says:

"It's not like you grew up in a trailer house."

"Yes, I did," I warned her.

"No you didn't," she scoffed.

"Yes, I really did," I insisted.

"Well, it's not like your house was in a trailer park." She looked for a loophole, but I didn't give in. She picked up the check as though I still was that person, even though she was only an intern at Christie's and had been to my apartment for dinner and knew that I had long ago left the aluminum siding and wheels behind me.

Every day I struggle with how to impart to my children a sense of reality. We all want to give our kids a better childhood, more opportunities, clothes that aren't all hand-me-downs (though Andy really did look good in my Garanimals), a good education. Hell, it's practically mandated in the Constitution that they should have a better life than the one we have lived. But without some sense of how the other half lives, I fear I run the risk of setting the bar too low. And how do I make them believe that I was once the other half? Cheryl had two children from her first marriage who are a couple of years older than Andy and I. That made six of us in a very small double-wide. Sardines, can.

When you're tall, blond, and reasonably good-looking, people don't stop to think that you might have waited in line to get a five-pound block of government-issued cheese when you were young. Nor do they think you've ever had to work for what you have. They instead assume that somehow the world treats you just a little bit better, that good things just come to you. And you know what? For the most part, they're right. It's much easier to shake off your past and remake your identity if you clean up nice. In high school, when I was stuck behind a fence of braces and a hedge of bad perm, no one thought I could be pretty or popular or anything but trailer trash. You don't have to wear a tank top and cut-offs or sleep with your daddy to earn that designation. In fact, if you've ever been called it, you'll know it doesn't mean what most people think it does. It's much closer to "worthless piece of shit" than "clever theme for my new restaurant."

Ah, but I'm not bitter. I bloomed myself out and I dressed in D&G knockoffs and dated high rollers. I lived well, nightclubbing with the club kids, eating at four-star restaurants with celebrities, and taking Manhattan for all it was worth, learning quickly that you only have to put yourself in the right place with the right atti-tude to fit in with a wide array of very rich people. In the early eighties in New York you could sleep with a famous person every night of the week, if you were so inclined. Eventually I got tired of living a superficially fast life and decided to go back to school dur-ing those long Heathless winters. I paid my way by waiting tables—Heath never offered, I never asked. And then I met Thom, got a good job, and we settled in and had kids. We've somehow managed to earn our way into a high tax bracket and live in a fantastic loft. When we first looked at this place, though, it was a fright—whitewashed brick, painted cement floor, no kitchen or baths—but somehow the way it was laid out felt just right to me, and I con-vinced Thom that it was going to be perfect. After a complete over-haul, it emerged as a jewel. I was so excited to show the finished place to Cheryl, who took one look around and said:

"It's really nice, honey, but did you happen to notice that the layout is exactly the same as our old trailer?"

Maybe I'm overestimating how far I've come and underesti-mating how much further Georgia and Max may someday go. Maybe on the moon or Mars there will be a fantastic complex of buildings that my daughter has designed and my son has built, and just the way our children are fractals of Thom and me, their new homes will also echo this lovely nest we've lined for their temporary comfort.

Thirteen

MAX HAS ALWAYS HAD a fondness for Asians. When he was first big enough to ride face out in his BabyBjörn carrier, nothing would bring him greater joy than a walk through K-town or Little Japan or Chinatown. And so it comes as no surprise that he is desperately in love with his new friend Lily.

Sven arranged with the Y to return our baby swim fee so I could pay him directly for our lessons. Between countless attempts by Sven to get me to put my head in the water without pinching my nose, he told me that he'd brought his daughter Lily along to help me learn how to hold a slippery guppy. After a disastrous hour of flushing out my sinuses with chlorine we went to get the kids from day care, where I found Max sitting on the floor, his mouth slack and drooling, staring at a Chinese girl a little smaller and a little older than he is. As a way of thanking Sven for taking us on, I asked him back to my house for a playdate after the lesson—and told him he could bring Lily, of course.

I'm still in the flower of my romance with Sven, and I find I've never been so nervous around a man. It's almost as though just knowing we will never have sex sets the conversation bar higher. I mean, if a guy's just looking for a quickie, he'll think everything you say is brilliant. But this is different. I have to use something less tangible to lure my catch—wit, whimsy, bon mots. Sven is not a particularly stylish gay man, favoring lumberjack flannel and Levi's, so I'm not worried about my ridiculous-looking stretch pants and big sweater. . . . Even so, I'm feeling even more bulky and hairy than usual.

If you can't beat 'em, bake for 'em, I always say, and I've whipped up a cheese soufflé for lunch, the one thing I really mastered in the egg portion of my cooking class last summer—an anniversary present. Thom thought it would be nice for me to get out of the house one night a week. What a thoughtful husband. What a great way to honor our marriage. And now, like any good wife with a buried resentment, I am using what Thom has helped me learn to impress another man.

"You know how to make a soufflé?" Sven asks as he unhitches Lily from her backpack.

"Oh, it's easy, really, I've already put it together, I just need to fold in the egg whites, bake for twenty minutes, and voilà." See, I knew that French would come in handy.

"Wow. I never learned how to cook, but Tom thinks I should take a class. You know, give me something to do one night a week." I almost drop my soufflé.

"Tom? Your partner's name is Tom? I'll be damned. Mine too. Do you think it's too early to drink to that?"

"You wouldn't have any Lillet, would you? It's almost like not drinking."

"Not only do I have Lillet, I have oranges." He is my soul mate. Now if only I had a pack of Gitanes, two tickets to Paris, a penis, and ten fewer years around my midsection. "So tell me, Sven, are you of Scandinavian descent?"

"No, but that's a funny story. When I was a kid growing up in

New Jersey there were seven Stevens on my block. Seems there were a lot of Sondheim fans in my neighborhood, too bad none of them could spell his name right. When I moved to the city I dropped the *t* and *e* at my coming-out party. Hey, look at this," he says, turning my attention from his slate-blue eyes to the designated play area.

When we finished the loft, Thom and I promised each other that it wouldn't turn into another Toy Town nightmare, as our last apartment had. That there would be one playroom and that the rest of the rooms would serve their God-given purposes. And yet somehow, alas, you can't walk two feet in any direction without twisting an ankle on a block or a tiny car. We are not known for our resolve.

Sven, having been told poolside about my son's inability to crawl, holds up one hand in a stop sign and directs me around the kitchen wall with the tease of a curled finger on the other hand. I press myself against the wall and crane my neck around the corner, one eye at a time. And I see paradise: not only is Max crawling, but he is following Lily around the furniture like she has him on a leash. I press myself back against the wall and squeeze my eyes shut, freezing this picture for later when I describe it to Thom over the phone. He's in Russia delivering a priceless Fabergé egg to a co-dealer. Sometimes I think he's little more than Bjorn's overpaid courier.

"Oh, the soufflé!" I have forgotten to put it in the oven, which is a smaller sin than forgetting to set the timer, which I now do, stopping to cross "soufflé" off my to-do list on the counter. We take our drinks into the living room and Sven roars when he sees Max flop onto his stomach at the sound of my shoes. Lily is busy hand-feeding Cheerios to Max, who sticks out his tongue like a supplicant. This girl could heal him of anything.

"When did you get Lily?" I've been dying to know this story but am not sure what the etiquette is when asking about adoption. At the mention of her name, Lily looks at me, her hair cut straight across her eyebrows and short in the back like a boy's. She is wearing a perfect sky-blue wool jumper over a white turtle-neck, and I find myself falling for her as well.

"We adopted Lil six months ago, when she was just a year; isn't that right, sweetie?" She climbs into Sven's lap, placing her delicate feet with the agility of a rock climber, and puts her arms around his neck. Max rolls onto his back to get a better look—no doubt up her skirt. I pick him up to keep him from looking so positively lewd. "Believe it or not, she was already potty trained, which was my biggest worry about having a girl. I mean, who would teach her how to pee sitting down?"

"I know what you mean, it took me months to train Georgia. I think we waited a little too long. She especially didn't like to poop in the toilet, she felt it was a part of her. We're starting Max on his second birthday, I don't care what the books say. The whole 'let them tell you when they're ready' is criminal." Oh my god. Here I am, talking to my secret gay boyfriend about poop within ten minutes of our first playdate.

"Speaking of books, did you read *Disco Bloodbath*?" I change the subject. "They based the movie *Party Monster* on it—you know, the club kid killers, and all that. I'm dying to see the movie; there was a shot of me in the documentary." To my relief, Sven's face lights up.

"Really? Me too! I didn't know you were a club kid!" He puts Lily back down on the floor, and I just as quickly relieve myself of Max. We scurry back to the kitchen, where we can use more colorful language and refresh our drinks.

"I wasn't a club kid," I say. "I worked the door at the Slime-light for a while, taking people's money."

"Hey, were you the girl with the lemon yellow hair? Wait a minute, didn't you go by "Lemonfur"?" He's leaning in for a better look now, and I tilt my chin up to stretch out the sag.

"The one, the only. I can't believe you know that, I thought only my friend Penny called me that. And who might you have been?" I hold out my hand.

"Sven Svensson, né Steven Tanen, Olympic swimmer." He takes my hand and licks it, I pull it back in mock disgust. "I've gone back to Tanen, the other being too gay for even me. I was only in the clubs on the weekends, and I couldn't drink what with all the training. I never medaled but did make out with Louganis once or twice."

"God, I thought he was so hot. Totally my type."

"Lemmy, I don't know how to break it to you, but he's on *my* team."

"So? I like them gay, you got a problem with that?" We talk a bit about all the man crushes we have in common, recount our conquests, celebrate our fabulous younger selves. We don't talk about all the men we lost, or how utterly decimating the eighties were, or how lucky we are to be sitting here, drinking ourselves silly. When the conversation lulls into that hallowed ground, Sven does the smart thing.

He comes around to my side of the kitchen island and starts singing "Crazy," dancing me into his arms. Lily runs into the room, and we pick her up to join us as Max crawls in after her—in full view of his mother. We are all swept off our feet as the timer rings.

Sven and I have scraped the bottom of the soufflé dish and nearly finished the bottle of Lillet. We've put the babies down for a nap, and I feel more relaxed and happier than I have in a very long time.

"Do you ever regret quitting your job?" he asks me. Sven has been a SAHD for six months now, having left his sports marketing job when he and Tom brought Lily home. "I mean, Lily is my world and all, but I'm finding I have less and less to talk to Tom about when he gets home. I find myself telling him the plot of the *Baby Einstein Nietzsche* DVD." We laugh, but we know it's not all that funny.

"Trust me, it's hard at first, but it gets much easier, and no, for the most part I don't regret it." I sense a qualifier in what I've said, and hope he doesn't notice my complete lack of confidence on this front. "I mean, I do sort of regret not trying to go back, at least for a few months. So I'd know whether I regret it or not. Sort of."

"You know, it's not the boredom or the repetition or the constant neediness so much as it is the way it seems to drain my libido." He looks down at the bottom of the dish and pretends to scrape a little more.

"Um. Really? Even though you're, well, you know?" I've lived in the city for twenty years and I suddenly can't say *gay*.

"Gay?"

"Yeah, you know . . ."

"You think that gay men are just horny all the time, don't you?" He's got me there.

"Well, not horny exactly, just more capable of getting horny when you're not. Horny." What is it about me that encourages people to reveal things that make me uncomfortable? I want this to be a sexless relationship. Entirely.

"It's just that Tom always wants to, and since having the baby I'm just too tired all the time. What does he expect? For me to fake it?" There's a new one.

"Okay, let me tell you a little secret. All the girls fake it every now and then. There's no shame in it. And you'll see that it's a much quicker train to sleepytown if you just give in than if you put up the 'closed' sign. Something about that sign just makes them want it more." I don't really mean any of this, as Thom and I have a great, if infrequent, sex life, but I just have to commiserate, that's what my new best friend wants. Besides, if he follows my advice, he'll most likely discover that he is horny after all.

"I'm sorry, I'm such a mess. I really don't know why I told you all of this. I'd better go wake up Lily or she won't sleep tonight."

"Look, why don't you leave Lily here and go out for a romantic dinner? She can help me entertain Max. . . ."

"You'd do that? How can I thank you?"

"Go get laid, and never mention your sex life again."

"Done."

Fourteen

THE FIRST TIME I THREW UP after missing my period, I said a little prayer asking for a boy. My baby brother is a boy. My husband is a boy. All my gay boyfriends have always been boys. Except for Madison, who became a girl. I had only babysat for boys and my friends had given birth only to boys and, well, I just loved the way little boys do little boy things. I was terrified the baby would be a girl. Girls are shrewd, manipulative tiny things who come out of the womb one step ahead of you. When people asked me, "Do you care if it's a boy or a girl?" I couldn't say "None of your business" or "Frankly, if it's not a boy I'm sending it back," so instead, to shut them up, I'd say, "I don't care if it's a boy or girl, as long as it's gay."

At first I said this for the shock value, but after a while I realized that a part of me really meant it. If, god willing, it were a boy, and if, god willing, he were gay, then he'd never ever leave me for another woman. Except maybe a cross-gendered Madison. Vera was mortified by my harmless joke, but Cheryl, she of the surprises, used the opportunity to reveal that her first husband, father to my step-sibs Judy and Vince, left her for many reasons, but most of all because he was gay. And being gay in the sixties in a small town in the Catskills was not something he had the wherewithal to battle.

When we tried to conceive our first, I followed all the tricks for getting a boy: I had sex standing up, lay on my right side afterward, timed conception with both a quarter moon and an odd day of the month, and put all my cosmic thinking power into the word *boy*. You can imagine my surprise at the twenty-week sonogram when there was no penis to be found. How did I feel when the doctor pointed out on the screen that these were the labia and that was the clitoris? I have only one word: *Georgia*.

A lot of newborn girls look like their fathers, and she certainly did. In spades. Luckily, Thom is a very pretty man, and she got his dark brown curls and piercing hazel eyes. She's more like me on the inside, with her keen sense of fairness and inability to lie when it's important to do so. Unfortunately, she's also got my inwardness and can be painfully taciturn, particularly around strangers. I've worked hard to overcome my introversion, but it is difficult for me to have to relive the old days through her. She's a lightning rod for other people's emotions, a deeply sensitive child with nerve endings that jut straight out of her skin, or so it seems. Yes, she may be manipulative, and she may be shrewd, but I hope she learns earlier and better than I did how she can use these attributes as protection from those who will hurt her.

My defense was a good offense, not letting anyone in, steeling myself against heartbreak after feeling the pain so keenly so many times. I became an island of one, deserted by my need for affection. It was easy: Heath was always away, shooting a sitcom pilot in Vancouver or doing a tour of a Broadway musical. I rejected attention, made plans only to cancel them, staying home with a bowl of cereal and a baseball game instead. I knew all the stats of all the Yankees three summers in a row. Eventually I began to suffer migraine headaches and a vertiginous out-of-body feeling that was eventually diagnosed as "dissociation." After first seeing my GP, then a headache specialist, a neurosurgeon, and countless healthcare professionals, I took Portia's suggestion that I go to her therapist. I went to session after session insisting that everything in my life was perfect, until one day he simply asked me, "Why are you so unhappy?" and all those years of tears came pouring forth, all those missed opportunities to feel, to be felt. Not long after that I met Thom, and his direct approach to love was such a shock that I finally knew what I had been missing. I worry that his leaving now will cause me to close down again. It does occur to me that he's taking the Singapore gig to give me some time to figure myself out, but is that really what I need most right now?

Fifteen

I WANT ELLA AND EMMA and Amelia and Amy and Emma—"

"Sweetie, you already said Emma."

"Emma Shapiro, not Emma Jones."

"Oh, sorry. Go on."

"And Donovan and Matinka, and Brendan and Clarissa."

"What about Chloë?"

"Between you and me?" Leans in, whispers. "Too stuck-up."

"Well, I can't argue with you there, but I thought she was your bestest friend."

"*Best* friend, J. She was last week."

"And who's it this week?"

"Matinka. Can we got a Chez Emilie cake?"

"What's wrong with Cupcake Café?"

"Too nineties."

"G, you weren't even born in the nineties."

"Yes I was. 1998."

"It's a figure of speech."

"I really really want a Chez Emilie cake. Puleeze?"

"How 'bout I make you a cake?"

Eye roll.

"Come on, you used to love my cakes."

"That was when I was *little*. *Please* don't humidify me."

"Humiliate. When did you turn fourteen?"

"I'm almost five, I need to dood it right."

"Okay, okay, don't cry."

"I'm not *crying*, I'm *stressed out*."

"The party's not for a few months—why don't we get ready to go to Penny's for Halloween?"

"We need to order the shirts."

"What shirts?"

"For the soccer game." Stupid.

"Okay, I'll bite, what soccer game?"

"The one at the *party*."

"You don't play soccer."

"But it's a soccer party."

"Since when?"

"Half pink shirts and half purple."

"Pink, purple, got it."

"The pinks write on them Georgia, and the purples Aigroeg."

"A what?"

"A-I-G-R-O-E-G."

"What's an aigroeg?"

Eye roll, arms crossed.

"Well?"

"My name *backwards*."

"How clever. Really."

"And no babies."

"We can do that."

"I mean it. Don't change my mine."

"Why would I do that?"

"Because you *like* the baby."

"So do you."

"And he has a *penis*."

"So you say."

"And he's a *baby*."

"You got me there."

"Okay, okay, he can come."

"Not if you don't want him."

"Okay, *okay*."

"Don't invite him on my behalf."

Eye roll, hug.

Sixteen

WHEN I WAS A CHILD, having a birthday party was pretty much unheard of. At least in my house. Most years, Cheryl would bake my favorite cake (angel food, icebox frosting), we'd put some candles on it, I'd open some presents, and voilà, another year's passing marked. And I felt special. Now I end up spending a large portion of my time either planning a party, shopping for another kid's party, or writing thank-yous for parties and playdates. Yes, that's right, a thank-you note for hosting me and my child for an hour. Some of the mothers go a step further and send me thank-you wine, or thank-you flatware. This in the form of a Tiffany silver spoon with a note: "Maybe this will help you get Max to open his mouth!"

It wouldn't be so bad if I were able to draw any vicarious pleasure out of these parties, but because they stress out my child, they stress me out too. These are the days when I seriously consider moving out of the city and going off the grid. Although quite recently, when the grid went off the grid, the blackout put an official end to nursing, as both my pump and my baby decided not to suck anymore. Twenty-four hours of sweating by candlelight, not flushing the toilets, engorged breasts, and cold pizza. Were we any happier, really?

I never thought of myself as idealistic or crunchy until I got pregnant with Georgia, and suddenly there seemed to be carcinogens hiding in every deed. Shoulds and shouldn'ts were everywhere, and I had nowhere to turn. Vaccinations cause autism, diapers choke landfills, child-care centers are run by child molesters. Sleep with your child, don't sleep with your child, keep her squeaky clean, dirt wards off asthma. If you don't put your child in day care, he won't be socialized. If you do, he will be aggressive. Revive Ophelia, raise Cain, don't father a bully, don't mother a Heather. Give your children time-outs, listen to their needs.

Last week Georgia's teacher called, saying she was worried about G. She seemed sad, was there anything I wanted to talk about? Yeah, I'd like to talk about how teachers used to spend more time engaging children and less time calling parents. Don't call me because she's sad, I wanted to say, call me because she has a fever, or a boo-boo. From a very early age Georgia has been able to pull a long face, sigh, and say, "I'm sad, Mommy." Whether it was a ploy to crawl into bed with us, get me to read her a story, or simply to get another cookie, this hot-button phrase worked wonders. At first it broke my heart, but very quickly I learned that the little shit was using me. Miss Cartwright (yeah, all those years of work getting people to call us *Ms.* and some schools still won't do it) hasn't been burned yet. Soon. If I know my daughter, very soon.

God knows, I have tried to figure out the secrets of child rearing. I kept the kids off refined sugar until the issue went out of my immediate control, and even still Georgia would give her left arm for a pastry. We don't watch TV, though now it is one of my guilty pleasures to pop in a DVD and buy with it an hour of peace. And yes, Max and I occasionally watch shows about the seventies. It's good for him. He needs to know about Lite-Brite, bell bottoms, *The Dating Game*. My nostalgia for my childhood helps me take it easy on my children. I was raised by wolves. They gave me meat at two weeks. Watered down in formula, but meat nonetheless. I watched far more television than anyone I know, and I watched it close. I ate sugared cereal right out of the box and slept in my clothes. Meanwhile, I haven't had as much as a head cold since I quit smoking to have Georgia. I'm told my mother smoked a pack a day when she was pregnant with me and that when her doctor recommended she switch to "new" low-tar cigarettes, she increased to two packs. I weighed in at ten pounds. When the surgeon general reported soon after that smoking lowers birth weight, she said to my father, "Thank God I didn't quit."

I always wanted a birthday party, I just didn't think it would take me almost forty years to admit it. I don't want one now, though—I want to go back to being five and have one with all my friends from kindergarten and get a nicely wrapped box of new underpants with the days of the week embroidered right on them by Joanie's mom. And a Scarlett O'Hara birthday cake, her hooped-out skirt frosted in lavender, a ribbon-tied bonnet on her doll head. We'd play pin-the-tail-on-the-donkey and drink punch from little glass cups. Best of all, I'd wear the kind of lacy dress other girls wore at their parties, with the satin ribbon at the waist, and buckle shoes. All my friends would be there: Patty, Joanie, Holly, Candy, Julie, Dorothy, Missy, Barbie, Jackie. No Emmas or Cassandras or Chloës, just simple little girls with pretty little names having fun.

But if I give Georgia a plain party, she will be treated as a plain girl and may think herself one for the rest of her life. I worry nightly how to manage her expectations as I reevaluate my own. I want to be the mommy other mommies envy, the one other kids wish were theirs. But at what price? Literally. I would stick to my guns, bake Georgia a cake, have paper party hats and balloons filled with my own breath, but I can't risk her being humiliated, can't risk her hating me for humiliating her. So I'll be the kind of mommy she thinks I should be for that one day, even if it means hating myself in the process.

Seventeen

THOM'S SISTER IS HAVING her fifth baby in six years. Honor, Chastity, Pryde, and Prudence. Felicity is no doubt on the way. A veritable virgin suicides in the making. The four girls so far are simply stunning, and though I relish Georgia's chestnut spirals, these blondies will one day cheer my daughter's Goth ass into a corner. Thom's sister, meanwhile, is the kind of radiant at eight months pregnant that only the very rich can achieve. I've read somewhere that pregnant women have started taking diet pills to keep from gaining too much weight. I'm not saying Theta is one of them, I'm just saying.

As this shower, like the others, is to take place at Vera's club, I know the level of care I have to give my appearance, and frankly, I just don't have it in me. I went shopping yesterday, but after about ten minutes in the dressing room at Eileen Fisher I started to melt down. Max did what he could to help, clapping hands at the sight of my naked thighs, but I fear it was his fondness for cottage cheese and not an Oedipal reaction. I mean, if I can't look good in clothes that make fat women svelte, then what's left for me? As luck would have it, the rain was pouring down when I left the store, and there were no taxis to be had. Max was happy as a boy in a bubble in his plastic-draped stroller, but I had left my umbrella at home and was not looking forward to a good soaking. So I went around the corner to wait out the storm at City Bakery. Though my pretzel croissant—a sinful, unholy marriage of baked goods—dunked in rich hot chocolate no doubt contributed to my ungainly form, at the time it seemed the only balm for a bruising day.

After trying on every stitch of clothing in my closet over size 10 this morning, I opt for a simple black-tunic-with-black-pants look. When I finally emerge from the bedroom, Thom is up to his elbows in children, making the most of his last weekend at home. I have to say this for my husband: he may not be here all the time, but when he is, he rarely complains about the kids—he just plunges right in and takes over entirely. I also have to say this: he has no control over what comes out of his mouth.

"Hey, babe, you look great. Are you going to wear that to the shower?" I go up on my toes at this.

"Um. Yes. Is there something wrong with it?" He has barely looked up from Max and Georgia. Maybe he didn't get a good look.

"Well, no, there's nothing wrong with it, you look great. But isn't this a shower? At the club?" I see stars.

"Yeah. So?"

"It's just that you know how these things are, and I want you to be comfortable." Georgia, who has developed the mommy sonar of a nuclear submarine, lures Max under the coffee table.

"I am comfortable."

"Okay, then never mind. You look great."

"No, I want to know what you mean. You don't think I look great enough for your mother's club, do you?" Old arguments die hard.

"Sweetie, I mean it, you look really great. It's just that you know how those women are, and I don't want you to feel bad if you're not as well dressed as they are. What about that red suit you have?"

"What red suit?"

"You know, the one you look really good in?"

"Oh, the one that's a size six and I haven't worn since before Georgie? Great idea. I'll go see if I can find it."

I internalize my rage, frustration, and self-loathing and slip quietly back into the bedroom, where I proceed to sob for twenty minutes, the first ten in the bathroom, eyes red-rimmed, as I blow out my hair into Waspy-straight perfection. Damn him and damn his sister and their damn mother. I approach the bed, where I am met by a two-foot pile of already discarded clothing, clearly not enough cotton, silk, and wool to absorb the deluge. In the end I pull on a New You minimizing panty—what Cheryl would call, quite simply, a girdle—and like the good little sausage-in-law that I am, get myself into a size 10 black skirt with elastic waist, a black silk blouse, and the jacket from the red suit, decidedly unbuttoned. If *comfortable* means not being able to sit, breathe, or swallow, then I am now completely at ease. I use the standard club formula and apply twice the makeup I usually would and choose the most gaudily tasteful earrings from Vera that I can find. When I reemerge from the bedroom, Georgia gasps.

"Mommy, is that you?" She tries to hide her fear, but I see her take a step back. Max starts to cry.

"Wow, Jen, you look *amazing*." Thom clearly has no recourse but to support his choice in my clothing. Or maybe he really means it. Either way, I have officially ceased to care.

"Great, I'm glad you think so." A button pops off the blouse and flies across the room. I crumple onto the ottoman, face in hands. Okay, so maybe I still care a tiny bit. "I can't go. Call and tell her."

"You're beautiful, I'm sorry I made you feel bad." Thom kneels in front of me and the kids join him, hugging my legs. "Why don't you go change and I'll get the kids together and we'll drive you up there and wait outside for it to be over?" My knight, his shining armor.

I walk into the club and see Vera—a not-much-younger version of Barbara Walters—waiting at the door to the restaurant, along with Theta's mother-in-law, who could be Vera's clone. There is no getting around them, no back way in. Chin up, I decide to not let anything get to me. Not let anything get to me. Not let anything get to—

"Jennifer! And just in time. Don't you look lovely! I always say you look better with a little color around your face. I don't think I've seen that jacket since Theta's wedding. You remember Mrs. Stebbins, of course?" How could I forget her? At the shower for Pryde I was seated at her table—the women-over-five-foot-nine table—and she spent both courses talking to the woman on her left, a professional basketball player who had grown up with Theta.

"Yes, of course, Mrs. Snubbins, how good to see you." I truly can't help myself sometimes.

"Excuse me, dear?" Vera pinches my arm.

"Sorry, Altoid caught in my throat. So good to see you both." I scan the room, but there isn't a soul to save me.

"I was just telling Mrs. Stebbins about you taking Max to swim class, dear. Caroline, can you believe anyone would try to teach a little defenseless baby to swim? Well, I went right out and bought that child a life vest, but you know, Jennifer has her own ideas, and I do not like to interfere. At least it will not be on my head if anything happens to that sweet boy."

"Why don't we catch up later, I really should go find my table." Either that, or I turn around and find the nearest pawn-shop to trade in my earrings for a Colt .45.

"Why don't I take you there myself?" There is no escaping Vera, so I buckle up for round 2. "Please try not to embarrass me today," she whispers, though it comes out as more of a growl, a gritted smile pasted to her face. "I have spent too much time planning this party for you to fuck it up."

I know what you're thinking. But Vera really isn't a cliché. She's a bitch of the first order. A dry drunk, she found God about ten years ago but misplaces him when it's convenient. And it wasn't an Altoid stuck in my throat; it was a much smaller pill with a curiously strong sedating power.

"I'll make you a deal," I whisper back. "You stop telling people that I'm out to kill my son, and I'll behave like the daughter-in-law you wish you had."

"I'll bet you fifty bucks you can't keep your mouth shut." She also has a gambling habit, one that none of the women in this room knows about. As we approach a table of Heathers, I sud-denly see what she has planned. I recognize one of them as Thom's high school sweetheart, and the other two look familiar from other showers and Theta's wedding, but since Vera likes to keep things interesting, she always makes a theme-seating, and I've never come in contact with any of them.

"Make it a hundred." I know where she lives.

"You're on." We stop at the empty seat. "Ladies, I'd like you to meet Thom's wife." There are three of them, and they look hungry. They are dressed in a medley of autumnal colors: rust, ochre, chocolate brown. I look like a cardinal that forgot to fly south. I really should have taken Thom's advice and changed one last time, instead of sewing the button back on my shirt in the car.

"Jennifer. My name is Jennifer, and I couldn't be happier to meet you." This is not going to be the easiest C-note I've ever earned.

"Hi, I'm Treena. Thom and I dated in college." The blondest one puts out her hand in one of those begging-dog handshakes. It's limp and slightly moist, and the fingers taper into my grasp as I try to avoid a damp Kleenex buried in her palm. "Sorry about the cold, my babies have been sick all week, passing it around." I wipe my hand on Vera's sleeve in what looks like a pat of affection.

"And this is Clara. She and Thom were sweethearts in high school, even though she was *much* younger." She turns me to face my nemesis. "Is she not perfection? She graduated top of her class at Barnard—maybe you know each other from school? Oh no, that's not possible, you two are at least ten years apart . . . and you went to that night school at Columbia—what was it called again?"

"The School of General Studies."

"How very quaint." I have the sense that Vera would pat me on the head if she could reach that high.

"Hi, Jen, I've heard such interesting things about you." She *is* perfection. A rope of flaxen hair brushes against her waist and I am struck by Thom's recent campaign to get me to grow my hair long again—what he refers to as "boyfriend hair."

"And I'm Peggy, Theta's roommate from Princeton." Though I probably shouldn't, I take an instant liking to Peggy, her broad face and clear blue eyes beaming into me her knowledge of how I must suffer at Vera's hands. She's got a butterball in the oven herself and is incandescent in a bloated, big-faced way. She wrests my arm away from Vera and draws me into the chair next to hers. "Thanks, Mrs. Bradley, we'll take good care of her."

"So did you date Thom too?" I ask Peggy as I line up my knife and forks, trying to figure out the theme of the table.

"Yeah, but only once. No offense." Ah yes, the more successful exes table. Charming.

"That's okay," I tell her. "He's much more offensive these days."

Vera likes to seat tables of four at the club, to keep the conversation flowing, and also to make it easier to transition to a rollicking round of bridge for money later in the afternoon. I was raised playing pinochle, so I tend to leave before the real fun begins. But just in case I get drunk enough to stay, Thom's given me a roll of cash to go crazy with. Only one hour to go, if I know my mother-in-law's inner game clock. I decide to have a glass of wine to help pass the time with Thom's assorted exes.

"So, Jen, do you live in Westchester?" Clara's heart-shaped face is doll-like, but I detect a hint of the dark circles she's tried carefully to conceal.

"Nope, the city. Chelsea. And you?" Not that I care, but I do hope that it's another state.

"We just moved out of Boston to the suburbs. Now that I've

got another one on the way . . ." She shrugs and points wistfully at her flat stomach. "Well, I made partner last year, but the firm wants me to take over the domestic part of the practice—you know, family law—and I'm going to have to tell them no. I love criminal defense too much to go over to kindergarten court. It's okay, though: I feel like now is my time to give my all to *my* kids. Jack and Marcy are just three, so I'll have plenty of family law at home!"

"Hey, it's not as bad as it looks," Treena snuffles. "I've already got three and we're working on the fourth. The great thing about stepping out of the career track is that it gives you the opportunity to have more kids and really devote yourself full-time." Her meticulously ironed suit is a bit shiny at the elbows. I realize it's most likely a holdover from when she did whatever it was that she stepped out of.

"I don't know how you guys do it," Peggy says. "This is my first, and I'm really torn about leaving work." It's a regular breeding ground here. I cross my legs. "Fact is, I don't think I'd miss producing commercials. I've done it better than anyone and killed myself to get to my level. If I do decide to step out for a few years, I've got the kind of résumé that will throw open doors. Right?" She wants to believe all of this, but her eyes are a bit misty, and I wonder whether she has taken a beta-blocker to get through the afternoon.

"Oh yeah," I say, "I'm sure Christie's is holding my job five years later." Christy, my old boss, told me she'd welcome me back, but I haven't exactly kept up on the current trends in art and antiquities—apart from following Thom's career, that is.

"What did you do there?" Clara asks.

"I was an antiquities appraiser, mostly," I say. It's always hard to explain exactly what you do and make it interesting at the same time, especially when you haven't done it in almost five years.

"My grandmother has this amazing china teapot that's been in the family since the Civil War," Treena says. "Maybe you could take a look at it for me and tell me how much it's worth?"

"Or better yet, you could take it to *Antiques Roadshow*," I reply. This is another reason I never talk about my work—people just don't get it. "They're more experienced in Americana. My specialty was, as I said, antiquities—you know, ancient stuff. But I'm not doing that now either. So . . ." I emit a strangled laugh, and the table goes quiet. I take a deep breath, and no one else knows how to fill the gap left by my inability to help Treena with her teapot.

We remove the napkins in front of us and see that Vera has been kind enough to have pictures of our kids printed onto our chargers. Clara and I have two, Treena three, and Peggy has a cartoon of a stork. As a way of covering over our silent regrets, we pass our plates around to each other and introduce our pancake babies. Vera has done me the favor of picking a simply gorgeous shot of Georgia, one Vera had taken by Richard Avedon when G turned four (me: "You took her *where?*"). The photo of Max is recent; he's wearing the bike helmet Vera brought down to me when she heard he had stood for the first time (Vera: "I just know he's going to crack his head open on that concrete floor you insist on having in your *loft*"). The stork is rather handsome compared to Clara's kids. She really should have stuck with Thom; I can only hope she married money along with that nose. Treena's kids are rugged in an entirely anemic way. The girl is a sweet kind of beautiful, but the boys will need some eyebrow-waxing tips and soon.

"So, Peggy, you *are* going to breast-feed?" Clara has a mean streak, I just knew it. It mystifies me why people think this is an appropriate thing to ask a pregnant woman, though I'm pretty sure I can predict Peggy's response.

"Well, yes, of course. Unless it doesn't work. Or I don't like it. Which I'm sure I will. Like it. Won't I?" Yep, the first-timer's waffle.

"You must breast-feed!" Treena says. "How could you deny your baby the most natural, nurturing thing you have to give?" I didn't expect Treena to be La Leche, but then she did say she's really thrown herself into this.

"I loved breast-feeding!" Clara chimes in. "I'm so glad I'll be home full-time with this one so I don't have to deny her myself whenever she wants me. You'll like it, you'll see. Don't give up if it hurts, I promise it's just so wonderful to look down and see your child getting nourishment from you and you alone."

"Um, yeah, I want that, I really do. I've heard it's very power-ful," Peggy says, clearly trying to make the boob Nazis happy. "Jennifer, how long did you breast-feed?" I'm feeling guilty about having scoffed at Peggy's desire to step back into the track and am smarting a bit at my own inability to do so, so I decide to make amends by saving her from this line of questioning.

"Let's see, two weeks with the first and a year with the sec-ond." I'm lying, of course, but I feel the need to teach someone a lesson.

"Why only two weeks, if you don't mind my asking?" Treena says, reaching into her pocketbook for either another Kleenex or an *Adverse Effects of Formula on Babies* brochure.

"Mind? Why would I mind?" Do I really need a hundred dol-lars so badly? "I couldn't get the hang of it. I'd had a C-section, so my milk didn't come right in. Georgia was an enormous starving baby, I was exhausted, my one nipple was inverted and the other oozed a green-colored liquid. After two weeks of trying, we both developed an excruciating case of thrush, and I just threw in the towel. I knew when I'd been beaten." Peggy sits back in her chair, knowing the heat is off her for good.

"Wow, that's an amazing story," Clara says. "But you know, with the right help, you could have succeeded. Are you Jewish?"

"I'm sorry?"

"Are you Jewish? I've heard that Jewish women don't like to breast-feed. I mean, it's okay if you didn't like it, not everyone has what it takes to stick with it through the first learning curve."

In the name of all things decent and pro-Semitic, I've decided not to answer Clara's question. However, in the name of all things you-don't-know-what-you're-talking-about-you-sanctimonious-bitch, I decide to finish spinning my tale.

"Yes, well, then I had Max, and even though I had another C, the little fucker just latched right on and wouldn't let go. But just so you know, Peggy"—I turn to her and lean in a little—"it hurt like hell for weeks, and my nipples cracked no matter how much lanolin I applied, and I will swear to you as I sit here that Max will never be as smart as Georgia. It's just not going to happen. So if you decide for whatever reason to formula feed, then god bless."

"You know what I miss?" Treena knows when she's beat and changes the subject. "I really miss my breasts." Well, almost changes the subject.

"Me too," Clara says, stroking her chest. "They used to be so perky. I never needed a bra. Now I have to do a nipple check before I leave the house, just to make sure they're pointed in the same direction."

"Right? I mean, mine used to be up here." Treena lifts her okay-looking breasts improbably high up her chest. "Now, if I don't wear a bra, they look like used condoms."

I refuse to talk about my breasts in public, much less handle them. There is something about a woman who has nursed that makes her lose all sense of how inappropriate this behavior is. Peggy has gone very white, and I quietly reach under the table to pat her hand. Seems I'll have to break my own rules.

"Don't worry, Peg, I've barely noticed a change, and Thom says I have the best breasts he's ever met—can't keep his hands off them." I shoot Clara a look, daring her to reveal some sordid second-basing under the bleachers. "In fact, I have some make-up-sex obligations to fulfill, so if you'll all excuse me, I've got to go home and fuck my husband."

I pick up my plate and on my way to the door drop a Ben Franklin on Vera without breaking stride.

Eighteen

WHEN I WAS A JUNIOR in high school and an ugly duck-
ling, Todd Peterson asked me to the prom. He was
scrawny, shorter, and the opposite of the type of guy I wanted to
ask me. I told him I already had a date. Near as I can figure, that's
when the love curse began. I didn't have a date, or a dress, or the
money to buy either, but figured I'd better come up with something fast or risk being the liar I was. Through my church I knew
an older boy in another town who had always been nice to me at
Bible camp, and so I wrote him a letter, asking him to take me to
my prom. He accepted. Cheryl bought me a dress—an indescrib-
ably ugly flouncy thing that was modest and gray—and I bor-
rowed a pair of shoes from Judy that were a full size too big. All
this to avoid the humiliation of going with a nerd. I was Samantha Baker a good two years before Molly Ringwald was Samantha
Baker. Only I didn't get the fairytale ending.

My date showed up in a rusty old pickup truck that had seats
upholstered in dog hair. I hadn't seen him in a few years and was
surprised to find he'd grown to well over six feet, his acne had
worsened, and he had lost a good deal of his hair, even though he

was only nineteen. His suit was, coincidentally, gray—but woven of a very large, shocking wool plaid that on his lanky frame looked like it had just walked out of Hicksville General Store. No other way of putting it—he was the beast. Not that I was any great beauty, but I did rank myself a tiny bit higher on the unhomely scale. He was nice enough, sure, but nice like Jesus, not nice like Rex Smith. When we got to the prom, Todd was alone in a corner. It might have been my imagination, but I swear he watched me all night. As soon as the prom was over, I asked my date to take me home—yes, I've had a splendid evening, but no, I don't want to go to any after-prom parties, I'm too tired, my head hurts. He dropped me off; I changed clothes and went out partying by myself.

For the next five years I had maybe ten dates, all disasters. Even after I moved to Manhattan, men didn't seem to find me interesting. The clubs provided a great refuge, and the kids who were misfits and nerds ruled the night. I knew better than to sleep with any of them, though. AIDS hit hard and it hit fast, wiping out many of my gay and bisexual friends. Wiping out all of them, actually. It was around that time that Cheryl had Andy ask me if I was gay. I told him to report back that I wasn't gay, I was a fag hag, and to please try to explain the difference.

At my five-year high school reunion I sought Todd out. He hadn't changed, and apart from my yellow hair, I guess neither had I. He was already married and had two kids—his wife was a large, glossy, truck-driving brand of pretty. I told him the truth about the prom. He told me he'd only asked me on a dare and had been relieved when I'd said no.

That summer the curse lifted and I met the real Rex Smith at a bar—don't ask. We went out on a couple of dates, but when I found out from his best friend that Rex was engaged to his pregnant girlfriend, I stopped fooling around and started dating the friend—otherwise known as Heath Monroe. I didn't think a name could get any cheesier than Rex, but clearly I was wrong. Heath actually told me that his first agent was a fan of Brontë and felt "Heath" would have a better chance than "Keith" of getting a part on the vampire soap opera *Dark Shadows*. It worked, and the name stuck.

I had slept with exactly four men by the time I met Thom. That should surprise you. It surprises me; these were the go-go eighties and safe-sex nineties, after all. Call me old-fashioned, but I fell in love with every man who slept with me, and only two of them returned the favor. It's a short list, but oh so sweet: the Chippendale's dancer who broke my heart, the Psychedelic Furs backup guitarist who stole it and took it back to England with him, the nice Jewish doctor who tried to heal me, the adult child actor, and my one true love.

Nineteen

IT'S BEEN TWO WEEKS since Halloween, and Max refuses to go anywhere out of costume. It may have something to do with Thom's departure, but I doubt it—Max is simply one of a kind. His delicious little Dalmatian suit is so dirty that he looks like a grungy black Lab. The mechanism in the snout/hood that once barked when squeezed now emits a hiccup that so scares Max I've had to remove its battery. The good news is that Max has taken to walking. The bad news is he's also taken to falling. He prefers to fall backward, and though we've lined almost the entire apartment with rugs, he seems to have a magnet in his skull that seeks the hardest, barest bits of flooring. We had a wrestling match this morning, and he threw his head back against my lip and split it wide open. It's amazing how my first instinct was to throw him across the room. Luckily, my second instinct followed quickly and did not involve babycide. In any case, it made me less worried about his head and more concerned for the floor.

We picked Georgia up from school and took the subway down to Madison Park. G has decided that "the baby" is entirely insufferable now that he is a puppy, and ignores him completely. She is acting out over Daddy going away, reverting to some of her more anxious behavior—lisping around strangers, clutching my hand whenever we go out. Max is sound asleep in his stroller, so we decide to walk around the paths to prolong his nap before we meet Sven and Lily at the dog run.

"Mommy, why do people have other gods than us?" I look at my watch, which is practically attached to Georgia, as she's clutching my hand with both of hers. Damn. Fifteen minutes to kill. Not enough to launch into a proper discussion of religion. Too much to distract Georgia onto another topic. Like any good mother, I choose to throw it back onto her.

"What do you mean, sweetie?" I wonder when she'll catch on that "sweetie" really means "pain in the ass."

"Well, some people have differnt gods than us. Gods like, um, Ally and Yowie." Ally? Yowie? This is new to me. Maybe she's not asking about religion after all. Wait a minute. Allah. Yaweh. Aha. I stop at the fountain and kneel down in front of her, saving my shoulder from being dislocated from her weight hanging off me.

"Okay, kiddo. Here goes. There are many different religions in the world that people believe in. 'Our' god, as you put it, would have to be considered the Christian god, though we are not practicing Christians."

"Why not?" Why not. Let's see. How to make this sound as simple as it is complicated.

"Because Mommy and Daddy don't believe in God. Per se."

"But Granna says that God is love." I thought I smelled a well-coiffed rat. Vera took Georgia to Serendipity for hot chocolate the other day, to "help me out." I should have seen this coming.

"Too true. Too true." I hug her closer to me. "What else does Granna say?"

"That other people's gods are smaller. That Ally is darker and Yowie don't eat pigs." Though Georgia may sound ridiculous, my guess is she's got it pretty much the way Vera's telling it. Now for the damage control.

"Huh, okay. Ally, or, better, Allah, is the Muslim word for God. And Muslims simply have a different approach to God, as do the Jews, who call God Yaweh. The main difference is Jesus. Christians believe that Jesus is the Son of God, the Messiah, but Muslims and Jews are still waiting for their Messiah. There are many different types of Christians too, Boo, but we're going to be late for our date if we don't get moving. Can we talk about this later, gator?"

"How many?" She doesn't budge.

"How many what?" I stand and start rolling Max, who stretches and yawns.

"How many Christians?" She's still by the fountain, looking up at me with don't-take-another-step-or-I'll-scream eyes.

"How many Christians what?" Probably not the answer she's looking for.

"How many Christians are there?" She starts to shiver. "More than Muslins and Jews?"

"I haven't counted them all recently." Much to my surprise and horror, she starts to sputter. A woman passes pushing a Bugaboo stroller, takes in Georgia, dog-Max, and me, and throws me a "You should be ashamed of yourself" look at me.

I wheel Max back to the fountain and lift Georgia up. "What's the matter, baby?"

"Granna said we're not going to heaven with her and Granda if we aren't Christians." Seven ways to Sunday, this woman finds a way to kill me and send me burning to hell through my kids.

"We are christians, baby," I comfort her, rub her back. The small *c* is for my comfort. "But we can be other things too, if we decide it makes more sense. As long as you're kind to other people, you can believe in any faith you want. Wanna go see the dogs?"

She nods her head once, a look of sheer relief on her face that can only be mirroring my own.

Lily and Sven are already in doggie heaven when we round the corner. They have rescued a five-pound Pomeranian and renamed her Suky. This is her inaugural trip to the dog run, though we've been coming for years. Both Georgia and Max have an outsize love of all things dog and would have one by now if it weren't for my deep fear of having to explain death to them. We got Peeve before the kids, and with any luck she'll live forever. You've seen how smooth I am with the big issues. Georgia scrambles out of my arms and runs over to our friends, who are all three dressed in matching peacoats.

"Swenja!" Georgia screams as she's twirled into the air.

"Peaches!" he screams back, mimicking her voice perfectly. Max struggles against his shoulder straps as I push him the last few feet to his beloved. Suky starts barking like a hellcat, no doubt thinking that Max really is a dog. Sven winces at me and mouths, "Nice lip." I point at my son.

"Hello, ladies," I address my adopted brood. "How's tricks? Or should I say ticks?"

"Jenfur." Georgia lets out a little groan and rolls her eyes. Seems she doesn't want to be humidified in front of her secret gay boyfriend. She has a point. "Hey, Swen, can I aks you a question?"

"Depends. How personal?" He sits her on a bench, then kneels down and leans forward to meet her eye.

"Are you a Jew?" Silly me, I thought we'd finished Religion 101.

"G," I say, "that's really not how we ask people . . . Um, what I mean is, we don't really ask people . . . Help?" I look at Sven, who hasn't yet taken his bemused eyes off Georgia.

"Yes. I'm a Jew."

"Me too. I haven't met my own personal Jesus yet." She's a quicker study than I thought.

"Me either." This seems to finally satisfy Georgia, and she wanders a couple of feet away to look at the bigger dogs, while we set Suky free in the miniature-dog run. They don't let kids in the dog runs, but since Suky is the only small dog right now, we bend a rule and let Lily and Max run around with her. Penny was right about Max: once he got his feet under him, he went right to running. He looks completely ridiculous in his dog suit, yet somehow he carries it off. Maybe he is gay after all.

"So, how'd it go yesterday?" Sven asks me.

"Well, it could have been worse. Georgia dragged around for hours after he left, but Max doesn't know the difference—he's so used to Thom coming and going that he probably won't realize something's up for at least a week. But it's only a matter of time before they start blaming me. I've started a therapy fund to go alongside their college savings. Just in case."

"Good idea, wish my folks had thought of that. Not to change the subject to me, but I have great news," Sven says, leaning on the fence next to me.

"G, come here, baby, and stand inside with us." It's a good park, a safe park, in fact, I call it "Maclaren Park" for the trendy stroller of choice of its patrons. Still, it only takes a second, a "She was only a heartbeat away." I offhandedly memorize what Georgia is wearing. "What kind of news? Animal, vegetable, or mineral?"

"None of the above. I'm going back to work."

"Wow."

"Yeah."

"Wow. What about Lily?" What about Jennifer?

"That's the best part. I've been approached to be a commentator for next summer's Olympics, the swimming and diving, and all the qualifying meets before then. It's a hectic schedule, but I get to take Lily with me when I'm on the road, and when I'm here, it's only a couple of days a week in the studio for editing and redubbing and putting together color commentary on the athletes, so we'll only need to hire a part-time sitter." He wants me to be happy for him, I know he does. I try. But, damn it, they can't all get their lives together and leave me here with the children and the dogs. Even the gay ones are breaking my heart. They can't keep forcing me to look at my own choices in their absence and make me admit I've fucked up my life.

"Wow. That's great. Really."

I beat back a couple of tears. I haven't fucked up anyone, not me, not Georgia, not even Max, regardless of how it may occasionally look to passersby.

"Aw, Jen, don't be upset. We'll still have playdates. I want you to be happy for me. This stay-at-home stuff is okay, but I'm losing my mind. And it's a lot of money, not to mention a chance at something bigger." He puts his arm around me, and through the blur of tears I see Lily riding Max like a horse—a dirty Dalmatian horse—and I try to laugh in spite of myself. He's losing his mind? He's only been at it three months. Just think what kind of coleslaw I've been making with my cabbage.

"Okay, I'm happy. See, happy." I doubt that he believes me, and I don't care. A chance at something bigger? What could possibly be bigger than shaping the mind of a child? Jawing on about someone's diving form? Cataloging rare antiques? Opening a field office in Singapore? I go completely silent, and Sven respects my mood.

Twenty

Let me come right out and say it: I'm not happy. But I don't know whether this is a new "I don't like staying at home with kids" kind of not happy or the same old "I don't like being a creature of this planet" kind of not happy. Depression runs in my family—not deep but sort of *surface* depression. For my father, it is routinely dismissed by Pabst Blue Ribbon. For my brother, the occasional puke-your-brains-out variety of flu masks a deeper woe. For me it changes with the seasons, and as we're soon to cross the winter solstice, I have to consider that my relative unhappiness is light-affected. I need a vacation. I'm asking for a spa trip for Christmas, which reminds me: I'm sick to death of asking for things from Thom. Sure, I have the house budget to run everyday things, but if I want to do anything other than buy cat food or diapers, I feel compelled to ask.

Here's the rub: Thom and I never discussed what would happen if I didn't go back to work. My salary simply disappeared, and with it my Barneys card. Even when I was living with the adult child actor I held my own accounts. Cheryl, having been robbed blind by her gay ex-husband, always told me to keep my

money my own, but I thought throwing in our lot was more romantic. It never occurred to me that once I stopped throwing
anything in I'd feel this bankrupt.

I don't blame Thom for this, and unlike some of my more
complicated friends, I do not withhold sex as revenge. On the
contrary, I dole it out to get what I want. And what I want is a little peace and quiet. I had somehow erased the hell Georgia's
teething was, and now that Max is chewing up the furniture like a
rabid puppy, waking every couple of hours at night for a chilled
chew toy, a dose of Tylenol, or simply to be held, I honestly think
I'm going to lose my mind. He's also managed to contract lice
from God knows where. He's added two new words to his reper-
toire: *bug* and *ouch*. His pain slices me in two even as I wish to hell
he'd shut up about it. I think it's the worst around four in the
morning. I sit here in the rocking chair, singing lullabies to his
low whine, searching his scalp with my fingers, while outside the
window I can hear clubland emptying out and streaming past my
door. I don't miss that life, but I do miss the girl in me who could
stay up all night, then sleep past noon. I miss going to the movies,
strolling through Central Park by myself, indulging in a two-
hour workout, sweating vodka out of my pores.

I cannot remember the last time I was completely alone.

I'm also deeply envious of Sven's news. I feel betrayed, like
he's dipped his toe in the rusty waters of stay-at-home and decided he'd rather remain on dry ground. Discarded me and Max,
just when we need him the most. Thom's going to miss Thanksgiving but be back for Christmas Day. We try to talk every night,
but there's really not that much for either of us to say. Maybe he
already has another family in Asia. A beautiful, well-kept wife
who folds napkins into cranes for their dinner table. A spotless

little girl with ebony braids and a toddler who likes his women Caucasian. It's been known to happen. In fact, it happened in *Coffee, Tea, or Me*. Karen Valentine had a husband in L.A. and one in London. Of course, being characters in a TV movie, they found out about each other, but until they did, everyone was really very happy.

There's that damn word again. Okay, I have healthy living parents, a man who loves me, two beautiful and perfect children, good friends, a roof over my head, food on my table, all the clichés are in place for me to be happy, happy, happy. Could I have affluenza? Could it be that I'm overserved in the luck category, that I have way more than my share and now have nothing left to want? Should I call Dr. Kreigsman and restart my therapy? But then I'd have to ask Thom for the money, and Dr. Kreigsman always said that if I'm not paying for my therapy, then I'm not owning my issues. Fuck him.

Okay, gloves off, I'm bitterly mad at Thom. Not for leaving me home alone with the children, though I'd have every right, but because he stole my job. My future. My earnings. And he used my love for babies to do it. I know antiquities far better than he does and have tutored him through countless acquisitions for Universal Imports. Without my expertise, he wouldn't be opening the office in Singapore, wouldn't be Bjorn's right-hand man. I could have gone the commercial route, beaten him at his own game. But no, I had to teach him to be the breadwinner, how to hunt and gather, so I could stay home and pick nits. This really isn't half as much fun as it sounds. Maybe that's all it is, though—I'm just suffering from a mid-lice crisis.

Twenty-One

CHERYL AND DAD HAVE COME down for Thanksgiving weekend and to take some of the pressure off of me while Thom's away. I've only had a couple of weeks alone with the kids, and though I've managed not to kill either of them, I could use a break. It was nice putting up the tree last night. Dad was sober the whole evening, and when everyone was tucked into bed Cheryl and I hung the more fragile ornaments on the upper branches. As quiet settled over the room, I found I didn't feel much like talking.

"How's single motherhood?" Cheryl asked, trying to coax me out of my shell. It was her idea to get this ridiculous jump on the holidays.

"Not much better than it was back in your day, I reckon," I said, unwrapping some hand-blown globes.

"You never call to chat—is everything all right?" she asked, not meaning to make me feel guilty, just putting her finger right on the hot button.

"Does it look all right?" I shot back, my anger surging back up after a calm evening.

"Yes, yes it does. Max is walking and Georgia is speaking above a whisper. Looks pretty good to me." She dangled a crystal angel from its red cord. "Oh look, baby, remember when you got this for Georgie?"

"Her first Christmas. How could I forget?" I took the ornament from her and sat down on the couch. "I can't do it anymore. I just can't."

"Do what, sweetie?" She sat down with me.

"It. All of it. Any of it. It." I wanted her to say it for me, wanted her to break the ice.

"Of course you can, you always have."

"Exactly. I always have. And now I want someone else to. I'm tired of it. I'm just so tired." I started to cry, and Cheryl hugged me to her—not something either of us is all that comfortable with, so it took me a moment to lean into her and let go.

"Once, when you were very little, you wanted more than anything to follow your dad to work in the next town, and I said, 'No, you have to take a nap, now lie down with me and go to sleep.' You waited until I was asleep and then you snuck out of the house, remember?" I mumble an *mm-hm*. I've heard this story a million times on a million occasions, but each time Cheryl has found a way to make it sound new. "So you walked toward where you thought Will had gone, but you went the wrong way and ended up in a cornfield outside of town." I put my feet up on the couch, let the tears subside, the anger die down. "And the corn was so high that you got lost in it, and we had to get your dad's uncle out in his spray plane to go looking for you. When we found you, you were rolled up in a ball, sound asleep in the middle of that field. I was so frantic that when we found you I tried to scare you with stories of foxes and wolves that might try to eat you, but you wouldn't scare, you just kept saying, 'I'm sorry, I'm a good Jenny, don't tell Daddy, be a good mommy.' Point is, Jenny, you didn't give up on what you wanted, even though I told you no. You're a very stubborn girl, baby, and I wouldn't have it any other way. If your instinct is to follow Thom, then go out there and get him." She stroked my hair, thinking. "If not, then go out there and get you. Foxes and wolves be damned. But be sure to give the man a chance to prove himself, that's all he wants from you. Now go to bed and don't get up until you feel like it."

After sleeping until *nine* and sitting down to a *breakfast* of French toast at the *table* with my children and parents, I make a list of how to spend the day.

"So I think I'll get a manicure this morning," I say to no one in particular as I jot that down. "And then go to Barneys for lunch at Fred's and some light shopping. Then I'll go see them decorating the tree at Rockefeller Center—"

"Mommy, I want to see the tree!" Georgia slams her fork on the table, clearly unnerved by my use of the personal pronoun, a commodity that she cornered long ago.

"Honey, we can go see it next week, when it's lit."

"I want to see it today!"

"Okay, Dad, would you mind taking them to see the tree?" I realize how much more calm I am with eight hours of sleep under my belt. There's no ruffling me today. I say good-bye to the wolves and foxes and go about my selfish schedule.

I get that manicure, and I eat at Fred's. I have a Cobb salad, and I make them hold the onions, chop the ingredients, and put the dressing on the side, just like any good lady luncher. I sit at the bar and drink a dirty martini, reading a copy of *The New*

Yorker. Having eaten the last vodka-soaked olive, I wander down to the Co-op and buy myself a pair of size 8 Prada pants—incentive for the New Year's resolution I've yet to make. I pick up a few little trinkets for friends and family, then hop in a cab down to the Angelika for the two o'clock showing of some seedy, terrible French movie that should already be cast into obscurity.

When I walk out of the theater, my eyes have barely adjusted to the glare of a snow-white sky when I see Thom waiting on the sidewalk with a dozen yellow roses and half a grin on his face. I blink a dozen times, trying to make him go away. He appears to have completely forgotten that I don't like surprises. My impulse is to run from him, but then I remember Cheryl's advice, and I decide to give him a chance to lure me back to him. He escorts me into a waiting cab (a rented checker, no less), ties a silk scarf over my eyes, and I'm thrown against the backseat as the car jerks to a start.

"Okay, Mickey Rourke, very funny. Where are we going?" I attempt to play along.

"Now, why would I need a blindfold if I was just going to tell you? I know you don't like surprises, but where's your sense of adventure?"

"Um, I don't know, have you tried looking in the clothes hamper?" Even as I start to suck the joy out of the moment, I fall a tiny bit for the old Thom magic. No matter how mad I get at him, he always finds a way to undo me. I will resist as long as I can, but ultimately I will fall, and gladly. But not before putting up a good fight. Though this is very romantic, whatever it is, I have to admit I was really grooving on being alone.

"Jen, would you rather I take the blindfold off?" He sounds crushed. But that could just be part of his game.

"No, no, by all means, leave it on. Have your fun, don't let me spoil it." I've found a teasing note in my voice. I'm making nice.

"I have been stationed in Dara for three and a half years." His breath is hot against my ear, and I like it. "If I were posted to the dark side of the moon I could not be more isolated. You don't have the slightest idea what I'm talking about, do you, Lawrence?"

"No, effendi," I whisper back, my pulse quickening.

"Do you? No. That would be too . . . lucky."

The taxi stops and Thom eases me out of it, taking the scarf off to reveal the Inn at Irving Place, where he brought me the night he proposed. We have tea in front of the fire in the parlor, all the finger sandwiches and scones with clotted cream that I can stand. We also have our first bottle of champagne, nectar of the gods-who-abhor-self-control. Without champagne I wouldn't have Thom, certainly wouldn't have Georgia, and probably wouldn't have Max. It's the one thing that consistently works to get me out of my own head, which frees me up to say what I need to say, feel what I need to feel. In short, it's a miracle that I'm not an alcoholic. My resolve slowly melts and I remember quite clearly every little thing I love about this man: how he once gave his winter coat to a homeless woman on the street in subzero temperatures; how he loaned Andy enough money to build onto his house and never asked for a dime back; how he has long conversations with Cheryl when she calls, instead of saying a polite hello and handing the phone over to me; that he gained weight along with me when I was pregnant with Georgia so that I would never outweigh him.

Once we're stuffed and tipsy, Thom guides me up the stairs to the same room we had last time. The roses have been put in a vase for us, and I see that Thom has decked out the room with early Christmas spirit. There are poinsettias of every hue, and cinnamon-scented candles warm the room.

"When . . . ?"

"I did it this morning, after getting the red-eye in from L.A. I've been flying pretty much nonstop for the past twenty-four hours, and boy are my arms tired!" I roll my eyes. He pops open another bottle of bubbly, and I feel the witchcraft in this room.

"How . . . ?"

"Cheryl. She called me this morning with your planned itinerary. I started stalking you at Barneys and even sat through most of that terrible movie." He hands me a glass and runs a drop of champagne across my lips with his fingertip.

"Why?"

"Because more than anything else in the world, Jennifer Ann Bradley, I love you. I can't live without you." He finishes his toast with a clink of glasses. "Thank you."

"For what?"

"For saying yes." He takes a step closer. "If the camels die, we die. And in twenty days they will start to die."

"There's no time to waste, then, is there?"

We drop our glasses and lunge in for the clutch. We haven't kissed like this in years, and I am stunned by how much I just need to get laid, and fast.

Everything goes as planned, shoes off, clothes off, onto the bed, rolling this way, then that. We're worked up like teenagers when Thom suddenly jumps off the bed.

"Shit!"

"What, are you hurt? Did I hurt something?"

"Goddamn it!" He's up off the bed, kicking his overnight bag.

"Come here and tell me what's wrong. Honey?"

"Fuck fuck fuck fuck." He's winding down now, after swigging from the bottle. "I forgot to bring the fucking rubbers!"

I'm not sure why, but this strikes me as hilarious, and I start a low giggle that bursts into a full-on fit.

"Fucking . . . rubbers . . . no . . . fucking . . . rubbers . . . for . . . fucking . . ."

"Very funny. Hahaha." He's trying not to laugh, but he can't help it either, and we're right back at it. I tell him that we're in the clear as long as he pulls out. I'm about to get my period—that might explain my anger-management issues—and can always tell when I'm ovulating. I don't like the idea of going without rubbers, but since I gave the green light, there will be no stopping this man who has always been more than diligent with the birth control.

As I listen to Thom snore a bare fifteen minutes later, my love for him washes over me and puddles in my heart. He would lasso the moon for me, if I asked him, which is why I never have to ask. I also realize I haven't thought of the kids in over five hours. I'll take good wife for tonight and work on good mommy tomorrow. Good Jenny will just have to wait until Monday.

Twenty-Two

I DIDN'T INTEND TO TAKE THOM'S name. In fact, I don't think I've ever quite made the change legal. It was just one of those things that happen when you're not looking, and the next thing you know, you're no longer Ms. Probstfeld, you're Mrs. Bradley. When I was a kid, I couldn't wait to unload my unspellable name for something simpler, more elegant. It never was about keeping my identity or making a statement, I was just tired of having to spell it out for people: No, *b-s-T*, *T* as in Toy, *T* as in Tell me when you're going to stop Torturing me.

When I was living with the adult child actor, I dreamed of the day I'd sign my name Jennifer Monroe. How simple. How elegant. But that day never came, even after six years of cohabitation. To be fair, he didn't want to have children but was willing to wait to see if he might change his mind. He didn't, but I did. While he was on a coast-to-coast tour of *Cats* ("Now and Forever"), I realized that if I was going to have children, I'd like them to start out as babies, and not as adult child actors.

After we got engaged, Thom asked me whether I would take his name. I said sure, why not, Bradley is a lovely name. I quibbled a little, saying I wanted to keep my name for the time being because my career was just starting to percolate and I didn't want to send the message that marriage would make me less serious about my ambition. As for hyphenation? How very eighties. Besides, think about it: Jennifer Probstfeld-Bradley. Sounds like a disease. "I'm sorry, I can't come out and play, I have Probstfeld-Bradley syndrome." Or like a white-shoe law firm. I had it clear in my mind that by day I would be Jennifer Probstfeld, Junior Specialist, Antiquities, and by night, Jen Bradley, wife and homemaker.

In the year it took us to get married, something strange and complicated happened. Thom and I had decided to plan and pay for the wedding ourselves, but slowly Vera's touch started to creep into the event. Nothing I noticed right away, but small things, like Vera's insisting on her uncle's band during the cocktail hour, or the engagement diamond being Thom's grandmother's—very thoughtful, but an enormous burden. I had my heart set on a very simple gold band, a tradition from the Scandinavian side of my family. I had discussed this with Thom and he approved. Next thing I know we're at the Inn and he's cracking open the velvet vault to reveal what can only be described as a headlight. Weighing in at two and a half carats, it had all the understatement of a bowling trophy. It yelled, *"This is how much my husband loves me!"* I blanched at the sight of it, but not wanting to ruin the evening I didn't express my shock and horror.

I wore it for a week. It was an honor, really, that Vera would entrust such a priceless jewel to me. She and Theta took me out to lunch at Le Cirque to celebrate—to celebrate the ring, no doubt—and it was there I learned that not only was Theta's ring a matching stone but that the two rocks had once been a pair of earrings that Thom's grandfather had bought for his wife back in the late thirties on a business trip to Austria.

One of my dad's hobbies has been collecting World War II memorabilia, from books to guns to medals. I remembered reading a book of his about how the Jews in Austria were, let us say, relieved of their possessions in an attempt to make paupers out of them and force them to emigrate. I was wearing a dead woman's diamond, and not the dead woman I had thought.

Suddenly, I was less enamored of sporting anything Bradley, and as discreetly as I could I asked Thom to return the stone to his mother. We made up some story about how forgetful and clumsy I am, and how I was so terrified of losing it that I just couldn't bear the responsibility. There were more, smaller hurdles we encountered, and I learned about their truly fascinating family history. It seems that Bradley was also Vera's maiden name. Her people were Irish Catholic from the southern reaches of County Tyrone. Thom's father Skip's family were Ulster Bradleys, descended from the Scottish Presbyterian sect. A Gaelic Juliet and Romeo. Vera clearly saw Skip as her ticket out of Lace Curtain hell and into the country clubs that had denied her father entrance through the front door but were happy to have him behind the bar. She's the worst kind of Wasp: a Catholic one. Turns out the only name she changed was her first one. From Mary Teresa to Verity—Vera for short.

In the end, I quietly reneged on my promise and only changed my name on our marriage license. But over time, after quitting my job, giving my name as Jennifer Bradley in the hospital so there wouldn't be any confusion with the babies, and countless invitations and Christmas cards bearing "Mr. and Mrs. Thomas

Bradley III," the name change sort of happened on its own. I feel like this name is now paving me over, absorbing what little originality I brought to the relationship. In trying not to become a Bradley on the outside, I've made myself unrecognizable on the inside, letting go of who I once thought I was. Really, I'm no better than Vera, my hard-earned identity of career woman/neofeminist thrown out with the baby's bathwater.

Twenty-Three

SVEN HASN'T QUITE ABANDONED me after all. His job doesn't start until after Christmas, so we're still dating. Thom and I had a really good time over the weekend, and during brunch at the Inn after our night of reckless debauchery—two more times, if you can believe it—we talked about making some changes to improve our life. As soon as the new office is open, he's going to make a play for a bigger job here with less travel. He's paid his dues and can take his expertise elsewhere if Bjorn calls his bluff. It's a start. We've set up a separate account in which Thom will deposit money for me to spend as I see fit. Hello, Canyon Ranch. We have also decided that I need more time to sort out my head and to figure out what I want to do once Max is in nursery school.

To this end, I have hired the neighbor's nanny, Veronika, to take care of Max on Tuesdays and Thursdays, from ten until two. Her main charge is in school from nine until three now, and the Mercers have docked her pay but still have her around all day to do their laundry and make their beds in the morning. She's ecstatic to be earning an extra hundred a week, but even more she likes having something interesting to do while Joseph is at kindergarten.

Like any good explorer, I have set out well-equipped on this my first Tuesday, pencils sharpened and backpack full of empty notebooks, ready to cozy up in a carrel at the public library and pick up my research on Hannibal where I left off, thanks to Penny's well-intentioned suggestion. I figure I should use this time to find out whether I really want to write this biography or not.

But first, Sven and I decided to have a celebratory Starbucks playdate across the street. I'm waiting for him, keeping an eye on my freedom clock, when I hear:

"Hey, JP." I feel a light touch on my shoulder. I know who it is, even though I haven't seen him in six years, and as my blood turns to boiling ice in my veins, I take a long glance down, turn my head at a jaw-defining angle, and reply:

"Why, Heath, what are the odds?" I look into his eyes as I use my peripheral vision to check out the rest of him. Still taller than any man in the room, still carved from Calabrian marble, still smelling like the most exotic blend of spices a private cologne maker could contrive, my Heath, my adult child actor, is every bit as magnetic as the day I met him.

"The odds are pretty good, considering I'm in a play just a block from here. The question is, what brings you to Times Square?"

"This isn't Times Square, it's Bryant Park." I won't let him get away with anything. Ever.

"Details. You always were so German with the details. Good to see you haven't changed." Oh, if it were only true. I've had two kids, cut my hair, and gained at least twenty pounds. Not exactly the sylph he plucked off the nubile shelf.

"I've had two kids." Smooth, Jen, very smooth. Why not just lift your shirt and show him the scars?

"So I hear. A boy and a girl, right?"

"A girl and a boy, yes. Georgia and Max. Almost five and just over one. Sorry I don't carry their pictures, I'm usually too loaded down carrying the actual items."

"I always knew you'd have kids." He smirks. Heath the All-Knowing. The wonderful wizard of Heath. Heath Almighty.

"You're very clever, there's no denying it. What play are you in? I didn't know you were on Broadway." No need telling him that www.heathmonroe.com is on my favorites list. That I've been following his career very closely, and even gone to a couple of his nightclub shows downtown, disguised in a black wig.

"I'm taking over for John Stamos in *Nine* next month. Right now I'm understudying and filling in for the Christmas Eve and New Year's Eve shows."

"Hey, didn't Stamos get his start on TV, too?" Heath hates being reminded of his origins, how his second sitcom, *Getting Bigger, Baby!*, was always a point or two behind *Full House* in the ratings.

"Yep."

"And now you're subbing for him? Isn't that ironic?" It's amazing how bitter I am, even after all this time. Bitter, and yet if he offered I might just go around the corner for a quickie.

"Yeah, he's a really nice guy, though—has taught me a lot." He laughs, bulletproof as ever. "I seem to be following him around Broadway. First *Cabaret,* now *Nine.* I can only hope he keeps getting good roles. It really takes the pressure off me to open a big show."

"Don't be silly, you could open anything if they let you. And they will—just wait, you'll see, and then Stamos will be subbing for you." He's done it again, turned the tables so that I'm supporting his insecurity, giving him morsels of can-do spirit to feed his feral ego.

"Hey, listen." He leans down, nearly whispering in my ear. "It's *really* good to see you. Can we have dinner sometime soon and catch up?"

"I'd like that," I say, like I mean it. What surprises me is that I really do mean it, and I scribble my number and e-mail on a piece of notepaper.

"Hey, what's up with all the paper and pencils?" He's seen into the dark confines of my backpack. "You look like you're on your way to school. That's kind of hot."

"Um, well, yeah. Going back to school. Again." I can't believe I told him that, a complete bold-faced lie. "But right now I'm working on my Hannibal book."

"That's great, Jen, I always knew you'd write someday. You've got so much talent."

"Really? You think so?"

"I always have." He brushes my cheek, and I'm hooked into the old Heath, the one who fed me while I was finishing my degree, the one who took me for a long weekend to Tokyo just because he could. "Gotta run." The one who was always leaving me to go on tour and fuck some bus-and-truck ingénue. The one who wouldn't marry me. "I'll call."

I watch him saunter out the door, passing Sven on his way out. Sven plays it cool for a moment but registers Heath out of the corner of his eye and does a full swivel pivot to get a better look. He sees me in the sweep and rushes over.

"Was that . . . ?"

"Yeah."

"Heath Monroe?"

"On a scale of one to ten, just how bad do I look today?"

"What was he doing in here?" He looks over at the door.

"Focus, baby. On a scale of one to ten, how bad?" I turn his face to mine.

"One being good or bad?"

"Bad."

"Seven, maybe eight."

"This is no time to lie. I'm going to get you a latte, now watch me as though you don't know me, and give me your full dive-commentator's attention." I take my time, pick out a pumpkin scone, order another latte for myself and one for Sven. I turn to see him holding up a notebook with a 6.5 scrawled on it.

"You're being kind," I say on my return.

"You slept with him, didn't you?" he says.

"Guilty."

"How could you!" He slaps me on the leg.

"Pretty easily, as it turned out. Met him in a bar, went home with him, insert H. into J., etc." The more interested Sven gets in this discussion, the more bored I get. But as I've been down this road a few times before, I know it doesn't end until all the tires are flat.

"No, I mean how could you keep this from me? From Sven? I call not fair on you. I told you about Louganis, and what do you do? Throw it in my face." He's so cute and gay when he pouts. But he's right, I should have told him.

"Sorry, boyo, it just never came up, you know? Here's the long and the short of it. We met, fell in love, lived together for six years, and then went our separate ways. The end. Do I look old and fat to you?"

"Yes. Very old and hideously fat. And greasy. Stuffed. Like

every day is Thanksgiving. Like every day is Thanksgiving at the old people's home, prechewed, digested, colorless, and lifeless. And drooling." He's turned his stool away from me, and I know he's just looking for me to throw him a bone. Though I have to admit I'm enjoying his insult stream of consciousness.

"He likes boys." It's not really true, but the rumors have been floating for so long, what difference does it make if one more gay guy thinks Heath is on their team?

"*I knew it!*" He actually high-fives me, he's so happy.

"And Heath isn't his real name, it's Keith."

"A name-changer too—he is my soul mate." He swoons into his seat.

"Who doesn't change their name?" I wish I had. The world could do with one less Jennifer in New York. I always liked the name Claire. So elegant, so full of light. "Satisfied?"

"You don't look greasy." He sips his latte.

"Neither do you."

"I saw him make eye contact with me. I loved him in *Big Baby*, that was the best sitcom ever. Remember that one time when he wet his bed, and his stepdad was really mad, but then he made that face and all was forgiven?" The inevitable ride down memory lane tends to reveal more about the fan, I've learned.

"I never watched the show, it was opposite *Happy Days*," I say, getting a dig in at Heath though he's not even within earshot. No one could hate Scott Baio more than my ex. "But trust me, after a drunken, black-out night on the town, the whole bed-wetting thing isn't quite so funny."

"Yeah, but you gotta admit, he was *très* hot in *Getting Bigger, Baby!* I had all the *Teen Beat* mags from that period. What a god." He glances off in the direction of Heath's exit. It's possible that

Sven has the worst case of Heathitis I've encountered. I make a big show of looking at my watch.

"Wow, time really does fly, doesn't it?" I say, collecting my notebooks, my 6.5, and my pencils. "I've gotta get to the library before my free time is over."

We walk out together, and Sven makes some lame excuse to go off toward Heath's theater, no doubt hoping for another glimpse. I know, I've been there, and I still feel the pull of that six-foot-four magnet even as I push off in the other direction.

I sit down at a large oak table, nod to the homeless man to my right, and unpack the tools of my new trade: five number-two pencils, perfectly sharpened, three notepads, my laptop, the thirty pages of notes on Carthage and Hannibal that I accumulated ten years ago, and a medium-point blue Bic. I unstrap my watch and lay it next to the pencils. Only forty-five minutes before I have to leave to pick up Georgia. How can I possibly get any work done this way? Focus. Focus. Focus.

I open my notes and flip past my diving score. I tip my head back and look at the light fixtures. They're large. And pretty. I open my laptop and turn it on. Blue screen. Up pops Georgie and Max wallpaper. I miss them. I look at the time in the corner of the screen. Exactly forty-two minutes to go. I pick up the library's wireless signal and sign on to the Web. Retrieve my e-mail. One note from Thom, says he loves me. That's nice. A note from Sven saying he'll meet me at Starbucks. Done. A couple of Viagra offers.

The homeless man starts snoring, and I get to thinking about what he might have done in his life to lead him here. Drugs, probably. He seems to be sleeping off a nod. Nice of them to let him stay here. The smell of urine is starting to get to me, but I pretend it's a diaper and try not to offend a sleeping homeless man by moving to another table.

Forty minutes. Tick. Tick. Tick.

Okay, so I don't want to write a book today. I decide to use the remaining time productively and make a list of what I would need to do to get back in the job market.

1. Cut and color hair.
2. Lose twenty pounds.
3. Borrow money from Thom to buy new suits.
4. Get up to date on antiquity.

I give myself a mental pat for being so clever.

5. Call Christy.
6.

I tap the eraser against my teeth. What's 6? Get a clue? Mr. Homeless wakes up, sniffs in my direction, and moves his paper bags to another table. I try to discreetly smell myself, lean my nose against my shoulder. Ew. I forgot about Max throwing up his milk this morning. That must have made a good impression on Heath. Yes, good to see you, I've really got it together, I'm writing my book after all this time. No, I've got the babies completely under control. I even bathe regularly. Ye gods. Thirty-five minutes.

To hell with it. It's a beautiful day outside, so I shut down my laptop and pack my bag. Writing is a lot harder than it looks. There's always Thursday.

Number five. Call Christy.

No time like the present. I go outside to the steps and turn on my cell phone, dial the number I used to answer.

"Good afternoon, Christy Bloomington's office. This is Francesca. How may I help you?" Not Christy. Damn. Of course not: she's never answered her own phone, why would she start now?

"Uh, hi. Hello. Is Christy in?" The wind blows into my ear, causing me to hunch behind one of the lions.

"I'm sorry, she's at lunch. May I take a message?" Francesca sounds like she's never eaten lunch in her life. I bet she's half my size, a willowy Paltrow wannabe.

"Yeah, could you please tell her that Jennifer Bradley called?"

"And what is it regarding?" Good question. Your job. Better watch your back, Frances, I'm a living legend.

"Nothing, just an old friend. Tell her Jennifer called, would you?"

"Hey, you're not *the* Jennifer Bradley, are you?" Her voice loses its icy froth, and I detect a hint of Long Island in her accent. "Like, you used to work here?" I'd bet she's never dared start a sentence with *like* in front of Christy.

"So it would seem," I say.

"Hey, Christy talks about you all the time."

"She does?"

"Oh God yeah. 'Jennifer made the best coffee, Jennifer could spot a fake a mile away, you should have seen how fast Jennifer wrote her copy, never needed a redraft.' It's kind of hard living up to your reputation, it's like you were the queen of all assistants ever." I made the best coffee? That's how I'm remembered? "Can I get your number so she can call you back?"

"She has it."

"Are you sure? She likes me to get a number whether she has it or not." I know, I'm the one who spoiled her that way. She never once had to look up a number under my watch.

"I'm sure. Thanks." I press END without waiting to hear more from this young woman. Maybe I had it wrong. Maybe Christy wanted to keep me so badly because I made her look so good, not because of my potential. As I rush off to get the subway uptown, part of me hopes that Christy doesn't have my number, so she can't call me or my bluff.

Twenty-Four

I FEAR THE HOLIDAYS. I resent the rush to buy presents, the crowds that gridlock the city, the complete absence of the true Baby Jesus, and the pressure to eat everything everyone makes or sends me at the same time that I'm desperate to lose the ten extra pounds I gained at Thanksgiving. My stepsister Judy makes the most delicious peanut butter cookies dusted with sugar and imprinted with a Hershey's kiss, and she sends me two dozen every year. One dozen for me, the other for Thom and the kids. I put on two pounds just signing the UPS receipt.

This feeling of complete detachment tortures me every December. I go through all the motions, but underneath it all I feel like Scrooge. Well, not Scrooge exactly, as I'm all for other people diving into gift wrap and getting frisky at the office party. It's just me. Maybe it was the day I realized that we didn't have a chimney in our trailer house, that Santa couldn't squeeze his red girth through the tiny heating vents. When I was five, my parents had us take a nap a couple of hours before we opened presents on Christmas Eve, so "Santa could come." Oh, don't get dirty, that's not what they meant. I know, because I did a Cindy Lou Who on

them and snuck out of bed, looked under their door, and saw
them wrapping the doll I had asked for. When I opened the package that night, I knew they'd been lying all along. I didn't let on,
though; that wouldn't have been a smart move, especially since
Andy clearly still believed. Judy and Vince were too old to care by
then but gave us a good show anyway.

Okay, so here's the thing about the Baby Jesus. If my parents
told me that Christmas is about Santa and the Baby Jesus, but
then I find out they're lying about the first guy (lives at the
North Pole? canvasses the earth in one night?), what right do
they have to expect me to buy into the other, much bigger lie (a
Virgin birth? the Son of God?)? Sure, you say, we all had to re-
adjust after those first disappointments. No big deal, it's the
spirit of Santa that's important, the *holy* spirit of the Baby Jesus.
Forgive me, but somehow I find eight days of Hanukkah oil easier to swallow.

I don't want to lie to my children. Not big lies, anyway. Perhaps the little lies can do them good, but the big ones, not so
much. On Georgia's first Christmas, I told Thom that I couldn't
bring myself to indoctrinate her into the cult of Christmas, and
we had a fight that nearly wrecked our marriage. He grabbed the
"innocence" high road, I reluctantly set out on the "honesty" low
road, and he somehow got to Santaland before me. I sulked on the
couch as he put up a tree, wrapped packages, and walked around
in a red-and-white hat saying "Ho, ho, ho." I dismantled my argument and began reconstructing it for the next year, when the
effects of lying to an almost-two-year-old would far outweigh the
negligible damage done the first year.

Living a lie is easy only so long as you remain blind to the lie
you've told yourself. When I look back on my youth and think

about how much time I spent in church and in religious activities, it's as though I'm looking at two people: I see the Jennifer who lights the Advent candles and recites John 3:16, and the Jennifer who has learned lines and acts the part of a religious girl. That's not to say that I would go outside after services and smoke and drink. I really was a good girl. And I prided myself on convincing everyone just how filled with the spirit I was. But I now know I didn't have the spirit in me at all. Here's the best way I can explain it: it was as though I was gay and the whole town was straight, so I pretended to be straight too. It never occurred to me that my hollow feeling was in conflict with the hallowed feeling I was faking. The minute I left Tannersville, I left the church as well. Funny thing is, I never gave it any thought; I just slept in Sunday mornings as though this was who I always had been.

I want my kids to have a meaningful relationship with God, or a god, or some gods, I really do. I want them to find joy in the beauty of creation and give the Creator a high-five. But I can't hand them what for me is an empty belief. Sometimes I wish so desperately that I could simply believe in God, since with belief must come some sort of solace that is denied me, but I see those who do, and many of them are suffering. So I will stay silent as the night and let Thom take Georgia and Max to church at Christmas. I'll hope that it really is the spirit that will impress them, and perhaps they will find the meaning that I have not.

Meanwhile, Georgia and I have an understanding—I never tell her a big lie, and she never asks me to tell her a mean truth. Last year I started a new tradition. I explained to her that Saint Nicholas was a charitable fellow who lived a long time ago, and that he has been turned into a very special character to give children joy and hope. On December 6 we go to the post office to pick out a Santa letter and then spend the afternoon shopping and mailing a gift to a child who has so much less than we do. We make cookies for us and Saint Nick, and I share with her stories about good deeds well done.

This year I will explain to Georgia that I love the Baby Jesus and that we are lucky that he lived such a momentous life. We will also light the candles for her newly Jewish soul, and once I've read up on Kwanzaa, I'll give her a play-by-play of that too. It may in the end be easier for me to lie to her. If she's very lucky, she will find something beautiful to believe in, that one thing I seem to wholly lack. I choose to hide this emptiness from her— from everyone, for that matter. I like to think of it as my invisible cross to bear, and in that small way, Jesus is my personal savior. Now if he could just get me to stop taking myself so seriously.

Twenty-Five

ONE OF THE REASONS I rarely left the house for four years was the sheer velocity it requires. Take today, for instance. Georgia has a new best friend again, and we have a playdate at her house this morning. I made myself a little promise when I started down this social road that we would keep Saturdays for ourselves, but since it's a mere week until Christmas, Georgia has insisted on fitting this into our schedule. I'm not stupid—I know this is a very slippery slope: once a child gets her way, there's no turning back. It is nice, though, to have something to do on a Saturday other than explaining once again why Daddy still isn't home.

I have discovered that the after-school playdate is most desired, as it does not take the entire Italian army to get both kids ready and on mass transportation during their favorite cartoons—more specifically, their favorite ads interrupted by asinine cartoons. I've actually seen Georgia mute the shows only to restore sound for the latest Barbie. It wasn't that long ago that we didn't even have a TV in the living room, but part of letting Georgia play with other children is letting go of what your child does in other kids' houses, and once Geege realized what she was missing, the whining, pleading, and begging set in. It occurs to me that she's winning a lot lately, and I'm not entirely surprised. Mainly, I'm just getting tired of being the enforcer with Thom away, as he always says yes on the phone, good-copping me at too many turns. So sometimes I say yes, even when I mean no.

"Georgie, you really need to brush your teeth, we're going to be late." She's sitting in front of the TV, chewing on her thumb. "Don't be a zombie, sweetie, it doesn't become you." She's only just gotten out of bed and is curled around her sleep-warm blanket, pajamaed and pouty.

"Don't wanna."

"Don't wanna what?" Max and I have been up for hours. We've both had our coffee and read the paper, and but for shoes we are ready to set the world on fire.

"Don't wanna go." She sneaks her thumb into her mouth even as she throws a tepid glance my way, daring me to uncork her.

"Well, what if Max and I go without you?" Max leaps at me and just as quickly cruises away, attempting to scale the coffee table in his pursuit of Peeve's tail.

"'Kay." She doesn't mean it. I see one foot creep out from under the blanket in the direction of her clothes, which I have laid out on the couch for ease of access. This has been a new battle lately, as Georgia's sleeping habits have dramatically changed. She's decided on her own that she needs to stay up later than the baby, so she's gone from her normal seven-thirty bedtime to, sometimes, eleven. Don't tut me, I still put her to bed at the same time as always, but I hear her in there for hours talking to imaginary people or just softly singing. I wouldn't care if it didn't make her such a pill in the morning.

"Tell you what. If we get going toot sweet we can stop for hot chocolate on the way home." Maybe this is how I've been losing lately, instituting a reward-for-snitty-behavior system, but I'm becoming all about the shortcut as my patience and energy to outwit my little minx are on the wane.

"At Saradipty?"

"If you're ready in five minutes, hair combed, teeth brushed, shoes tied—" And she's off.

"Can we take Ella?" Jammies off.

"We'll have to ask her mommy." Leggings on.

"And Miles?" Shirt on.

"Who's Miles?" Sock on.

"Brother." Sock on.

"Again, we'll have to ask their mommy. She might not want them to have hot chocolate. Or she might have some waiting for us, we don't know." Shoes on. She's chosen the clogs to shave seconds off her time. She runs to the bathroom and attempts to brush her hair, while I wrestle Max into his sock-moccasins.

"*Ouch*, can't do it, Mommy. You do it!"

"Okay, get the teeth, I'll get the hair." When we exit the bathroom, Max and Peeve are licking the floor, Max's shirt, pants, and moccasins coated in a slurry of orange gunk. He has somehow managed to get into his stroller snack sack, silently unzip the Goldfish-and-Cheerios combo baggie, and spill the already leaking bottle of milk in the process. All this in maybe thirty seconds. Georgia peeks around my leg, only to fall into hysterics.

"Mommy, look at Max! He's funny!" It's all I can do not to haul off and hit her. My frustration and rage have her caught in the crosshairs, and I blame this whole messy episode on her. But since hitting a child is no longer common practice, I pull a stay-out-of-jail-free card instead.

"Go to your room, Georgia." I don't look at her, and my voice doesn't modulate.

"But I didn't do anything!"

"Exactly my point. Go now." I don't have to yell, she gets it, and she goes, quietly shutting the door behind her. With a sure grip on what is left of my quickly diminishing sanity, I whisk Peeve into the bathroom, take off my own sweater and pants, and pick Max up under the armpits. Dressed only in my bra and panties, I stand him in the kitchen sink and peel off his now soaking, food-speckled clothes. Once I get him undressed, I take him to his room and figure I might as well change his diaper while I'm at it. There, next to his penis, is one last Goldfish, mocking me with its insipid half-smile.

Somehow, we all make it to Ella's door in our respective whole pieces. This is all I know about Ella Little: she lives on Park Avenue in a swanky doorman building; her birthday is the day after Georgia's; she smells, according to Georgia, "like cookies"; she has a brother named Miles; and she's not related to Stuart. I've never met her mother, Angela, but we did speak on the phone for a few minutes to set up this date. I hoist Max onto my hip and let him ring the bell.

I'm not expecting the nanny to be working on a weekend, but when a black woman opens the door, I automatically say, "Hello, is Angela home?" To which she replies, "You must be Jennifer. Please come in." I park the stroller in the hallway as directed and she leads us into a spotless white-on-white living room with sweeping views of northern Manhattan before ex-

cusing herself. We're alone for a couple of minutes as we all
look around with our hands hovering over the various shades of
cream, linen, and ivory and try to "make ourselves at home," as
instructed. Georgia walks over to the full wall of windows and
peers out at the traffic coming down Park, Max scrambles
down me only to sit on the floor and pat the shaggy rug. I give
him his lucky toy bag; he ignores it and starts the hunt for
something to smash. The nanny returns with a tray of cookies
and small mugs of hot chocolate, setting it on the glass coffee
table. She sits down and sings out, "Ella, Georgia is here!" and
it occurs to me that she is not the nanny. I've never been very
good at concealing embarrassment, and today is no exception. I
break into an instant sweat, feel the heat creep up my face, and
start coughing on air. Thanks a lot, Georgia. "Smells like cookies"? How about "Is black"?

"Nice place. I mean home. Nice home you have. Here," I manage, and reach for a mug. "You really didn't need to trouble over
us like this." I sip, manage some more. "Delicious, did you make
this yourself? I mean from scratch? It tastes like it's from
scratch." None of my best friends have ever been black. I'm
afraid it shows on my face.

"You didn't know we're black, did you?" Angela smiles, a mix
of compassion and fortitude.

"Um, no, not exactly. I'm sorry." Ugh. I try to save that misplaced apology with a wan smile back.

"It's cool. Ella didn't tell me you were white, either."

"I don't remember ever seeing you at Park Street." Could be
because I never hang around long enough to encounter the other
mothers.

"Oh, I'm never there. I have a job. Had a job, I mean." The ice breaks a little with Ella's arrival. She is perfectly dressed in a tartan plaid wool dress, her hair braided in a zigzag pattern that descends into numerous free braids at her neck. "Say hello to Mrs. Bradley, honey."

"Hello, Mrs. Bradley," she says, taking my hand and giving a small curtsy. She smells like vanilla, not cookies, and has already lost one of her front teeth. She's so pretty I want to bite her.

"Hello, Ella. Have you been to see the tooth fairy?"

"Yes, ma'am, and I got a whole dollar." She and Georgia share greetings, and G introduces her to Max before the three of them settle in to their cocoa and cookies. I'm impressed not only by Ella's manners but by my own daughter's as I see her exhibit a much more refined behavior than she uses at home. They chat and giggle like ladies at lunch, and I have to strain to catch what they're saying.

"Gonna . . . soccer . . . Chelzy Piers . . ."

". . . cool . . . day later . . . circus . . ."

"So, Jennifer, how do you like Park Street?" Which lie do I tell? That I love it and wouldn't dream of sending Georgia anywhere else? That we're so lucky to have her on the "right track"? I opt for opaque.

"I don't know. The teacher is nice, and Georgia seems happy. You?" I've only noticed a handful of black kids at the school and have wondered why they chose it.

"If it weren't for the education, I'd switch in a minute. It's so full of snotty little girls and spoiled little boys, I'm having a tough time with Ella. She's really learned how to manipulate me. Girls are hard enough to rear without bad influences. No offense."

"None taken. So why did you choose it?" I nibble on a gingersnap, even though sugar is not on the South Fork Diet, which I have decided to follow to the letter in order to lose weight before I

see Heath again, if he ever calls for that dinner. Ginger's a root.
I'll look up roots when I get home.

"The senior partner in my husband's firm got her in, all his kids
went there. We couldn't say no. Ty wants her to have everything
he didn't." I hear a baby cry from somewhere in the apartment.

"Oh, that's Miles, I'll be right back." Angela takes the empty
tray with her, removing it from Max's reach one last time. Georgia gives me a wary look that says "Don't you dare talk to us" and
ushers Ella over to the window. They now talk in hushed whispers and I feel like Rosemary in the Dakota.

"Hey, Jennifer, little help back here?" comes from the same
direction as the now-hysterical baby. I follow the noise until I
reach the nursery, Max at my heel. The smell hits me before
I even see Miles—he is a poo bomb that has recently detonated. I
walk into the room, undaunted, while Angela stands frozen near
the changing table, Miles flailing on his back in the crib. He's
not really crying now, just sort of staring up at his mother in a
standoff.

"I know that in a few months he will be smiling, laughing,
hugging, and all that, but right now he's just a bundle of nerves
wrapped around a shit factory." Angela exhales. I move her to the
glider and proceed to clean up Miles. The shit has seeped out of
his diaper, up the back to his shoulder blades, and up the front to
his nipples. It's soaked through the sheet and gotten on the
bumper. I put down a couple of layers of cloth diapers on the
changing table before I move Miles there. Max greets him with a
"Baby."

"I just got fired." She's near tears, which makes her eyes glisten
in the low light of the nursery. "I've maybe changed ten diapers
up until last week. If I timed it right I wouldn't even see shit on

the weekends. Now he suddenly shits all the time. I don't put that much food into him, how could he be so full of shit? I mean, the first poop was kind of cute, and when he's constipated it's nice to see some shit, but Lord, what a stink! I can't help but think his ass is a metaphor for my life right now."

"What should I put on him?" I've got Miles shit-free and diapered, and I pull out a sleeper from where Angela's pointed under the changing table. I completely forgot how easy it is to fix a baby when he can't fight back. Once he's dressed, I hand him over to Angela as I proceed to clean up the shit crib. Max is now opening and closing the door, saying "bye-bye," and repeating a mysterious pattern.

"God knows I wanted another kid, but I can't stay home with him. They cut me after maternity leave, can you believe it? My stupid bitch of a boss tells me the guy who's been picking up my slack is doing such a good job that they're handing the job over to him."

"What do you do, Angela? Or did you do, I guess." I lean against the crib, giving her my full attention.

"It's Angie. Sorry to unload. I know you just met me, but I'm working a pretty short fuse right now and I don't know what I'm going to do if I don't talk." Miles is already back to sleep; it's clear she's doing something right.

"It's okay, I seem to have that effect on people. So what happened?" I do have that effect on people. And I'm secretly thrilled that I might actually be starting a friendship with someone as cool—and as black—as Angie. I mean, her *tongue* is pierced.

"I was creative director at Brent, Brad, and Barrow. Place was straight out of *thirtysomething*—you know, great bennies, chill atmosphere, take-out Chinese, pool table in the lobby. I worked my way up from copywriter to a pretty sweet position, reporting directly to the CEO. When I had Ella they were cool about it. I took three months off and came back four days a week for the first year. I worked my ass off those four days, let me tell you. And even on the fifth day I was doing work from home."

"Then what?" Not that she needs the encouragement to tell me, she's so clearly on a roll.

"Well, then one of the women that started at the same time as me, who was always my girl and ate lunch with me every day, she gets promoted to overseer, and I do mean overseer—they created a managing director position and had me report to her. I've never seen a woman get so power-happy and so nasty in such a short time. She even put some streaks of silver in her hair to look older. She got all high and mighty on my ass. Started telling me how to do my ads—for accounts I'd been working on for fifteen years. Says to me, 'Angie, your client doesn't want Malcolm X in their advertising. No one cares about Malcolm X.' No one cares about Malcolm X! What's she, smoking *crack*? *Then* she has the balls to say, 'See if you can work in Michael Jordan. Now, *he's* sexy. You know, Angie, there's one thing you have to remember. You're black, and you need to try to appeal to the black market more. That's what makes you so valuable.' I have to remember that I'm *black? No brother Malcolm!*"

"Wow," I say, nodding in what feels like agreement, even though I have no idea what it's like to be told that I have to remember that I'm white.

"So I got pregnant. Figured it was as good a time as any, girl might actually mature a little while I was away. Went to the CEO, got my maternity leave all sorted out, showed my assistant the ropes—the conniving little Eve—and worked out the same deal I had the first time. I should have seen this coming, you know?

That's the worst part." Now she does start to cry, and Miles wakes up and cries with her. Max starts crying too, even as he tries to open the dirty diaper silo. I try to stuff the new diaper in, but it's full, so I unload it. "That undermining bitch gave my accounts away while I was gone. When I come back she sits me down and says, 'Now, Angie, don't take this personally. You know how much I value you. It's just time to try some new things here.' Truth is they couldn't keep paying both of us a quarter mil, so they got rid of the one who didn't kiss ass. I'd better feed this baby so he can shit himself again. Wanna hold him, since you cleaned him? I'll take the shit sausages to the garbage." She hands me the baby, picks up the sealed diapers.

"Sure, I'd love to. I miss the little baby stage." As you can imagine, this makes the big baby instantly unhappy, so I pick him up too as I follow Angie back down the hallway to the kitchen. I think about how great Christy always was to me, how she mentored and encouraged me, and how hard she tried to change my mind the day I decided to stay home. I get a pang of guilt, a feeling like I've somehow insulted Christy and how much she believed in me, how much she invested in me.

We pass Ella's room, which is quite possibly the pinkest room I've ever seen. I poke my head in and Georgia rushes over, trying to climb up the baby tree. Ella seems to find this funny, and joins in from the other side. I crumple to my knees and we all get the giggles, as I hold Miles with one hand and tickle the three bigger kids in turn with the other. Angie comes back and joins in, as there's nothing a good cry needs like a good laugh.

"Have you ever stalked your nanny?" I ask Angie in the kitchen as she heats up Miles's formula. Max has been allowed into the pots and pans and is banging up a storm.

"What?" she says, and she snorts.

"Withdrawn. Hey, the water's boiling. You should invest in a cheap bottle heater, they're much easier. Not that I ever heated things for either kid. If they only ever have room temperature or cold out of the fridge, they're never the wiser." Bang. Bang.

"Wait a minute, don't try to deflect. What's this about stalking your nanny?" Fair's fair—she told me hers, I'll show her mine.

"Well, I've recently hired a babysitter twice a week to watch Max so I can get some time to myself, but then this past Thursday I was on my way to the library, and I caught a glimpse of them in the park. It was weird, like I was watching a parallel universe and here was my baby with his other mommy." Bang. I shoot Max a "stop it" look. He ignores me. Bang.

"Uh-huh. . . ." She hasn't decided if I'm crazy. Neither have I.

"So next thing I know, I'm following them around. And not because I don't trust her—not that, she's great. I just couldn't help myself. I watched them thinking, 'And this is what they do while I'm at lunch, and this is what they do while I'm at the library.' Anyway, I shadowed them for a good hour, and then once they got back to the house I hung out across the street and watched her turn lights on, ducking under an awning when Max spotted me out the window. I had to pretend that I was just coming home. I mean, do you think that's weird?"

"Look, girl, what's weird is having kids. It's completely unnatural fucked up and weird. The way they physically rip us open, then go on to emotionally tear us to shreds even while they're shitting all over us? And then they grow up, leave, blame all their weirdness on us, and tell us how to live our lives. What to eat. That they're going to put us in a nursing home if we're not careful. That's what's weird. I'm going to make a lot of money, then put it in an iron-clad will that Miles has to change my diapers until I'm dead before he sees one red cent. I'm tough. I'll live to be a hundred." She's officially my new idol.

"Okay, so following Veronika around is okay, then. Thanks."

"No, man, that shit's fucked up too. But if it makes you feel better, then go ahead and stalk your nanny. It's hard as hell being at work all day not knowing what they're doing. I'm lucky my mom looks after Ella and Miles. She takes the train in from Brooklyn and I pay her the going rate. They love her, I love her, and I know she won't beat them, because she never laid a finger on me I didn't deserve." She takes Miles from me and gives him the bottle.

"Shis fud up. Up. Up!" Max puts down his pot lid and starts pulling on my pants hard enough to almost yank them off. It might slow him down if I gave up elastic waistbands. I pick him up; he instantly wants back down.

"Oops, sorry about that," Angie says. "I didn't know he could talk."

"He can't. Besides, he heard worse this morning. You're so lucky your mom's close. Mine's two hours away. But she makes it down as much as she can."

Georgia and Ella come flying into the kitchen, all lit up with what is no doubt a bright idea.

"You ask," Georgia whispers behind her hand to Ella, who clasps her hands behind her back and looks up at her mother.

"Can we go to the carousel?" she rabbits out as fast as she can.

"Is that how we ask?" Angie replies, more kind than correcting.

"May we go to the carousel, please, Mommy?" Ella and Georgia bounce in place, and everyone looks at me. I nod to Angie and the place erupts. As we scurry into jackets and mittens and assorted strollers, a note deep within me resonates with this new tribe. And as Angie gives me a sheepishly beguiling grin as we roll down the street, chatting away about who we are, I feel like I've known her all of my life—or, at the very least, will know her for the rest of it.

Twenty-Six

U P UNTIL GEORGIA, I had always worked. It never occurred to me that my pay was unequal or that my boss might be plotting my demise. When I worked at Christie's, I never gave a thought to whether I was on a career track, I was just driven by my joy at finding a job that I truly loved. Feminism as a principle was never discussed in my house: instead, the message sent by my hardworking, and occasionally hard-drinking, parents was that if there was work to be done, you'd better get to doing it. When I was just out of diapers, Cheryl took in other people's children in a makeshift daycare. I helped her by picking up toys and passing out snacks. All I remember from those days is one little boy named Bobby who would wipe his always-running nose on his sleeves until they were slick. When I was a little older, I would spend the afternoons with my grandpa out on the farm, helping him trap gophers for a quarter a tail. By the time I was eleven I was very tall and mature enough to take a summer babysitting job for a four-year-old girl.

My first salary job was for the county welfare office my senior year. I was their clerical help for two hours of school—I was paid minimum wage and was graded for work-study credit. I had taken two years of typing because where I grew up a girl was very lucky to get a good secretarial job out of high school. Dad wanted me to go to beauty school instead of college so I could get a job at Connie's Cut and Curl and trim his hair for free. It's good to push your kids.

The welfare office was new and exotic to me, as I never knew that people could fill out forms and get money just for turning them in. During my daily filing I learned many secrets about my neighbors—the Trehorns in the trailer to the right were on full welfare benefits, and the Jarvises in the trailer by the park entrance were being investigated for child abuse, just to name two. But I was most astonished to realize that my family qualified for assistance. This was life-altering—a cheese line was one thing, but Aid to Families with Dependent Children quite another. To this day Cheryl will deny that we were ever poor—one of her more quaint affectations.

Cheryl set me the best example of how to find odd jobs and collect a paycheck. For a while in the seventies she lectured for Weight Watchers in the church basements of Tannersville and neighboring towns. She was paid a dollar for every new member she enrolled and fifty cents for each member who came to be weighed every week. On a good night in January she could bring in thirty dollars, but during the summer she'd be lucky if two women showed up. To supplement this income, Cheryl taught herself how to bake party cakes. These were good days for us kids, as there was always a bowl of frosting in the fridge. There were the Tupperware years, followed by the Mary Kay months, not to mention an ongoing stint as organist for the synagogue in New Paltz—she was a Shabbas goy. When Cheryl turned forty, she did the unexpected and went back to school for psychotherapy. She became a couple's counselor and has had so much success that she's written two books on the subject and built a new house in the country with the profits.

My father, named Wilhelm but known as Will, spent a good deal of time on the road, selling insurance on commission for State Farm to the rural folk in the Finger Lakes, back before ice wine changed the bruised farm economy up there. A good man known for his silence, he was beaten routinely as a child and vowed to never lay a hand on any of us. This translated as any kind of hand, including hugs and piggyback rides. He harbored a rage that revealed itself only one time, during a blizzard when the furnace went dead and he spent two hours under the house trying to fix it. Suffering from what turned out to be frostbite, he came into the house and said to Cheryl, "Get the kids, I'm going to let the fucker blow."

My people are not career-driven, they are job-driven. Judy did become a beautician and is now the owner of Judy's Cut and Curl—having bought Connie out late last year; Vince bartends at the ski saloon where Dad drinks; Andy moved to Rochester after getting an associate degree from a junior college and works for Kodak in their development department, whatever that means.

Was I on a career track or am I on a baby track? If I had stayed at Christie's, would I be hitting the glass ceiling by now? From my first clerical job to the time I had Georgia, I was never unemployed. Even in the lap of luxury that was Heath's *Big Baby* bankroll, I continued to bring in my own money. I sometimes feel that my prenatal vitamins must have had "drink me" writ large on the label, for at some point during my pregnancy I gave up any thoughts of work as a definition of my character. Maternity leave was the first time in my life I was not working. You know what? I liked it. My dirty little secret is that I found being at home in sweats preferable to showering, dressing, and being measured by my daily interactions with the people who employed me. Georgia wasn't equipped to give me an annual review, didn't care how I wore my hair or what kind of shoes I bought. She just opened her mouth and latched on.

But now the sad truth is that Georgia doesn't need me—she's got friends of her own—and Max . . . well, Max is a strong little fucker. I feel less and less useful as the days go past and I find myself thinking "what if" more often than not. Do I wait another four years for Max to be in school full-time and sign up for twelve years of bake sales and after-school activities, only to find I'm pushing sixty and empty-handed, waiting another dozen years for grandchildren to fill the empty space? Yeah, I could do that. But I could also go back to something I really know how to do. Work.

Twenty-Seven

CHRISTMAS IS A TIME TO SPEND with your family, a time of magic for children, surprises for all. Which is why I'm glad it's now January. This morning Max and I are nursing a holiday-size hangover as we prepare to go to Chelsea Piers with Sven, Lily, Penny, and Mikhail. We've got a date later this afternoon to go over to the toddler gym, a place in which I have refused to set foot up until now, even though Thom assures me it is not the germ-saturated petri dish I've imagined it to be. I dare you to put thirty drooling toddlers in an absorbent-foam-lined box, do a random swab for E. coli, varicella, acellular pertussis, or pneumococcal conjugate, and then show me it came up clean. The early vaccination rate is plummeting due to a handful of studies that show a possible, but not likely, link to autism, so god knows what kind of superbug is waiting to bite my baby in the ball pit.

But right now it's feeding time at the zoo. Max has suddenly transitioned from two daily naps to one, meaning I have to feed him at eleven before he crashes into a two-hour heap in the middle of the day. This isn't his biggest meal, but if I want him to sleep longer than an hour, I have to make sure he eats enough. Breakfast was a cup of oatmeal with Yo-Baby and mashed banana at seven, followed by a full eight-ouncer of whole milk, after which we raced uptown to drop Georgia at school, got home about an hour ago, did a little baby dancing, and now it's back to scratch. I thought I'd have more hours in the day once Georgia started school, but instead I've lost almost two to her transportation. None of her classmates lives in this neighborhood, but today Angie is going to pick her up for me. Us stay-at-home girls have to stick together.

I've drizzled a starter course of Cheerios onto Max's high chair tray, and he's running them around the perimeter, just before pinching them like tiddlywinks halfway across the kitchen. He's not exactly a self-feeder yet. When I give him the spoon, he tries to stick it in his ear before launching it over the side. Rule is, once over, bye-bye. I'm still feeding him from a jar. As far as I'm concerned, he can eat Gerber spinach lasagna at college. It'll store nicely in the dorm. I did once make a spinach lasagna, then pureed half of it in the blender, freezing it into Max-sized cubes. He took one spoonful, opened his mouth, turned his head, and let it slide off his tongue onto the floor. I threw out the entire ice tray.

I can get a jar or two of baby food into Max in ten minutes, in less time if he's really hungry. Today he's tired, so I have to jab his lip to get an opening wide enough to shove some cottage cheese in. At least he doesn't spit it back at me, he just uses his spoon as a blocker to keep my food-laden fork at bay. I thrust, he parries. I riposte, he counterparries. I try a flying parry to distract him, and he responds with a corps-a-corps, earning him a black card and an early departure to napland.

Now that he's asleep, I can try to figure out what happened last week. Cheryl dropped a bomb at the Christmas Eve dinner table.

"Will and I are no longer living together. He's moved into the guest suite over the garage," she told the gathered clan: Thom, Georgia, Max, and me; Andy, his wife, Teresa, their kids, Matthew and Mark; Judy, her husband, Carl, their daughter, La-Toya; and Vince. Then, like good Presbyterians, we looked at her, looked at Dad, finished our meal in our usual silence, and went to church. We're not talkers. I didn't even know that Cheryl wasn't my mother until I started going to school and other kids asked me why I didn't call her "Mom." When I asked her, she told me a few details, added some more a few years later, and eventually the puzzle pieced itself together out of a paucity of words.

Cheryl's church has a new pastor, their third in two years. To lead her congregation is to be a drummer in Spinal Tap—your life expectancy is greatly reduced just by saying yes. Reverend Monk has been with them since August, when poor Reverend Hammond's emphysema took a turn for the worst. Cheryl really likes Reverend Monk and promised me that I would not regret going to candlelight services. We have this confrontation every year— she wants me to go to church, I don't want me to go to church. This year I had no intention of going, planned to beg off with Max, but once she broke her news I didn't really have a choice.

Max was placid for the first three hymns, humming along in his sweet, tuneless way, but the instant the children were called forward for the Baby Jesus meet-and-greet, Max let out a squeal and began arching his back like a dolphin. I took him to the bad-baby room and listened to the rest of the service on the intercom. Reverend Monk—whose arm was in a cast for no reason Cheryl could explain—gave the strangest sermon about his talking dog that seemed to go on forever, "Silent Night" was sung, the candles were lit, and we passed the peace out into the chilly night air.

Once sugarplums were dancing in heads, I went downstairs to find a cup of tea already waiting for me by the woodstove.

"Hey, remember when we were kids and Andy and I would get into it?" I said, trying to avoid the subject of her and my father. "You'd yell, 'Cut it out or I'll get the knives,' or better, 'If you don't stop, I'll have to call Service Master to clean up the mess.'"

"I never said that. I don't even know what Service Master is." She sat on the couch and looked at me.

"Oh, come on, you know, they're that company you call to clean up after a murder or a suicide—they come and clean the blood out of the carpets, bits of brain off the walls." I took a sip of tea, burnt the tip of my tongue.

"Nope, never heard of them. I don't know where you get these ideas, but I must say, that's very amusing." She kept looking at me. We sipped in silence, me looking at the fire, Cheryl looking at me.

"You're going to want to know why," Cheryl finally said. Her long gray hair lay coiled into a braid on her shoulder. She'd always been a little on the fat side, but lately she has taken up walking and is emerging from her doughy fifties as a very handsome sixtysomething.

"Why Reverend Monk's arm is in a cast? Not really my business, I should think," I said, continuing my attempt to deflect.

"Very funny. You always were my most clever child." We sat and sipped our tea some more, taking in the trimmed tree and the heap of presents under it. "Well, it's not sex, if that's what you're thinking."

"No, can't say that I was." I've thought about my parents having sex exactly never. "I was thinking that there are too many presents under the tree. We really should start drawing names."

"Because I don't think I've gone a week since we were married without having sex with Will."

"Huh."

"That man must have the strongest libido in creation. But you know, it's rarely making love. It's just the act, the release, then rollover goodnight." Oh, how I longed for the days when we didn't share these kinds of details, but Cheryl clearly wanted me to play counselor to her patient. Rather than run to the bathroom and throw up, I decided to assume the role she'd assigned me.

"Uh-huh . . . and that's not what you want?"

"Don't get me wrong, it's nice to feel desired, but I'm getting too old. I know you will refuse to believe this at your age, but there comes a time when a woman simply does not need to have the mechanics of sex administered to her by a man. We are not designed to procreate beyond a certain age, and so we should not expect to continue the act itself for itself." Though she could have easily taken this from one of her own books, I haven't read them, and that was hardly the moment to admit it.

"I see. I'll have to take your word for it." I matched my tone to hers as well as I could, considering I was in full-blown out-of-body mode, listening to the woman who raised me tell me how bleak my sexual future is while using hers with my father as exhibit A. "Would you like some brandy in your tea?"

"I'll get it." She went into the pantry. I took the moment of quiet to mentally check on the children and to try and think of a way to change the subject without changing the subject. She came back and poured strong shots into both our mugs. She was preparing me for something bigger, something worse, I could sense it.

"He doesn't have another woman yet, but I've asked him to start looking." This wasn't exactly the direction I was hoping she would go, but at least now we were only talking about one of them having sex.

"Okay, and do you think he will?" My father has only ever slept with two women that I know of, my mother and Cheryl. So they were sisters; that's beside the point. "I mean, old dog, new tricks?"

"I hope so. As I've said, he's very virile, and a man needs to feel potent." Ugh. "Don't worry, honey, I've put a small bundle of money in a trust for him to pad his pension, and he's going to live in the guest suite above the garage for as long as he likes—forever, if that's what he wants. His drinking is under control, and God love him, he probably only has a good ten years left before his heart realizes all the liquor and nicotine it's pumped through his body. I just want him to be happy."

"So no divorce?"

"Heaven's no, no divorce." I relaxed back into my chair. They could do whatever they wanted, as long as they didn't make me a bastard. "I love him. I want to stay married to him. But I can't be tied to his needs anymore. I want to travel, have friends over, start a book club. He's so antisocial and I've let him fence us in long enough." There was not a trace of bitterness in her voice. "Sometimes we can choose to do the impossible."

"So I've heard."

"We can love and live at the same time."

"Okay." We fell silent for a while longer, and I thought about what she was trying to tell me until her soft snore woke me from my reverie and I went to bed, leaving her on the couch where she's preferred to sleep for years.

Max screams from the other room just as I am nodding off on my own couch, sorting through how I feel about the un-divorce. I check my watch—he's been asleep for only half an hour, and our playdate is a good while off yet. When I get to his crib, there is nothing visibly wrong, he just sits there and screams in a dull and tearless way. When I try to pick him up, he slams himself into the mattress, heels drumming. His eyes are wide open, but he's not awake. I'm rattled, but I'm not al-lowed to show it, because that's my job. He flops over onto his stomach and I scratch his back until he relaxes and falls into a deep sleep. I wait a good five minutes to make sure he's down again before I run to the computer and type *baby scream nap* into the Google toolbar. Next thing I know I'm in a place I fear more than the ball pit—a stay-at-home mom chat board. After stepping on a couple of "How do I fight the boredom?" and "I'm envious of my friends who work" landmines, I find what I'm looking for.

It seems that Max might have night terrors, something that is much more frightening for the parent than for the child. I'm to do exactly what I did. I'll just have to wait and see if there are more of them. Having taken my anxiety down a notch, I do the un-thinkable and click on the boredom chat. Lots of helpful sugges-tions there, like write a book. Now, that's a good idea. Or how about doing a little yoga while the baby's asleep, or "start a scrap-book about the baby that s/he can then finish when s/he's older." Note to self: must start scrapbook. The one thing these mommies aren't saying is that the boredom is at its worst when the baby is awake. Many mornings I lie in bed with a creeping sense of dread over how I'm going to fill the day. But before I blink, I'm back in bed, wondering where that day has gone.

The phone rings, and I let the machine get it, as I'm deep into a chat on how to start finger foods.

"Hey, kitten, it's Daddy. Um. Hello, Jennifer, it's your father. Calling to say . . . um—"

I grab the phone.

"Hi, Dad, hi, how are you?" My father never calls. I tense up in my seat, half expecting terrible news.

"I'm fine, how are you?"

"Good, how are you? I mean, how's everyone? Is everything okay?" I try not to show my anxiety; try to make the call a normal event. But it's not, and he knows it as well as I do.

"Everyone's great. I'm just calling to say hello and see how you're doing. We didn't get to talk last week much." Or at all. Bad Jenny.

"I know, sorry, it was so quick and we had to get to Vera's and well, you know, with Thom away it's hard to get a moment. And then you went to bed early. So, yeah, I'm doing really great. Thanks. What's new with you?" Other than looking for a new woman, that is.

"I don't think you noticed, but I lost some weight. Debbie down at the clinic put me on a weight-loss pill and it seems to be working." My father has a full-term beer belly. Or beer shelf, as we like to call it, since he rests his bottle there when he watches the game.

"Wow, Dad, that's awesome. Really. But are you sure it's okay with your blood pressure pills and the cholesterol pills?" And the VO Cokes and the 7&7s?

"Yeah, well, we're monitoring that, aren't we? But I've lost five pounds already, and I was just sitting here sewing a button on one of my shirts that I haven't worn in a couple of years 'cause it's too small and I think I'll be wearing it again soon. I feel just great." I hear the wheel on his Zippo grind and a sharp inhale. My heart sinks a bit.

"So you think you'll quit smoking next?" We both force a laugh at this refrain.

"One thing at a time, kitten, that's what I'm working on. Speaking of, I need to tell you something." He takes a long crackling drag on his cigarette, and I listen as he sighs into the exhale.

"Yeah?"

"Well. It's just that I know there were a lot of things I missed. When you were a kid. You know. Plays, recitals. That sort of thing. When I was on the road. And whatnot."

"Uh-huh . . ." I get gooseflesh, sense where this is going, but refuse to enable him or comfort him until he gets there on his own.

"Well, I. Um." He clears his throat, takes another drag. "I just think that it was hard for you. But you need to know it was hard for me too." Hard for him to sit at the bar while I waited to be picked up from an activity he completely missed? Hard for him to pass out before the news on the nights he was home, beer after beer by his side? Hard for him to drive me home blind drunk in a blizzard, never noticing the silent tears that practically choked my fear that he was going to, this time, kill us both?

"Okay. But what do you mean by hard, exactly?" My voice breaks with the flood of these carefully folded and put away memories even as I force him to open more closets.

"I'm sorry, kitten. I'm sorry. I wish I'd been a better dad. I wish I could go back and see you in *Oklahoma!* I bet you didn't think I even remembered what show I missed, right? Well I do, and I'm sorry. Heard you were real good." His voice cracks.

"Uh, you know, I . . ." But I can't say anything, my throat is too tight.

"Don't say anything, Jenny, it's all my fault. I shouldn't have been drinking. I have no excuse. I just want you to know that you are very important to me and you were then too. Even if I didn't make it look like it." He takes another drag, and I imagine the smoke coming out his nose and mouth at the same time, the way it always has. "So, we good?"

"Um, yeah, I think so." Max wails from the other room. "Dad, I have to go get Max and take him out. Okay? Can we talk again later?"

"Okay, kitten. You know where to find me. Above the garage!" His jokey side returns with a small flourish. "I love you, kitten."

"I love you too, Daddy. I'm really glad you feel good."

"I think my dad's going to A.A.," I tell Sven and Penny as we set the kids free in the toddler gym. It's not that bad here, mostly mats and soft areas to climb; a plastic playhouse, a couple of ramps and slides. In the corner is a very low, very authentic balance beam, just in case you've spawned Bart Conner.

"It's about time!" Penny practically yells. "That's so great!"

"What makes you think so?" Sven asks me.

"Well, he just took step nine with me. Apologized. Owned up."

"Hey, remember when I step-nined you?" Penny asks as she helps Mikhail put balls back into one of the small pits. It looks like they've been washed recently; it's not nearly as dirty here as I had thought.

"How could I forget? You told me you got me fired from the Limelight, slept with my boyfriend, stole five hundred dollars from my apartment, and didn't feed my cat the week I went out of town and you were supposed to feed my cat. Did I leave anything out that you'd like to share now?" I spot Max at the door of the little house. Opening. Shutting. Opening. Shutting.

"Crazy times, crazy times." Penny shakes her head, impressed by her badness. "I don't know how you ever forgave me. So your dad is meeting with friends of Bill? Incredible. It's going to change his life, you know. When did he stop drinking?"

"He hasn't."

"You sure?"

"Saw him drink a cup of eggnog Christmas Eve." I'm beginning to wish I hadn't brought this up. I try to change the subject. "Don't you think that little girl over in the playhouse looks too old to be in the toddler gym?"

"She must be about fourteen," Sven says. "I think I see a bra strap."

"Well, maybe he's doing Al-Anon," Penny says. "Some people do that so they can keep drinking and lie about it. Yep, I bet your dad is one of those." She runs off after Mikhail and places him on the balance beam.

"I don't know why you're friends with her." Sven lowers his voice. "She's poison."

"Sometimes, which is why I take her in small doses." I lower my voice as well. "It's like this. I saved her from an overdose a long time ago and I feel invested—in a weird way, I'm her guardian angel. And she's got a great heart, she just doesn't think before she talks. You get used to it."

"You sure you're not enabling her behavior?" He's a little too new in my life to be giving me this sort of rhetorical advice, but I love that he's concerned enough to ask.

"You have to just trust me on this one, baby," I say, taking his hand. "I like having someone from the old days around, reminds me of where I came from. Besides, her kid looks like Howdy Doody—isn't that punishment enough?" Max tries to close the door but the big girl, whose name is Violet and whose dad is videotaping her every move, pushes him onto his butt from the other side. I cross over to sort things out.

"Okay, Max, let Violet have the house for now, come over and play with Lily." I take him by the hand and see Violet's dad shoot me a look. "What was that for?"

"Violet doesn't need to have the house, she can share with Max, can't you, Vi? Vi? Come back here. . . ." She's made it to the front door and yells over her shoulder, "I'm gone bowling." I could ask him why she's not in the bigger kid's gym or, perhaps, school, but he's gone after her, watching her through the little screen on his camera. He probably thinks she's smaller than she is from seeing her two inches tall all the time.

Lily has joined us at the playhouse, and she and Max move in together. Sven and I lean against the wall and people-watch.

"Hey, check out the Joan Lunden twins over there." I nudge him. "She's got her husband *and* the nanny in tow."

"More like the surrogate. Doesn't anyone work in this town?" Sven asks, as though we're here on a break from the stock exchange floor. "What about you, how's Attila?"

"Hannibal. He's good. Still dead. Still waiting for me to resurrect him, do for him what that guy did for Da Vinci. Let me put it this way, I've broken a lot of pencils." I look for a diversion. Though I've been to the library numerous times, I haven't written a word, and I'm far from ready to confess this to anyone. "Two o'clock, meltdown in progress." Sure enough, Violet's back with her dolly and won't share the soccer ball with Mikhail. This should be good. We lean forward as Penny approaches the dad.

"Just how old is your kid, anyway?" Penny says, snapping his viewer flat against his camera. He jerks back, not expecting her head to be life-size.

"Gimme, I wanna play with Samantha!" Violet rips the ball away from Mikhail, landing him on his ass.

"Um, she's, you know, just thirty-seven months. Give the baby the ball, Vi, that's a good girl." He takes it from her and she throws herself onto the mat, arms pinwheeling.

"Listen, pal." Penny drops her voice. "Maybe you should take shrinking Violet to the three-year-old room. This room is for *toddlers*, meaning children who have just learned how to *toddle*."

"Wow, did you hear the way she said *pal*?" Sven says.

"Yep, that's why I keep her around. She's like taking the filter off and letting it fly." Violet's dad, who is a good foot taller than Penny, quickly collects his daughter and carries her out of the room, closing the door quietly behind him. Sven follows Lily over to a large stack of foam blocks, leaving my flank open for unwanted mommy contact.

"Hi, I'm Kate, how old is your son?" a pretty brunette asks me.

"About sixteen months," I reply, trying to indicate with my lack of manners that I'm not in the market for a playdate.

"Wow, he's so big. Jax is nineteen months and he's much smaller. But it gives him greater dexterity. He was an early walker, but we can't get him to talk much. And now I'm pregnant, so he's going to have some changes ahead! I'm Kate. Oh, did I say that already? Silly me." She's sweet, really: delicately boned and pale as the snow. Her red hoodie sweatshirt makes her look like a high school student, even with the little bulge under the pockets.

"I'm Jen. That's Max. Two kids is totally doable. He'll be fine. What was his name? Jackson?"

"Oh. No, it's Jax, *J-a-x*. I wanted to name him Max—great

name—but my husband wanted Jack and so we compromised.
It's got a certain freshness to it, I think. So you stay at home too?"
I nod. "I guess it's because I stay at home that Jax doesn't really
talk yet—careful, sweetie, want Mommy to help you down?"
She's in constant motion, even when she's standing still. "I anticipate his every need, so he hasn't had to learn the words for things
or anything. Do you think that's okay? Anticipating?"

"Well, Max doesn't—"

"I know what you're going to say, Max doesn't talk either so
don't worry about it, but I do worry. I worry a lot. What will Jax
do when his sister arrives? What comes before preverbal? How
will I make sure they both get everything they need? Here, baby,
before you climb up that ladder let me help you down the
slide. . . ." When she moves to help him, I lead Max in the opposite direction and give Sven a good hard pinch.

"Hey," he yells. "What was that for?"

"Did I not say you're not to leave my side? Megamommy almost gave me a panic attack." Max and Lily throw foam squares
at each other.

"Why, what's her story?"

"She's nuts, that's her story. She's anticipating his every need,
penning him in. Naming him *Jax*." I don't know why I dislike
this completely harmless woman so much.

"Jax? That's kind of cute. Sounds gay. I like it." He tosses Lily
a ball, she rolls it to Max, he looks at it.

"You would. You'd probably like her too." I pick up the ball,
hand it to Sven. "I think she's smothering that child."

"You should know, right?" Of course he's joking, but that's
when it hits me. I'm disdainful not of her, but of myself. Ouch.

"Um, yeah, I guess so," I say. He tosses me the ball, which
bounces off my chest.

"Go easy, slugger, don't be so hard on yourself. It's not like Georgia was diagnosed with Stockholm syndrome or anything. When's Thom back?" We sit on a stack of mats and watch Penny try to organize the children into some sort of tumbling class. I wonder to myself what Georgia could possibly have in common with Patty Hearst. Quite a bit, I decide.

"He's not. I mean, he was back for Christmas Day, but then had to leave the next morning again. Do you think I was rude to her? Sometimes I wish he wouldn't come back at all. It's too hard thinking about him on all those airplanes. And he disrupts stuff, lets the kids do whatever they want. Bought Georgia an iPod, if you can believe it." Kate and Jax are over in the corner. I look at her, she glances away.

"How was the Queen of Darkness?"

"Oh, Vera? She'd be a lot more fun if she drank. After updating Thom on how successful Gina is—she made partner at her firm last month—she went on to fill him in on every other ex-girlfriend she could conjure. Worst part is, he let her." Sven pats my knee. "Can we get out of here? I think I've had enough fun for today."

We gather the children into the coatroom, and as we're donning our winter gear and swaddling the kids, Penny pulls me aside.

"Did you talk to Kate in there? Sheesh, she's scary. I felt bad for her—seemed kind of lonely, like she could use some friends."

"You're right, wait here." I go back into the gym and invite Kate and Jax to come have some cocoa with us at City Bakery. She almost bursts into tears, she's so happy to have something to do and big people to do it with. I know exactly how she feels.

Twenty-Eight

SOMETIMES I TRY TO IMAGINE what it would be like to have another baby. All of a sudden Max is starting to look like a little boy, and I'm already missing the tiny little baby phase. I'm hoping that this is temporary insanity. I did have the option to have my tubes tied the last time around. They didn't ask until Max was out—"Hey, while we're in here . . ."—and I was clearly not in a position to be questioning my future fertility, so I said, simply, no. But was it really that simple? Of course not. I only ever wanted two kids, and I consider myself lucky to have one of each and no pining need to push on . . . but . . . there's always that *but* hanging out there.

We discussed Thom's getting a vasectomy, and if you think the Santa argument was ugly, you should have been there for this one. It's true that the Pill has set women free in many ways, but it's also true that we have compromised our health in small ways because of it—ways that men never have to stop and consider. Will this give me a stroke? Will it put ten pounds on? Will it clear up my acne at long last? Will it make my eggs stale? Will it make me a raving lunatic a couple of days a month? I once went on the "mini-Pill" and it made me so homicidal that I told my doctor that if she didn't take me off of it, I might just have to kill her. If the point of taking the Pill is to keep you from getting pregnant and one of its side effects is hating men, well, then it works perfectly. All that being said, I was on the Pill for over a decade, and it was great. Now, though, I resist it as a means of birth control, as much as I resist restarting the vasectomy conversation.

Though I didn't realize it at the time, being pregnant with Georgia was the happiest ten months of my life. I do really well on high doses of estrogen. My hair was thick and shiny, my skin radiant. I was in a perpetual state of grace and harmony, my usual snarky edge honed to butter-melting warmth. Penny stopped talking to me for a while, she was so unnerved by my complete lack of sarcasm. I took full advantage of carrying Max, really wallowed around in that rosy glow. With Georgia, my ever-present companion, we spent day after day curled up on the couch reading books and coloring. We were so inseparable that sometimes I thought I'd made her up, that only I could see her. I anticipated her every need. She never cried, never threw a tantrum. Never asked for something she couldn't have. I pleased her and she pleased me, it was a beautiful, codependent symbiotic free-for-all. Bordering on the parasitic, it can be said, but we managed to keep that line drawn with my growing belly pointing to a different future.

Funny thing is, Max didn't change things between Georgia and me. She took our promise "This is your baby too" very much to heart. She was more four than three when he arrived, and she considered herself his other mommy. Thom was away a few days every week, and though both Cheryl and Vera helped out as well as they could, I found I did perhaps rely on Georgia a little too

much and in the process forgot that she was still just a baby herself.

It was around Georgia's fourth birthday that the panic attacks
started. Cheryl took her upstate for a weekend and by Saturday
afternoon Georgia's hysteria drove them back to me. She wasn't
loud about it; she would just sit by the window, tears streaming
down her face. Cheryl tried to tempt her out of her funk, got her
to bake cookies for me and Max, played with her new paper dolls,
but the whole time the tears continued, even when Georgia would
find the strength to smile through them. Finally, Cheryl asked her
what was wrong, and Georgia whispered the first and only words
of the day: "She's gone." Cheryl saw the warning signs and urged
me to take Georgia to the doctor. I didn't. She had another
episode with Thom at the park. I ignored it. Truth is, when she
was away I spent my time crying as well, and to admit there was
something wrong with her would be to admit there was something wrong with me. And my mothering. It was at the gynecologist's office that I finally realized how far this antiseparation
campaign had gone, when Georgie popped her head up between
my splayed legs and said, "Mommy, pretty, pink!"

I took her to the pediatrician, who confirmed Cheryl's diagno-
sis of very early onset panic disorder caused by intense separation
anxiety, and he referred us to a neuropsychiatrist at Columbia
University, Lillian Moore, who specialized in a drug-free expo-
sure therapy for her youngest patients. Georgia responded beau-
tifully, I fared a little less well, but now we are mostly recovered
and visit Lillian every six months so she can track our progress.

How is it that we don't completely fuck them up, left to our
own devices? Max is as independent from me as Georgie was dependent, and I sometimes worry that I boomeranged him into ad-

vanced separation. Yet at the same time, he didn't exactly crawl early, did he? When I sit down and try to sort out where I'm going wrong and where I'm going right, the two sides of my two darlings get braided into a knot I cannot seem to untie. There's still hope for me, and as long as those tubes are open, I can imagine giving it one more go, getting it right this time, being hands-on without overtouching. Nurturing without poisoning, caring so much that I don't care. Cheryl says it took her until Andy to get it right. But do I really count in her team of four? And if she didn't get it right until Andy, then what does that say about me, her third child? I once asked her what I was like as a baby, and she sighed and said, "Oh, I'm not sure. You got lost; there was a lot happening, and you got lost. But I can tell you that you were very pretty, and we loved you very much."

Twenty-Nine

I STUMBLE INTO THE APARTMENT, wheel a sleeping Max into the quiet of his bedroom—leaving him zipped up and over-heated in his stroller—take off my shoes, and collapse on the couch. Georgia is spending the night at Ella's, and I'm looking down the barrel of macaroni, cheese, Nemo, and baby sedative. Now that Max is getting six teeth at once, he's sleeping through the night entirely with the aid of a thankfully nonaddictive pain medication. I don't know why I didn't think of drugging him months ago. I had planned to take him for his first haircut, but instead we've spent the day racing all over the city to find the perfect contents for Georgia's birthday-party goodie bags. The big day is only a week away, and I feel seriously unprepared. I don't think she stopped to consider back in September that her birthday is in the dead of winter. We've had to rent out a space at Chelsea Piers instead of picnicking in Central Park, which seems much more sensible now that there are four inches of snow on the ground. She's currently obsessed with goodie bags, a curiosity that I had never encountered until Park Streeters entered our lives. Our haul so far:

Matinka Sullivan: two Pocket Pals with scooter, handmade maple sugar candy in the shape of a *G*, and hand-knit cashmere mittens.

Emma Shapiro: a box of Payard chocolates, a Steuben paperweight in the shape of a *G*, and a very retro Mary Kay pink cosmetics compact for girls.

Emma Jones: matching mother-daughter Kate Spade clutches, a tiny collapsible umbrella printed with *G*s, and Tommy Girl perfume.

Donovan Reilly: a 1/64th-scale remote-controlled Hummer and a copy of a children's picture book written and illustrated by Donovan's mom, about Donovan. I think she also printed and bound them herself.

The bar is set high, and I just thank god that Chloë's birthday is a month after Georgia's. We already got the invitation, to a store called American Girl Place. Something to do with wholesome dolls and high tea, followed by a mini-musical dedicated to Chloë in the American Girl Theater. Chloë's dad made it big in telecom something or other and has pull around town. His picture is often in the business section of the paper, which usually ends up under Peeve's litter unread. Hillary has called me three times since the New Year trying to schedule a dinner foursome—she really can't quite understand that Thom is not in the country, no matter how many times I tell her. I've offered her lunch with just me, but she hasn't responded.

I'm drifting into a disco nap when I see the red light blinking on the phone. It seems I have four messages. Four more than I usually have. I punch play.

"Hey, Jen, it's Kate. How are you? Thanks for the other day. It was really good to get out and spend some time with other mommies. I hope I wasn't too nuts. And that you'll, um. So, can we get together?"

"Yeah, yeah, Kate, got it, but you're going to have to call back, I don't have your number," I say to the empty room. I hit DELETE, PLAY.

"Hey, babe, it's me. I miss you. Hi, Georgie, hi, Maxabillion! Jen, call me tonight, I have to talk to you about next week, okay? We've hit sort of a snag, but I'll be home as soon as I can." I stab REPLAY. "Hey, babe, it's me"—stab FAST FORWARD—"about next week"—stab again. "I'll be home as soon as I can"—REWIND, PLAY—"as soon as I can." Great. Not coming home for Georgia's birthday. That's just fucking great. I punch DELETE, PLAY.

"JP, it's me. Been a while. Let's eat." REPLAY. "JP, it's me." What is it about men that it's always "It's me," like you don't know any other me's? "Been a while. Let's eat." Ever charming, oh so verbal. PLAY.

"Jennifer? I hope I have the right number. It's Christy. You haven't moved, have you?" I sit up straighter. "I'd love to get lunch and catch up. I might have something interesting for you. Meet me tomorrow at Takashimaya, noon sharp. Don't call back, just be there." REWIND, PLAY: "something interesting for you." REWIND, PLAY: "for you."

I look down at the notepad and try to decide in which order to return calls. It's just about five o'clock, so it's almost five a.m. in Singapore. He could have called my cell phone, the coward. Fuck, he's punking out about next week. He was due to return on Wednesday and stay through Sunday, then come home for good the first of February. The phone rings, and I let the machine get it, as I tuck Christy into the back of my head to deal with later.

"Hello? Jennifer? Hi, it's Kate, I forgot to—"

I pick up. "Hey, Kate, how's it going?" I cross her name off the list, doodle.

"Hi, oh, hi. I forgot to leave my number. Sorry."

"Yeah, I know, that's okay. We just got in from running around. . . ." Damn him.

"Oh, is this a bad time? Do you want me to call you back?"

"Max is asleep, so I have a couple of minutes." A couple of minutes to have a meltdown, that is.

"Oh, I'm so sorry, this is a bad time. Why don't I call later?" Her voice cracks on "later" and the next thing I know she's quietly sniffling.

"Kate, are you okay?"

"Yes. No. Yes, okay, I'm okay. I'm fine. Really?" She squeaks from trying so hard not to cry.

"You want to come over for dinner? It's just me, Max, and Nemo. We'd love the company." I look at it this way: it will keep me from slamming my head into the concrete from the sheer boredom of watching that clown fish for the hundredth time. It's the only video Max will watch. If only I had Dory's memory.

"You sure? No, I can't. Kyle's expecting dinner in an hour, and Jax has an unreasonable fear of Nemo." I hear Jax in the background scream, *"No Nemo!"* followed by Kate's cajoling. "Sorry about that, I forgot we can't say N-e-m-o out loud. At least he's talking, right? You know, Kyle works so hard so I can stay home, it's not much to ask to have a hot meal at the end of the day. And I need to pick up. It's amazing how messy . . ." Now she's sobbing in earnest.

"Okay, okay, calm down. Do you want to talk? Max is asleep— I have fifteen minutes at least, okay?" I curl my feet under me and rest my head against the arm of the couch. It's cold and windy outside and hot and stuffy in here. The change in temperature has rendered me lethargic. What I wouldn't give for a nap. I wait through the silence on the other end, letting Kate piece together her composure, decide how much of her interior world she's going to reveal. I hear the *Baby Shakespeare* music on her end.

"I just can't do it again," is what she finally offers.

"Do what?" I murmur, and though it's simply because I can't muster the energy to speak louder, it has the added effect of calming her even more.

"Childbirth."

"Oh, I see." I take a note out of Cheryl's book, offer little in the way of words, much in empathy.

"I know it's a little late to be thinking about this, but I'm only just four months, that's first trimester technically, isn't it? I mean, they count like an extra week or something. It's not even a fetus yet, really." Kate's voice has taken on an edge. I sit up, suddenly realizing what she's asking me to greenlight.

"Slow down, let's start over. You didn't want to get pregnant?"

"No, I mean yes, I wanted to get pregnant. . . . They say you forget. That even if you don't forget, then at the very least the hormones during the next pregnancy help you gain courage again. But I can't do it, Jen, I just can't. And if I'm going to remedy the situation, then I have to do it now." The phone line beeps, I ignore it. "Do you need to get that?"

"Get what?"

"I heard that hollow sound when call-waiting beeps. Go ahead, it might be important, this can wait." Kate is clearly in need of better counseling than I can give.

"Kate, it's okay, they'll call back. Probably a telemarketer. Go on."

"I just tell them I'm the babysitter. 'Cause that's what I am.

You know, the person who sits around with the baby." She attempts to laugh at her own joke. "I'm not crazy, you know. I should go. Kyle'll be home any minute and I have to get Jax cleaned up." I feel like we're acting a scene out of *Law & Order* and that something bad could happen if I don't step it up.

"I know how you feel." It's a cliché, but it's a start. "Can you tell me about having Jax? Would that maybe help?" Having had two circus-sideshow deliveries of my own, I think that maybe if I listen to hers, then tell her mine, it will make her feel stronger.

"Well. Yes, where do I start? Okay, so my water breaks, nothing happens for ten hours, so they induce. They use Cytotec to jump up my Braxton-Hicks into real contractions and within about five hours I'm in agony. I start begging for an epidural, even though I had really really wanted to have natural, and they tell me it takes a half hour of pushing fluid into me before I can get the needle. A half hour later, in blinding pain, I'm in the shrimp position, clutching a nurse as contractions continue to wrack me. I never swear, but I did then. They tried three times with the needle before hitting my sciatic nerve, and all I can tell you is I thought I was about to die."

"Wow" is all I can manage.

"Yeah, wow is right, but it gets better." Her anger is coming in waves now, and her voice has developed a slight shiver. "So I tell them to fuck off—excuse my French—and the midwife offers Demerol, which must be a really sweet drug if you're not being run over by a steamroller every two minutes. Did I mention that at this point I'm about three centimeters? How's that for achievement? So then they put me on Pitocin and the fun really begins. The Demerol wears off, and the needle boy comes back in, this time getting it in two tries. I'm out of the woods now, I think: just have to dilate. Which I do, to nine centimeters in twenty minutes. It's finally time to push, and I think, home run, no more pain, baby's coming out. An hour goes by. Then two. Next thing I've been pushing for five hours and Jax hasn't even crowned. They suggest dialing down the epidural so I can 'feel' better where Jax is. Seems like a good idea at the time. What they don't tell me is that once they dial it down they can't dial it back up. That's when it happened." She stops talking. I wait. She sighs. "I wished him dead, Jennifer. I wished with everything I had that he would just die so they could tear him out and stop the pain."

"But he didn't."

"No, he didn't. It took another hour of pushing, an episiotomy that turned into six inches of shredded skin—they had to reconstruct *everything*—and then suction to get him out. I couldn't look at him. I held him, but I couldn't look at him and I just wanted them to take him away as fast as possible. Then a piece of the placenta didn't deliver and they had to rush me into surgery. I developed a Percoset addiction that lasted months. My doctor tells me that Jax was sunny-side up but that they didn't know until he came out. She also tells me that the next time it will be much easier, since I've already ripped a Jax-size hole in my vagina."

"She said that?"

"Not exactly, but she's really high on me having 'the birth I deserve,' as she says."

"But you don't want that?"

"Do you want me to tell you my birth story?" This time we both laugh.

"Then why not have a C-section? I've had two, it's not so bad." Now, there's an understatement. Like telling a woman who has scaled Kilimanjaro that she should have no problem with an anthill.

"Kyle says we can't afford it. Unless it's an emergency, our insurance won't cover the bills. And my doctor feels that there are too many C's being done already. And it's more dangerous. She has faith in me that I can do it next time." I sense that Kate is coming back around to the idea now, that the temporary desire to abort has left her. "I'm feeling much better, Jennifer, thanks for listening, but Kyle's going to be home any minute and I really do have to go."

"Listen, Kate, you can have a C-section. It can't be any more dangerous than what you've already done. I'll loan you the money if you need it." I have no idea why I would offer someone I just met money. A lot of it. I want her to say yes and to say no.

"Oh, wow, gosh, no, really. I couldn't, geez, I mean. That's really nice of you, but I couldn't. Thanks for offering, but I'll be okay, and I'll get some therapy. I think I just needed to get that off my chest. I've never told anyone how I felt about Jax, not even Kyle. I've done everything I can think of to make it up to the little guy. I don't even know why I told you. Please don't tell anyone, okay? You're the *best*. Oops, gotta go, have a great night!" Kate sounds like her false-cheerful self again, and I hang up the phone with a creeping dread. I'm torn between wanting to save her and wanting to run far away from her as fast as I can.

I rest my head against the back of the couch and let my eyes slam shut. Just for five minutes. Please God, just five minutes. I should put a load of laundry in while I have the time, but the phone rings in my hand. I reflexively press TALK, put the phone to my ear, say hello.

"Hello, Mrs. Thomas Bradley?" a woman asks, her voice sounding far away and lightly accented.

"I'm sorry, she's not home right now," I mumble.

"Well, it's rather important, can you tell me when she'll be in?" Sort of British, but with a hint of Asia.

"Um, I'm just the babysitter, she should be back soon, can I take a message and have her call you?" Outsourcing. You'd think they'd find credit card people with less detectable accents.

"No, that's all right, I'll try again later. Just tell her I need her to answer some questions." I try to sit up, intrigued, but my head is just too heavy.

"Excuse me? Can you repeat that?" My voice drops to its normal tone, its I'm-not-the-babysitter tone.

"Is this Mrs. Bradley?" she asks again, thinking my cover blown.

"No, I already told you, I'm just the babysitter. Now, what are your questions?"

"Ma'am, I'm not sure what kind of game you think this is, but unless you can identify yourself, I will need to call back later." Uh-oh, she "ma'amed" me. This isn't a telemarketer, it's the government. Only one way to handle this. I hang up. Speed-dial Thom's number in Singapore. He picks up on the first ring.

"Hello?" he says, not at all sleepy for five a.m.

"Hey, it's me, a really weird thing just happened and—"

"Oh, hello, no, we don't need any of those," he says. I hear a woman's voice in the background but can't make out her words. "Yes, we have plenty of fish sauce, and we're very happy with it. Thank you." The line goes dead. Maybe it wasn't Thom. I dial back. No answer, not even the machine.

I stretch out on the couch, listening to the phone ring halfway around the world. I finally give up and just as I'm dozing into a fitful nap, Max yells, "A-dah!" I don't move a muscle other than

the one that picks up my left eyelid. He calls out, "A-dah-dah!" I
play dead. He's only been asleep for twenty minutes. *"Ma-ma!"*
Insistent, not hysterical. But hysterical is no doubt next. He goes
quiet. We're in a standoff. I'm made out of lead, he's spun sugar,
ready to roll another four hours. I drift into a hyper-sleep that
turns into a bout of lucid dreaming—I'm caught in a loop where
I wake up every few seconds, hang up the phone, and go to Max's
stroller and check on him. But when I get there, Jax is in the
stroller, blue-faced and cold. Each time I start to panic, I half
wake again, only to repeat this horror. When I finally wake for
real, an hour has passed, and I'm drenched in sweat. I rush into
Max's room and find him snoring softly, the curls of his too-long
hair pasted to his red cheeks. Fish sauce? Did I imagine that
phone call? I must be more exhausted than I think. I curl up on
the floor at his feet and watch him until he wakes.

Thirty

BEFORE I GOT KNOCKED UP the first time I had countless discussions with my friends about the intensity, duration, and quality of childbirth pain. I read a handful of books on the subject and heeded Naomi Wolf's warnings about the medicalization of childbirth even while dismissing her personal reflections, which were even more horrifying than her birth stories. I thought I'd heard it all, from back labor causing excruciating pain, to one friend needing reconstructive surgery—for a vaginal delivery. I weighed the advice from all sides and determined that I would need as much pain medication as early as possible when it was my turn. Hook me up, I said. Cut me open if you must. In all my conversations I found only one woman who had what I would consider an uncomplicated, pain-free birth.

I also knew to ask my friends within twenty-four hours to recount their experience, because so many women do choose to forget. Cheryl gave birth back in the days when they'd give you something called "twilight sleep"—a combination of morphine and scopolamine, a regular amnesia cocktail—tie you to the bed, and let you hallucinate your way through the pain, with the cruel promise that you would remember none of it. During her labor with Judy, Cheryl imagined that the baby had already been born even as she was still dilating, and that the doctors had taken it away from her, never to be seen again. She thinks she remembers the woman in the bed next to her screaming, "Hang up! Hang up! Hang up!" over and over again. Seems her birth story is only shy one Nurse Mildred Ratched. All that said, Cheryl did go on to have two more babies and insists that childbirth is the easiest thing she's ever done. No small wonder, considering her memory was repeatedly wiped clean of the experience. In fact, she told me recently that she would gladly be a surrogate for women who can't have babies, if only she were younger and still had a uterus.

A funny thing happened a few weeks into my pregnancy. Out of the blue I decided I wanted a midwife. I found a beautiful practice downtown, complete with rooms that looked like hotel suites—king-size beds, whirlpools, birthing chairs—and a staff of young, smart, strong midwives. By my second visit I felt completely in control of my own pregnancy and started to imagine what it would be like to manage my labor through self-control and fortitude. I have wide hips, I reasoned, and I was told my mother had me in less than ten hours, no complications—that she was a woman who knew no pain. Which is reassuring considering she died in a head-on collision a few weeks later. By month 7, I had decided that there would be no drugs anywhere near me, that a combination of yoga chanting, massage, and pressure-point focus should and could do the trick. I'd seen the videos, Thom and I had taken the birthing class, and now, thanks to a prepartum pair-up, we had our own "birth-counselor" who had done it all naturally—had actually given birth *in the water*.

Needless to say, it didn't work out the way I had planned, and within five minutes of my emergency C-section the estrogen levels had dropped, and I couldn't believe that I had put myself through this much pain and these truly scary turns of event. I told every woman I knew that they should never, under any circumstances, ever get pregnant.

A few years and many mai tais later, I found myself in Kate's shoes—two sizes bigger than normal to accommodate my constantly swollen feet. Seems I had forgotten my own edict. And here's the kicker—I once again became convinced that I could do it all-natural. Estrogen is a pretty drug; it makes you emotionally attuned and strong willed, and it heightens your senses to wolfish levels. It also encourages you to do the impossible while removing your ability to tell the difference between heroism and stupidity. At least this time I was smart enough to give up within a couple of hours of no dilation. As soon as I saw the banana peel on the floor in front of me, I called in the scalpel. Not that a C-section is God's gift to women, not by a long shot. I recovered pretty well this time, since I didn't exhaust myself with twenty hours of labor, but then a creepy thing happened—the incision wouldn't heal. This is not quite as disgusting as it sounds, but trust me, it was gross. They restitched me twice, then applied a noxious-smelling salve to the last inch or so that took a good six months to close up. A ropy scar is my reward.

Some look on pregnancy as a miracle, insisting that for a woman to make another human being out of two small cells is alchemy at its finest. I think the real miracle is that we survive the experience—and often plunge right back into the deep end of childbirth. When I stop to think about all my friends who have had kids and the problems they've encountered on the way, it overwhelms me to think that so many of the mothers and babies would not be alive today if it weren't for intervention. Including me.

Thirty-One

THE PHONE RINGS. I surface out of a dreamless sleep, note the time—ten p.m.—and pick up the receiver.

"Mph—hello?"

"Hey, beautiful, did I wake you?" Thom asks.

"Yes," I say, sitting up, as wide awake as I was sound asleep a minute before. "Where have you been? I've been trying to call you all night."

"I'm at work, babe," he says, his voice clear and sure. "Listen, I fucked up. I'm supposed to be at Georgia's school today—I mean, in the morning—to give a show-and-tell about ancient Greece."

"What?"

"I told Miss Cartwright back in September that I'd do it, put it in my Outlook, and forgot all about it until my Blackberry just went off." He sighs. "You have to go in my place."

"Thom, no, you can't do this to me. Call Cartwright and tell her you can't make it." I push the covers off, hot and mad. "Are you coming home next week or not?"

"Right, that's why I called earlier. I can't come home just yet," he says, as glass shatters in the background.

"Where are you?" I ask.

"Singapore, where else would I be?" he answers. "I'm in the office. One of the assistants just dropped a coffee mug." Sounded more like a wineglass, if you ask me. I distinctly hear a woman's giggle this time, and what seems to be Thom muffling the handset.

"Okay, but when I called earlier, you were really weird and then hung up on me," I say, paranoia prickling my skin.

"You didn't call earlier. I mean, I didn't talk to you earlier. You might have called, but I didn't answer because the phone didn't ring . . . and it must have been a wrong number." He goes quiet, and I roll over, exhaling into the phone.

"You were talking about fish sauce."

"Wow, that's weird. I mean, why would I be talking about fish sauce? I wasn't even home earlier, you should have left a message on the machine."

"I couldn't, the machine wasn't on. Wait, what time did you leave the apartment?" If I can't get him to tell me the truth, maybe I can catch him in a lie.

"Why are you cross-examining me? Jen, I said I wasn't here, so I wasn't here, okay? Trust me, I know when I'm here and when I'm not." His voice is so uncharacteristically harsh that I'm a little unnerved. "Now, will you please go to Georgia's school and give a presentation on ancient Greece tomorrow at ten?"

"I'm not prepared . . ."

"They're children, Jen, not a dissertation committee. You could do it in your sleep." He exhales. I try to remember what I have going tomorrow. Oh shit, lunch with Christy.

"But who will watch Max?" I ask. "I've already asked Sven to take him in the afternoon so I can meet Christy, but he works in the morning. . . ."

"What about Veronika?"

"It's her day off. And I'm not calling her the night before to work in the morning. That's not fair."

"Okay then, call my mother. She'd be happy to do it."

"I'm not calling Vera in the middle of the night, are you insane?"

"Don't worry, I'll call her. You know, Jen, one of these days you're going to need Vera. And it's not exactly the middle of the night." Now he's just being mean.

"Says you," I throw back. "You have all the answers, don't you, Thom?"

"Let's not do this," he says with the kind of exasperation you give a misbehaving child, not your wife of ten years. Unless you're hiding something, that is.

"Do what?" I hiss.

"Fight long-distance. You know I worry about you enough as it is."

"You worry about me? You worry about *me*? Then maybe you shouldn't have gone halfway around the fucking world if you're so worried about me." I restrain my hand from slamming down the phone.

"Jen, stop winding yourself up," he cajoles, a softer note in his voice. "I didn't mean that I don't trust you, I just worry about you, is all. You're taking on a lot of responsibility and I wish I were there to help. Do us this one favor and I promise to make it up to you. I just can't stand disappointing Georgia."

"Fine. Why not let me be the one to disappoint her, then? That seems fair. Very thoughtful of you, darling," I say. "Will you be making it home for her birthday next weekend, or do you want me to somehow disappoint her for you on that one too?"

"Okay, let's just call a truce. I don't think I can make it as planned, but I'm going to try my best. Say hello to Christy for me." The line goes dead. Did he hang up on me? I wait for the phone to ring, for him to call back and apologize. An hour passes, then two. I get up and make some Sleepytime tea, wash up the dishes, and straighten the house pending Vera's inspection. I get back into bed and try to read in *Yoga Times* magazine how to deep-breathe into sleep, but my head is buzzing so loudly that nothing works. Ancient Greece to four-five-six-year-olds? How could I possibly make it interesting? That was most definitely him with the fish sauce, and there was clearly a woman in the background on both calls. That's it, he's having an affair. It was cute and funny when I joked about it, but it's getting uglier and sadder by the minute. I think I forgot to put the clothes in the dryer, I should get up and do that. Mythology, tragedies, democracy, what angle to take? If I could just remember the name of the inner sanctum of the Parthenon . . .

"No, I don't wanna get up," I say as a very firm hand shakes my shoulder. I leap out of bed and pull the hair out of my eyes only to find Vera holding a plate of toast out to me. "What? How did you get in?"

"Thom gave me a set of keys in case of emergency, dear, and from the look of things here, this was the perfect time to use them." He gave her keys? That bastard. Adultery is one thing, letting Vera have free access to my house is quite another. "Here, eat something, you need to get moving if you're going to get Georgia to school on time."

"I have to get Max up first," I say, noting that it's eight o'clock. "He's bound to be soaked."

"He's already bathed, fed, and dressed," she says. The plate hovers between us. I take it from her and start toward the bathroom. "Oh, and I brought you something to wear, I think it will suit you." She moves a dry-cleaning package onto the bed from the dresser. "It was Theta's right before she had Sela, so it should fit you perfectly. It's a bit too baggy in the middle for her now. If you like it, you can keep it for your next pregnancy—it should get you through the first trimester."

I think I feel a tooth crack as I hold back a *fuck you*. No matter how many times I tell Vera that I'm done breeding, she refuses to stop dropping her unwanted innuendos. I head into the bathroom, hoping that a shower will clear my head enough to tell Vera that it is not my responsibility to cover for her two-timing son. Just as I've dropped my nightshirt onto the floor, Georgia bursts in on me.

"Mommy, Granna says you're going to be Daddy! Wait till the other kids see how pretty you are." Good thing they can't see me right now.

"You know, Georgie," I say, pulling my robe around me, "I was thinking about maybe not being Daddy today. Mommy's really really tired, she didn't sleep much last night. Maybe they can wait until next week when Daddy's home?" Her face collapses.

"But," she says, looking up at the light to keep tears from collecting, "please? One of the kids called me a orphan, that I'm adopted and a orphan." I sit her down on the side of the tub.

"Which kid said that, sweetie?"

"BJ. His daddy works with my daddy and his daddy told him I was good as a orphan." I really do have to get more involved in this kid's school; I had completely forgotten that Bjorn Jr. was her classmate. Usually I drop Georgia off as early as possible to avoid the coffee klatchers and stay-at-home nannies, then slip away undetected and unmolested, so I've never seen Bjorn dropping off his son. He probably has the driver do it, anyway.

"Well, you're not *an* orphan and you're not adopted—look, here's the scar to prove it." I open the robe, give her a peek. "Now go play with Granna so I can get ready to take you to school."

Couple of peas in a pod, Thom and Bjorn. I should have seen all this coming. Of course Thom's proximity to the slug would eventually have consequences. How could I have been so unprepared? I turn the shower off and reach for a towel, only to realize that the shampoo is still in my hair.

When I get out of the shower, my bed is made and a white cashmere sweater dress is laid out across the duvet, along with an unopened package of nude-colored tights and a brand-new white bra and white slip. Well, if Vera is going to insist on behaving like my personal valet, the least I can do is humor her until I divorce her son and take him for every penny he has. I just need to make sure this isn't the Thom I married. Or is it?

I put on the bra and tights but decide to go without the slip. Something about it just feels too matronly. Because this is clearly a day when the wrong things will go right, it comes as no surprise that the dress is a perfect, flattering fit. I turn in front of the mirror one way, then the other, but I cannot discern any grotesqueries. The sad thing is that it's not even a maternity dress—Theta refused all things Liz Lange. It really is true that if you spend the money, you will look it. I'm tempted to lock myself in this room rather than let Vera see how right she was about this one.

After pulling my hair into a tidy twist and applying the basic makeup, I emerge anyway, to a round of slappy-hand applause.

I am standing in front of a room full of children dressed in togas. I am likewise draped in a white cotton sheet. Next to me is Bjorn

Olson, who arrived mere seconds ago with his cookie-cutter six-year-old son—proof that human cloning is already common-place. Thom, my bastard soon to be ex-husband, neglected to mention that I wouldn't be the only daddy here. Off to our left is a very twittery Miss Cartwright. Some of the children are seated in a beanbag semicircle at our feet, others are off in a corner finger-painting, yet another younger group is splashing their laurel wreaths in a large blue tub of water propped up on a small table. My daughter is in the farthest reach of the room, a slice of her visible between the papier-mâché columns of a mini-Parthenon. A fertility bull stuffed full of chocolate Greek coins is suspended from a sprinkler pipe overhead, waiting to be eviscerated by these little monsters. You would think that I'm about to say, "And then I woke up." You would be wrong; I'm clearly not going to wake up from this one.

"Children." Miss Cartwright claps her hands together. She's maybe a foot taller than the tallest child. "Children, pardon me, but if I may have your attention for a few minutes, please?"

"Hey, Jen," Bjorn whispers. "You're looking fantastic." I could say the same for him, because he's camera-ready handsome with his pink-pin-striped navy suit and wrinkle-proof smile, but no fucking way.

"Thanks," I say without turning my head.

A larger child goes over to the water table and dunks a smaller one. They both laugh, the smaller one saying, "Dood that again, dood again!"

"Simon!" Miss Cartwright bellows, and the whole room stops. "Enough!" She turns to us. "Sorry about that—really, I almost never have to raise my voice to the children, honest. Just some-times it's the only way." Her fine blond hair is pulled back into a bun so tight I can see her temples pulsing from the strain. She's wearing glasses with heavy black frames, but I'd be willing to bet they're an affectation and not a seeing aid.

"Now," she says, turning back to the room and smoothing her blue tweed jumper dress down the front, "who's ready to learn about ancient Greece?"

"Me! Me! Me!" the tallest girl practically screams. She's a pretty brunette packed into a pink-flamingo-colored Chanel-style suit. When I look closer, I see the authentic hugging *C*'s on the buttons.

"Okay, Jennifer, please take a seat, I love your enthusiasm!" Is it possible that I'm old enough for my name to have developed a retro appeal to a new generation? Miss Cartwright presses young Jennifer into a red beanbag, breaking the no-red-with-fuchsia rule. Whatever next? "Today we have with us BJ's dad, Mr. Olson, and standing in for Georgia's dad, Mrs. Bradley. BJ, Georgia, will you both please come sit down here in front?" She makes little circles with her hands, trying to herd them, even though BJ has yet to leave Bjorn's side, and Georgia, at the utterance of her name, has slipped into the dark recesses of the opisthodomos. See, I knew it would come to me if I didn't force it.

"Why don't we all take a little walkie over to Georgia's palace?" Bjorn says, covering the ten yards in three strides. I've never really noticed it before, but he has pretty classic Greek lines for someone of Scandinavian descent—his skin is a buttery brown even in the depth of winter and his hair hangs in loopy, finger-poking curls. I remember once stroking his arm in Egypt and remarking on the hairless smoothness of it. He catches me staring at him, winks, and nods me back over to his side. "The Parthenon—can you say Par-the-non?" The children try, Bjorn smiles wider. "Great, right, the Parthenon was started in 447 B.C. Who here knows what 'B.C.' stands for?" None of the children move. I raise my hand. "Yes, Mrs. Bradley?" Bjorn says in a way that makes it sound more like "Mrs. Robinson."

"It means literally 'before Christ,' which is an easy way to remember it, but a better way of thinking about it is 'before the Christian era,' meaning before there were Christians, or followers of Christ." Little eyes gloss over to the left of me. "This gives it a wider scope and sensibility, and sets it more effectively against A.D., or Anno Domini, or, literally, the year of our Lord." Little eyes gloss over to the right of me. "Though since the late nineteenth century many scholars and archeologists have preferred C.E. and B.C.E., which take Christ out of the counting, if you will, referring instead to the 'Common Era.' Any questions so far?" Ella raises her hand. It's always good to have a friend in the audience. "Yes, Ella?"

"Mrs. Bradley, may I go to the bathroom, please?" she asks, clearly in need of some fresh air and a cigarette break.

"Now, Ella, don't be rude," Miss Cartwright says. "You can wait until after daddy hour, yes?" Daddy *hour*? Only five minutes have passed. How about daddy half hour? There are two of us, after all. Bjorn takes me by the elbow, and it's as if I've freestyled into a pond of jellyfish. I jerk free, rub my arm.

"So yes," he continues, "the workers began building the Parthenon a very long time ago, when Athens was at the height of its imperial power." A little boy's hand shoots up as he pushes small wire-framed glasses up his nose with the other hand.

"Michael, it's not polite to interrupt the daddies, but as long as you don't have to go to the bathroom you may ask your question," Miss Cartwright says, looking back at Bjorn with *love me* in her eyes. I step into her sight line. She moves around to the other side.

"Yeah, okay, so like, is Athen like Darth Vader?" Michael says, a little out of breath for someone standing so still. "Cuz before the first trilogy, which is really the second trilogy, was after he got the imperial power, and I was thinking that maybe it's like that." His striped shirt pushes in and out, he's so excited to have made this connection.

"Just like that." Bjorn chuckles. I start to correct him, and he puts his hand in front of me. I want to bite into the muscular palm. "But let me just clarify one thing: Athens is a place, Darth Vader is a person. The empires were very similar, though, as the Peloponnesians were about to come together and topple the dark star that was Athens." He leans against the wall. "So, who wants to go break open the Minotaur and see what's inside?" The children all yell, "I do! I do!" and race to get in line for the blindfold. Bjorn starts to follow, I grab his coat sleeve.

"The dark star that was Athens? That's it? End of talk? We've got another forty-five minutes to fill, and there's so much more to tell them. Piñatas aren't even Greek, for god's sake."

"Listen, doll, they just want chocolate, they don't want to hear about the Common Era—or before the Common Era, for that matter." He moves in close. I can smell licorice on his breath, probably Sen-Sen. "They behaved for ten whole minutes. Look how happy they are. Besides, it gives us time to grab a cup of coffee before I have to be at work."

"Over my dead body." I take a step back.

"Nice cliché." He leans back in. He's not so much a close talker as a close seducer. At ten-thirty in the morning, in front of our children.

"Nice pocket square." It sounded better in my head, trust me.

"Nice husband," he says. So he knows too.

"Look, pal, you're the one who sent him halfway around the world."

"Maybe so, maybe so. But I didn't make him drink." He leans closer, whispers in my ear. I feel myself flush red. "Look, I'm going to take a swing at the bull, car leaves in ten minutes. Go dry your panties." If this were yesterday I wouldn't even consider spending one second more with this walking penis, but I need to know what Bjorn knows about Thom, even if it means admitting to myself that my underpants are indeed a bit on the moist side.

"Mommy?" I feel a tug on my toga, look down to see Georgia, her face streaked with tears. I fall to my knees and dry her cheeks with the corner of her sheet.

"Oh, Geege, what's the matter, baby?" Did she feel the tension between me and Bjorn? Have I finally won the Queen of Bad Mommies crown?

"I'm so proud of you," she says between sniffles. "You're so pretty and all the kids loved you."

"Then why are you crying, sweetie, doesn't that make you happy?"

"Yes, Mommy, these are I-love-you tears." I pull her close to me and our wreaths knock off our heads as we hug.

"You're my everything," I whisper, "my all." There's a sudden hollow *thwack* followed by a shower of coins, a few of which roll to where we sit. I pick one up, unwrap it, and hold it in my teeth. Georgia bites the other side and kisses me as she pulls away, backing into the Acropolis as she smiles and mouths "Bye-bye."

When I stand and turn around, Bjorn has left. I grab my coat and pull it on as I race past Miss Cartwright's chirpy thanks, throw her a "You're welcome," and dash out the front door. I look both ways down the street, but there's no car, no Bjorn, no salient proof of my husband's misdeeds. I stamp my foot, hear a low whistle, and there's Bjorn, leaning up against the school, shaking more Sen-Sen into his mouth. Trying to regain some cool, I walk over to him with my hand extended. He shakes a few tiny black candy squares into my palm. I toss them onto my tongue.

"I haven't had these since Egypt," I say, buttoning my coat against the cold. We both know what I mean. "I've got a twelve o'clock appointment on Fifth and Fifty-fifth, and I'm going to walk along the Park. You can join me if you want, but I'll be passing on the ride for today, thanks." There's nothing like a little hard-to-get around Bjorn.

"I'll just have the car follow us in case you change your mind," he says, motioning to a car I didn't even notice right in front of us. We walk a few blocks without talking, trying to get our blood working against the chill in the air. My dress begins to bunch up between my legs. I try to pull it down gracefully, only to have it bunch up again.

"So where have you been keeping yourself, Jenjy?" he asks when we get to Fifth Avenue, taking my arm as we cross the street to the Park. Again I feel an electrical shock, but this time I decide it's from the static cling generated by my tights. "I thought we'd see more of each other with Thom away."

"How's your new wife, Bjorn?" I ask. "She still escorting rich closeted gay men to charity balls, or did you let her quit her day job once you married her?"

"You're cute, I've always liked that about you. Spunky." He stops, turns me to him, catching my boot heel on a paving stone. I half expect him to lean in for a kiss right here in front of New York City. Worse, I more than half want him to. "Listen, Jen, I really don't want to be the one to tell you this." He looks past me, over the top of my head. "But Thom's gotten himself into some trouble."

"Let go of my arm," I say, making room to slap him if need be.

"Calm down, it's not what you think. Come over here." He takes me to a bench along the sidewalk, sits me down, and pulls out a flask as he stands before me. "Drink?"

"No thanks. He's having an affair, isn't he?"

"Okay, it is what you think, but it's more than that." He looks down the sidewalk to his left, then to his right, before sitting next to me. The skin down the entire side of my body goes hot; I move an inch away. "They've been forging antiquities and running them through my firm. I've turned a blind eye, but now that the feds are on their trail, I don't think I can help him. But I can still help you."

"Wait, wait, wait. You've got this all wrong. 'They' who?" I can suspect my husband of cheating on me, but he'd never cheat on the art world. It's simply too dangerous, and he's not made of that kind of moral fabric. Or is he? I look at Bjorn, waiting for him to respond. He watches a mother quickly pass with a jogging stroller as he takes a swig from the flask and puts it back in the vest pocket of his camel hair coat, extracting an envelope at the same time. I start to shake.

"Jen, you know we have a history. And you might think this is me trying to get even, but it's not. I care about you and Georgia and Max. I need to warn you to protect yourself and your kids." He hands me the envelope, then stands up. "I've loved Thom like a brother. I just didn't expect him to be Fredo."

"But he's not capable of hurting either of—" I chatter out before he silences me with a finger to my lips.

"Don't look at them now. Wait until I'm gone." He leans

down and kisses me tenderly on the mouth. I'm too confused to protest, and before I can come to my senses, he's gotten into his Town Car and pulled away.

I'm ten minutes late as I rush down the steps to the Tea Box in the basement of the Takashimaya department store. It is hushed and beautiful in here, with small tables and low lights. I hope that Christy won't be able to see how red my eyes are from scrutinizing the two small pictures in Bjorn's envelope.

As I approach the hostess I spot Christy in the back of the room, sipping from a bowl of tea. She looks up and waves me over. She hasn't changed at all since I last saw her almost five years ago. Still tiny, radiant, and dressed like her million-dollar Texas daddy would expect if he were still alive, she stands and gives me a big hug and two air kisses.

"Jen, you look divine," she says as I slip off my coat and hang it over the back of my chair, trying to calm my raw nerves and pretend that this morning didn't happen. "And a nice toga, too." I look down. Shit.

"Okay, right, I'll be right back," I say, nodding my head as I quickly make my way to the ladies' room. Luckily Christy is the only woman in Manhattan who's up early enough to be hungry at noon and the tea room is virtually empty.

It's about twenty degrees warmer in the bathroom, and I welcome the heat on my frozen and chapped cheeks. I tear off the toga and try to stuff it into the paper towel disposal, but it ends up hanging halfway out, so I lift my leg up onto the counter and try to stomp the damn thing in. A Japanese woman comes into the room, and when she sees what must look to her like the manic destruction of evidence, she enters silently into a stall. I pull the sheet back out and roll it into a ball, placing it quietly under the sink, behind a stack of extra toilet paper, which topples over with a dull series of thuds. I restack, notice my new friend isn't peeing, so I run the water to help cover her shyness while I try to fix my makeup. I look ridiculous with my dress scrunched up into my crotch and mascara smeared under my eyes from crying alone in the Park. I unzip my pocketbook to find a hairbrush and the pictures fall into the sink. I snatch them out and pat them dry with a paper towel. The Japanese woman flushes and joins me at the sink. I smile at her as though I'm not some crazy homeless person sent to this washroom in search of a warm French bath. I wet my hand and try to run it up my leg under my dress to get the damn thing to detach; she looks at me and blushes.

"Static cling," I say, trying to laugh it off.

"Please, take," she says, opening her bag and handing me a small can of Static Guard. "You keep." She bows and leaves the room.

I let out a huge sigh and pick up the soggy photos. One picture shows Thom in a clutch in front of the Inn at Irving Place, of all locations. She has straight black hair down to her waist and is about my height. It's not a thanks-for-the-teacakes hug, either; it's clearly charged with licentious sex. The second one is even worse. It's a shot of the two of them at River Café, hands entwined, heads bowed together in a shared intimacy. And here's the gut-kicker: she's got the exact same tennis bracelet he gave me. Score zero for originality, ten for audaciousness. Bjorn may be a skunk, but he's right: I have to protect myself and my family, I have to start preparing for the worst. Shit—Christy. I shove everything back into my pocketbook and wrap the photos individually in paper towels so they won't stick together.

When I get back to the table there is food already served.

"Everything okay?" Christy asks. "I ordered for you, I hope you don't mind."

"Yes, everything is great—sorry about that. Vera's watching Max, and I had to make sure he's still alive." I toss off what I hope sounds like a tinkling laugh, even as the reality of what the photos mean starts to sicken me. A piece of hair comes loose from the twist I secured it in earlier and sticks to my face. I attempt to smooth it back. It falls again. "I came straight from Georgia's school, where I gave a fascinating talk on ancient Greece, hence the toga."

"Naturally," Christy says, snapping apart a pair of chopsticks. "And how's Thom? Singapore, yes?"

"Thom? Great, just great. He's great." I pick up my fork and take a bite of tuna sashimi. Even though I feel like I'm falling apart, there is something about being back in Christy's presence that is calming, a natural fit on such an unnatural day. All my powers of professional lunching return as I speak around the morsels without breaking stride. "In Singapore, yes. Opening a branch of Universal Imports, but you probably know that, right? This is delicious."

"Yes, of course. Bjorn up to his old tricks, sleight of hand, don't look here—watch over there. It's perfect: he won't see it coming at all." She's practically got yellow feathers on her chin, she's so happy with some bit of quiet information.

"I'm sorry, I don't get it," I say as the hair on the other side of my face comes loose. "Won't see what coming?"

"I'm leaving Christie's." She puts down her sticks, folds her hands in front of her chest, perfectly framing a multicolored strand of freshwater pearls that echo the many highlights in her hair. "By next fall I want to have my own art dealership up and running, give Bjorn and his ilk a real run for it. I've done well for myself at Christie's, but it's just not *Christy's*, if you know what I mean," she says, pointing to her chest.

"Ownership."

"Exactly. You always were my brightest mentee. See how quick you catch on? I *knew* I was right to call you up." She slaps her hands together just like Max. "Over the next few months as I fade out of the auction world I have to get the new business ready, but to do that I need you."

"You want me to set up your office?" I ask, nodding as I think about how this could be exactly what I need, in case there's any truth to Bjorn's photos, and could be a way to start to support myself, should it come to that. I feel the sweat beading up under my arms, like a hot flash gathering in the distance. I also just want this for me. This is the what's next, I can feel it in my bones. The underwire of my new bra digs into my ribcage as I attempt to drape my arm casually over the chair next to me. "I could do that. Get the copiers and computers and office space picked out and delivered. Staplers, phones, whatever you need."

"No, no, Jennifer, I don't need an assistant." She laughs, shakes her head. That's it, I've blown it. "What I need is a *partner*."

"A partner? You want me to help you find a partner?" Well, temporary work is better than no work, and it would give me a foot up.

"I don't expect you to say yes right here right now—I'm sure you're going to want to talk to Thom about it and get to know more about how we would set up the partnership, which responsibilities would be yours, which mine. So why don't we do this," she says, checking her watch and flagging down the waiter. All other thoughts recede while I try to grasp what exactly she's saying. "Check, please—why don't we have lunch again next Wednesday so we can go through some of the details? You can give me your answer then, which I'm going to assume is yes, and then we'll get started the next week. I'm not going to let you get away again, Jennifer. You're too valuable to me. It's time to step up to the next level. Okay, partner?" Now I get it. The body moisture–cashmere combination starts to make my skin crawl, then itch. It's all I can do to keep from ripping this monstrosity off my body right here at the table. Instead, I keep my cool and try to focus on what Christy has just said. The pin holding my twist in place clatters to the floor.

"Christy, before we go any further, let me apologize for being late. It really wasn't in my control and it won't happen again." If she's serious—and Christy is always serious—then I need to mop up before we can get to dancing. I scoop the pin up and refasten my hair in one move. "I do want to work for you again, and I'll do anything to make it happen." Including obscuring the fact that my husband may be a low-life art forger. At least until I know for sure.

"Okay. Let's start by changing your vocabulary. Never apologize for being late. Your time is your own and you don't need to explain it to me—besides, you've not been late a day in your life. Second, you do not work *for* me. You work *with* me. It's a very important distinction to make. You're an adult now, pet: you need to sound like one. I've got to get back for auction run-through, but let me give you a quick idea of what we're talking about." She leans in; so do I. Our lunch lies between us, mostly untouched. "I'll be the front person, senior partner, giving a public face to a very exclusive and private company. You'll be the junior partner, managing the staff and putting together client and art portfolios, running research and facilities. It's time for me to make some real money, and I want you to benefit from my expertise even as I profit from your unmatchable skill set. You're brilliant, Jennifer, absolutely genius. Let's do it, yes? Let's take over the world and make a fortune doing it." Her phone rings; she holds up one finger and keeps it there while she answers. "Yes, Bruno, I'm ready, I'll be right out." She snaps the phone shut and pulls a wad of cash from her pocketbook. "That's my car. Here's some money, be sure to keep the receipt so we can run it through the company when we're set up. Capisce?" She puts her hand out for mine.

"Yes," I say, sweat pooling inside my boots around my ankles. I scratch at my right arm, pull up my sleeve to reveal a rash of hives. I pull it right back down and pretend that didn't happen. "Yes. I'd shake on it, but I really do not want you to know just how damp my palm is right now. Okay if we shake next week?"

"Come, let Bruno give you a ride home. You're a mess today, pet—are you sure everything's okay?" She stands and helps me into my coat. She never wears one, as there is always a car to take her to her next destination.

"Mostly. I think it might be early menopause," I say, trying to make light of my appearance.

"Oh, tell me about it," she says and fishes a pillbox out of her bag. "Take one of these, you'll never sweat again."

By the time Bruno drops me curbside at my apartment, I'm itching everywhere and scratching freely. Due to the high salt content of my sweat, the dress has shrunk at least one size since I put it on this morning. I'm starving and hurt and overjoyed and scared and furious and scared. I've only had ten minutes of quiet to con-

template the shit storm that my life suddenly is, and all I've decided is not to decide anything until I get out of this dress.

I let myself into the apartment to find Vera asleep on the
couch, the TV tuned to some Spanish soap opera with the sound
on mute, a copy of *Reader's Digest* spread across her chest. I drop
my keys on the kitchen counter.

"Oh, Jennifer dear, you're home," she says, collecting herself
and her possessions. "Good, I can catch the 2:05 and be home in
time for canasta at the club."

"Thank you so much for helping out at such short notice," I
say, taking off my coat.

"What have you done to that dress?" she practically cries, trying to pull it back into shape while it's still on my body. I find a
way not to slap her hands off of me.

"Cashmeres seem to be allergic to perspiration," I say, peeling it
off right in front of her, revealing the copious red bumps dotting
the top half of my body. Thank god for the tights. "The question
you might want to ask is what has this dress done to me?"

"Didn't I leave you a slip?"

"How's Max?" I say as I pull off my boots, pouring a few
drops of water into the sink. "Did he eat?"

"Yes, well, he's sleeping. We went on an adventure this morning and had lunch at the diner. You know, he can eat real food
now," she calls out as I move into the powder room to retrieve a
pair of sweats from the hamper. "It doesn't hurt to try it now and
then."

"Great. Okay, then. How much do I owe you?" We both
laugh at this old joke between us, this way of avoiding any real
conversation.

The minute the door shuts behind her I race in to check on the one man who will never betray me, only to discover a four-year-old sleeping peacefully in Max's crib. It takes me a moment to figure out what has changed, and then I realize where Vera's adventure took place. Kid's Cuts. She has scalped my son. And on his changing table is the trophy—a perfect golden lock sealed in a plastic baggie, stapled to a "Baby's First Haircut" certificate, along with a Polaroid of Max smiling in an airplane-shaped chair, curls littering the floor around him. Seeing my beautiful boy shorn of his baby locks is the straw that sends me into racking sobs. That's it, I want my mommy.

"Mmhello?" Cheryl answers on the first ring.

"You'll never believe what that woman did now." I'm not crying anymore, I am yelling.

"Jenny? Is that you?"

"*She cut his hair!* She didn't ask, she just took him to a complete stranger and had them shear him like a baby lamb." I slump onto the couch, the contents of my bag spilling out beside me.

"Oh, that's terrible, sweetie. Just awful. Did this just happen?" She sounds distracted and not nearly outraged enough on my behalf.

"Yes, it just happened, while I was out at lunch. Can you believe any woman would do such a thing to another woman's child?" I look at the paper-towel-wrapped time bomb, push it a few inches away.

"Vera was there again? Isn't that three times in the last week?" Now she's interested.

"She was just helping out, a last-minute thing."

"Oh, well, I could have done it too, you know," Cheryl says, more than a little annoyed.

"Don't you have clients?"

"Not today, it's my writing day, you know that. I would have helped you out, Jen, I don't know why you never ask me," she says, sighing.

"I'm sorry. It was just that Thom needed me to go to Georgia's school for him and it was late last night and he volunteered his mother." I unwrap the photos. They're dry but a little crumpled. A silent tear runs down my cheek.

"It would be nice if you brought the kids up here. The Thruway goes north, you know."

"I'm sorry, it's just too much for me to pack the kids up and haul them upstate right now. And besides, we were just there," I say, regretting having called Cheryl in the middle of the day, in the middle of her work. I pick up the envelope and bring it to my nose, inhale Bjorn's scent, wonder how and why he got this evidence.

"I know, I know, and I'm glad you came home for one day at Christmastime, really I am." She goes quiet, we wait out the silence together. "It would just be nice if I saw my grandchildren on an equal footing."

"Okay, how about this weekend?" I say, envelope pressed to my face. "I could really use your help on Saturday, I have a ton of errands to run."

"This Saturday? Honey, you know that this Saturday is my seminar up in Buffalo, I do it every year."

"Okay, then how about you stay the whole weekend for Georgia's birthday next week?" I stifle a small sob, remembering Thom's betrayal of Geege.

"I was meaning to tell you that I can't make the party. I've been asked to appear on a panel in Aspen for National Family Counseling Week. Maybe when I get back?"

"Sure, that would be great, whatever works—hey, how about a

week from today?" I ask, in one final attempt to make her happy, even as our conversation makes me more miserable. "I need to have lunch with someone and since it's your writing day again—"

"Oh, how I wish I could, but no, the Niedemeyers' daughter is going to be in town with their new grandchild and I promised them a special session. I can't wait to see the new baby! They've really come a long way together."

"All right, just let me know what works for you, I really need to go now." I put the photos back in the envelope and a tear splashes off my hand.

"Are you okay, honey? I mean other than the haircutting— which is really awful—is everything all right? I'm sensing a little distress in your voice."

"Nope, probably just low blood sugar, I guess." I sniffle. "Maybe a little cold I'm fighting off."

"Okay, if you're sure. I've got to get back to work, but don't hesitate to call if you need to talk about anything. I love you," she says, as much a question as a statement.

"Me too," I say, holding on to the phone after she's gone and sobbing outright, hoping to wake Max so I can begin to get on with my life.

Thirty-Two

Here's what you need to know: two weeks before I met Thom in Cairo, I met Bjorn in Tunis. It was an intense attraction, a die-in-a-cave-for-love kind of emotion that, after years of Heath, shocked both my heart and my body. We pursued each other, teased each other, and ultimately ended up in bed together—where I froze, freaked out, and left before any of the good stuff happened. He pursued me, I ran away, and by the time I got my head sorted out he had slept through all the women on the dig. I'm sensing a pattern emerging here, my attraction to men resulting in infidelity. Heath was a whore, there's no question, and Bjorn, who quite possibly could have fucked around with me for years, was more Alfie than even Heath was. But Thom? Beautiful, trustworthy, and, yes, even occasionally boring Thom?

The real question here, though, is where the hell have I been for the last six years? How did I become this trusting, dependent homebody when my training was survival-based, poverty-influenced, and feminist-leaning? I will not blame my children or my decision to have them or my choice to stay home with them for my own blindness, my shortcomings that have resulted in this corner I've painted myself into. No, it's not being a mommy, it's sacrificing all the other things I was so easily, so unhesitatingly. How could I just let everything go? How could I let my body, my mind, my ambition, my lust, my intellect, just sit and rust while I played endless rounds of Candy Land? Did I really never have time to read the newspaper, or did I choose not to burden myself with the responsibility of being a living, thinking member of the human race?

I feel like Snow White, and Bjorn's kiss has awakened the blood that's left in me, the fire that once made me move continents in search of knowledge and meaning and adventure. It's a poisonous kiss, to be sure, but now that my eyes are open to what Thom is capable of—not just the cheating but the lying, and the forgery, and the fish sauce—I need to make decisions based on what's best for me, Georgia, Max, in that order.

Then again, maybe all men are like this and all women are stupid. Or at least most of us. Maybe I need to trade infidelity with infidelity, even the score, sate *my* needs for once.

Thirty-Three

I'M STANDING IN A DARK entryway on Broome Street, holding my breath as my teeth chatter. I haven't gotten stoned since before Georgia, but I'm feeling a little reckless tonight, very high on myself after the week I've had, and I'm plugging back into the energy of bygone days, with a bygone Heath. I've tried calling Thom numerous times, but I only seem to get his voice mail or his housekeeper. If she is who she says she is, that is. The mysterious government woman keeps calling as well, but I don't want to talk to her before I talk to Thom. He's only managed to leave one message—that he won't be coming home tomorrow. Missing Georgia's birthday party is the last straw. He can leave me if he wants, but to hurt her is brutal. I'm feeling betrayed and lusty. Maybe not the best combination when huddled up with a dead-sexy exy. Unfortunately, the pot is going straight to my rhyming control center.

"So then I told her, 'I just don't think I'll ever find a woman who is as good as a blow job,'" Heath says on the exhale. "Of course, I didn't mean it, I was just giving her a hard time, she was such an ice princess. Hey, let's go to Raoul's, they'll give us our old table." He takes my arm and leads me down and across Prince Street, a real-life memory lane, considering he still has the loft on Broadway where we spent five years together. I haven't set foot in our old apartment since we split, but maybe later, gator?

While we walk and let the reefer goof on us, we fall silent, and my mind wanders. It feels good to feel good again, to be in the old hood. The post office is gone, the Dean & DeLuca coffee shop is no more. Thom was bizarre on the voice mail, saying he couldn't come home because of a "pending investigation." It looks like Bjorn might be right. I'm shocked to see how much like Mall of America my old neighborhood has become. The art gallery on West Broadway has moved up to Chelsea, replaced by Victoria's Secret. Thom was all cloak and dagger. Not since Egypt has he been so in love with his own drama, his importance. At least Mi-lady's with its cheap drinks, sticky tables, and neon-beer-sign decor is still standing. I can't believe Christy wants me to start a new business with her. She's leaving Christie's. I giggle. Snort. Christy's leaving Christie's. Christy's leaving Christie's. Christie's leaving Christy's. I laugh so hard I have to grab Heath's sleeve to keep from falling off the curb.

"Whoa, JP, go easy, what's so funny?" He starts laughing too, cold windblown tears reflecting on his high-set cheekbones. I bump off him; he steadies me, his hands sending a charge through my body, doubling me over in convulsive laughter. I try to tell him, but nothing comes out. Other than a loud snort and a bit of snot, which makes us laugh even harder.

"You," I take a deep breath, "wouldn't get it. It's a pun . . . Fun!" We collapse into the deeply lit warmth of Raoul's, where François greets us like we were just here last Friday and takes us to our old booth—the only open table in the place. We pass couples four deep at the bar, men try to slip François money, and women catch his eye over their Cosmos, to no avail. I forgot what celebrity fairy dust was like, liberally sprinkled on plebeians. I sit tall in the black-and-white booth so the rubberneckers around us can get a good view of my freshly cut and dyed hair and my ten-pounds-lighter frame while I read the menu. It's in French, but I'm so high I don't notice until Heath asks me to translate—possibly the first time I've read French without having to make sense of it.

"Don't think I can. I'm really, really baked," I whisper across the table, leaning over the small chalkboard. "Really."

"I know."

"Did you say something?" He doesn't answer me, just stares at the menu. "Did I say something?" Again no response. I throw back a glass of water, which slides down my tongue like ice-cold mercury. "Look, either I'm not talking or you're not hearing, which is it?"

"Both." We snicker. "Martini?"

"Dirty. Flirty." I wrinkle my nose, like trying to stop a sneeze after it's out.

"Just like you." I feel something brush my cheek and a warm flush envelopes me.

"Stop that, I mean it." Not really. I like it. He does it again. "I double mean it." Not at all, really. He goes to do it a third time, and I bat his hand away. "Anybody want a peanut?"

Over the course of the next twenty minutes, we flirt, order drinks, flirt, order dinner, flirt, eat some oysters, flirt. I feel the pot wearing off even as the vodka starts to mellow me out. It doesn't take much to fuck me up anymore. I've had one martini to Heath's three, and he's way behind me. At least I've stopped rhyming, something we can all be happy about.

By the time my hangar steak arrives, I've got my pacing back under control, and like a practiced deep-sea diver, I am rising to the surface without experiencing the paranoia bends. Heath is still on his way down, though, which puts me at an unexpected advantage.

"So, are you dating anyone?" I dip a *pomme frite* into the red wine reduction swamping my plate, warming him up with casual conversation.

"After the ice princess—believe it or not, she *was* a professional skater—there was one girl, but I found out she was a Republican, so I fired her ass." He carves into a triple-thick pork chop, perfectly pink in the center.

"I don't think I've ever been this hungry. Since when do you care about politics?" I'd be surprised if he's even registered to vote.

"When the Republican in question is also seventeen, pretending to be twenty. It was the only way to break it off without looking like a prude." Or a pervert.

"Twenty's old enough?" The wind goes out of my blown-dry sails. I was once young enough for Heath.

"Nah, she seemed a lot older, trust me. We met in a very dark club, she was really made up. She could have been your age." He looks up from his plate, stops his fork in midair when he sees my face. "You know, twenty-nine, thirty, around there." I don't break my look, forcing him to put the fork back on the plate. "Okay, sorry, I didn't mean it the way it sounds."

"Then how did you mean it?"

"Maybe I wanted to insult you a little. You just look so good and I'm such a fuck for having let you get away." I study his face for irony, never his forte, but even so I can't find a shred. His looks are starting to fade, let's admit it, and in a couple of years he's going to be in Vegas crooning to middle-aged moms from Nebraska.

"Ah, you didn't 'let' me do anything, remember? You pretty much shoved me out the revolving door." It's funny how history is rewritten by the wieners.

"Yeah, but I thought you'd leave the door open a crack, let me slip a foot in or something every once in a while. You know, what I said about the blow job earlier, what I really meant was you." He feigns a loss of appetite with this admission, pushing his plate into the center of the table so he can lean in a bit closer. "Nobody does it for me like you do, Jen."

Okay, so I'm sort of flattered, in a twisted way. Christy said a similar thing when we met again for lunch this Wednesday, going to a lot of trouble to convince me of her plan—even though I was already on board. She said no one collects and sorts information like I do; no one has the phone skills, the acute knowledge of antiquities, the flexibility. I'll start out on a junior level, but it's quite a step above where I was at Christie's. I guess this is one of the benefits of being with a small company; you're valued for what you're capable of and challenged to take on more responsibility. Sure, there's a lot more risk, but the benefits are already apparent. Christy asked me how I felt about competing with Thom, if he would keep my secret from Bjorn until we're ready. I told her that Thom may be a lot of things, but he's always kept my trust. Then I excused myself to the ladies' room and had another good cry.

"JP? Hello, you in there? I know it's a lot to take in, but . . ." He's lifting my chin with his finger.

"Sorry, what did you say? I think I slipped into a cow coma

there for a minute." It really was the most delicious steak I've ever tasted.

"Do you think there could be another chance for us? I really miss you sometimes, I'd do anything to get you back in my life. You just make everything so sane, so easy to bear." He seems sincere. Is it possible that I'm hallucinating? No, that's pictures, not words. It might be the pot giving me unasked-for clarity, but I really cannot remember what I ever saw in him. I mean, look at him—he's a washed-up pot-smoking child actor who's begging a fat married mother of two to give him another chance. And to think I considered sleeping with him again?

"Um, why do you think you deserve me?" I'm going to let him down, but I've waited a long time for this confession; he's not getting off with one Hail Mary.

"That's an excellent question. Why don't we go back to my place and have some coffee to discuss—"

"I like the coffee here just fine." There's no way I'm going into that lion's den. I have a soccer party to throw tomorrow morning, and I'm not doing it smelling of Heath. I guess the pot has officially worn off. I mentally execute a triple-Salchow—Sven gives me a 9.9, Penny a 9.4. She's always been my toughest critic.

"Okay, yeah, I didn't mean to rush you or anything. It's just that Thom doesn't deserve you. He's never home, he's left you barefoot and pregnant twice already, and now he's been gone for how long?"

"Two months . . ."

"Exactly, two months. That's crazy. How can he just run off to, where is it?"

"Singapore . . ."

"Right, Singapore, and leave you alone to raise those kids? I know I haven't seen you in ages, and this has to be coming out of left field for you, but I've been avoiding you because I can't stand to think of you not in my life. So I mostly just pretend you died." He cuts into his pork chop, relieved to fold his feelings back into hunger. I try to picture Thom in his rental apartment halfway around the world, pictures of me and the kids tacked over his desk, paper food containers strewn about. Perky little Asian housekeeper/whore dusting the bookshelf in a sarong. It's such a cliché of an existence: successful married man traveling out into the world to bring home security for his brood, neglecting and abandoning them in the process. Not in the least little bit like my father. Or Heath. Am I really so obvious?

"Do you have any idea how many days of our relationship you were out on the road?" I pop a cold *frite* into my mouth, chew it slowly as I wait for him to try to do the math.

"Okay, I know I was gone a lot . . ."

"Exactly 884 days."

"I know that sounds like a lot . . ."

"Out of a possible 1,887. That's twenty-six months. Almost fifty percent. Half our life together you spent on the road." I'm not mad so much as relieved to be saying these numbers out loud to the one person who needs to hear them. Shit, I should have never let Thom go away. What was I thinking? "So don't you dare tell me that Thom doesn't deserve me. No one deserves me. That's the God's honest truth." Except maybe Christy, who never took a sick day all the years I worked for her. No husband, no kids, no parents, no problems. She's an island of one and wants me to be her gal Friday.

"Maybe you're right, maybe I don't deserve you, but I deserve the chance to prove I can." The waiter comes by and clears our plates; I ask him for the check.

"Okay, let's not do this. We were having a perfectly lovely time. And you're drunk. And I have two very small children who need a mother and a father." The waiter slips the check between us on the table, where it stays.

"I can be their father. I can. I love playing with kids." He's looking at me with the most earnest eyes I've seen him manage, even more sincere than when he would say "uh-oh" to the TV cameras. I fear that he hasn't grown up at all, that the old child actor cliché is not only true but staring me in the face. He's no more real than his two-bit name.

"That's sweet, really it is. But no." I look at the check, look at him, and excuse myself to the ladies' room to give him time to think about paying.

At the top of the spiral staircase leading to the restrooms is a tarot card reader, tucked into a corner of the landing. She's been here for years, same table, same deck of cards, or so I imagine. No one's in the customer chair, so I slide into it, placing ten dollars on the red cloth. She takes her time, hums a little, lays out some cards.

"Confusion has settled around your heart, there are small things and bigger issues that are pulling you in many directions."

"I only have a couple of minutes, tell me something I don't know," I say, glancing at the stairs, hoping that Heath is sobering up even as I know he's doing a shot of tequila.

"You're planning a journey." Her eyes roll up in mock divinity. "One that will take you far away without ever leaving home. I sense a new beginning, a new life blooming inside of you. One that will surprise someone you love very much."

"Okay, that's pretty good. What else?" She's got to mean

Christy. We had discussed calling the company "Bloomington Bradley." This can't be a coincidence.

"Someone very close to you has a secret you need to know, for it will change the way you think about yourself." Her eyes roll down; she takes the tenspot and sits back.

"Hah! That's it?" I know ten dollars doesn't buy you much these days, but come on.

"That's it. The field has gone blank. You must have faith that you know what you know." With that she gets up and washes her hands in a sink that's oddly located outside of the bathrooms. I ease my way back down the spiral, the rabbit hole, trying to memorize every word she's said.

"You okay? You look like you've seen a ghost." Heath looks up from the bottom of an empty shot glass, dried salt on his hand. He pushes a full glass across the table to me. "I got you a little something."

"Back a little quickly to pretending that I'm dead, aren't you?" I throw the shot back. The check still sits there, unwanted. I turn it over.

"You want to split it?" he asks. Ever gallant, my millionaire ex-boyfriend.

"No, this one is definitely on me." I slap my card down and slide both to the edge of the table. "Did you hear that Neil Patrick Harris is going to be starring in *Assassins* when it finally opens on Broadway?"

"Um, yeah, I kind of lost the role to him. It's okay, I always thought *Doogie Howser* was underrated. Thanks for dinner. And, JP, it was kind of a joke, you know—the whole wanting-you-back thing. Just a way to make the evening more interesting?" He's no longer the Heath that I fell in love with, the one who could torture me up-close and long-distance with his inability to commit. And the beautiful thing is that at long last, I really don't care.

"And a very funny one at that, my pet." I sign for our meal.

After a soft kiss on the cheek, we go our separate ways. It's still early and not as cold as it was, and since I'm having that post-pot-and-martini buzzy feeling I decide to walk home. When I get there I'm going to call Thom and tell him to get his ass home so we can sort this out together. If Bjorn doesn't like it, he can go fuck himself. Then I'm going to call Christy, who is never asleep before midnight, and tell her I'm ready for what's next. Men have let me down for the last time.

As I walk up Sixth Avenue, I notice a Town Car keeping pace with me. At Fourteenth Street it pulls over and the door opens. I'm half expecting Mr. Big, but no such luck, it's only Bjorn.

"Get in," he says, leaning across the seat.

"No." The light changes and I keep walking. He gets out of the car and follows, giving me a little space.

"Jen, we need to talk. About Thom," he says, pulling alongside me. He offers the flask. I stop walking, take it from him, and throw my head back. I screw the top on and move in close to Bjorn's face. It's a good thing I wore heels.

"Listen," I slur a little. "Listen. To. Me. I'm done with talking about Thom, there's nothing more I want to know." I lunge in to kiss him and he stops me.

"Not here, get in the car," he says, opening the door of the ever-present Lincoln. I slide across the seat, he gets in next to me. It smells like a heady combination of Scotch, Bjorn, leather, and just a hint of sex; I'm intoxicated. We could do this, right here, right now with the smoked windows and the silent driver and no one would ever need to know. Heath, Bjorn, who cares, any whore in the storm. I move my body as close to his as I can get it. He moves an inch away.

"So what is it this time?" I ask. "Thom's into little boys? He's painted a Van Gogh and sold it on eBay? He's stolen the Eiffel Tower? Go ahead and tell me, I really don't care."

"It's Stephanie, my wife. They've run off. She's the one in the photos." He tries to light a cigarette, the match revealing what just might be tears in his eyes, but his hand shakes so badly he throws both out the window.

"Stephanie? That's her name?" I don't know what's more alarming—that I never knew Bjorn's new wife's name or that she's run off with my husband. Between the booze and the shock of the moment, it almost escapes my attention that I've never even seen Stephanie, other than in the photos.

"So you knew when you gave me the pictures?" I ask.

"Yes, but I didn't think you'd believe me. I wasn't even sure if I believed me."

"Is there any other proof? How do you know they've run off?"

"You know the funny thing, Jen?" he asks, sniffing and laughing at the same time. "She was the first woman I met who made me forget you. And you know the real kicker? They knew each other from college. They've been screwing us both over for years."

I instantly run all the Thom videotape I hold in my head, scouring my memory for the mention of a Stephanie, a photo of a raven-haired beauty. Nothing. Something about this whole story seems a bit off-center. I know Thom's history, I've met the women he's dated. In fact, his mother has never mentioned a Stephanie, and you know that she would. Bjorn hands me the flask, I take another swig. When I hand it back to him, he grabs my wrist.

"What am I going to do? I love her." He starts to sob; I take him in my arms and try to comfort him.

"We could kill them, I guess," I say, trying to laugh over Bjorn's head, which is firmly nestled in my cleavage. If he weren't in so much pain, I'd swear he's copping. I lift his head, look him in the eye. "Let's just wait until it runs its course. Why don't we both sleep on it and talk again tomorrow?"

"You'd do that for me, really?"

"Sure, why not." We stop outside my apartment as though this whole scene were perfectly timed. The symmetry makes me uneasy. I smell a rat of unusual size. "Call me in the afternoon, okay?" I ask as I get out of the car, shutting it behind me without waiting for Bjorn's reply.

In the elevator I replay the entire evening in my head, or at least the parts that I remember, and keep snagging on Bjorn's confession. I know I should be upset, cursing Thom for being such a total scumbag, but something in me refuses to take Bjorn's side until I can talk to Thom. Is he really capable of setting up his best friend and running off with his wife? The pictures don't lie, and there's the real problem for me. That—and Bjorn's first true show of emotion over a woman. Not even he can fake that.

I'm still puzzling over the jumble when I let myself into the apartment. The acrid after-smell of vomit hits me immediately, and it's all I can do not to hurl myself. I realize that I'm a bit more drunk than I thought; in comparison to Heath I may have been sober, but next to my mother-in-law, I'm a lush.

"Oh good, Jennifer, you're finally back," Vera says, wiping her hands on a dish towel. She's spotless in silk pajamas with a matching cream-colored quilted silk robe.

"Which one?" I ask, wriggling out of my coat.

"Georgia. She's been at it a good hour now. Only a low-grade fever, 101 degrees last time I checked fifteen minutes ago. Max has slept through it, but I'm concerned that he shouldn't stay here if Georgia has the flu." Though she's probably right, I still balk at this woman's giving me any advice, even if it means making all of us sick.

"It's okay, I'll have her sleep in my room, and if you would be so kind, please sleep in Max's room with him, in case he turns up sick in the middle of the night." I feel like Vera can smell the pot on my coat, the vodka/tequila/scotch on my breath, the men's cologne in my hair. The one night I go out without them, Georgia has to get sick, just my luck. This snaps me back to the reality I'm most comfortable with—mothering.

"You're sure? I can have Skip come in and get Max, then stay and help you take care of Georgia. You're looking a little pale yourself, dear." She takes a step toward me, AA bloodhound sniffing out the trail of evidence. I dodge around her.

"I'm sure. We can handle this. We'll wait to see how she feels tomorrow." I spy the gift wrap on the counter. "Aw, shit. Her birthday party."

"I think we should call the doctor. She could have that flu that's killing so many kids this winter. Did she have a flu shot?" Merely because we put both kids on a slower course of vaccinations, Vera thinks that we didn't give them any shots at all, when in reality they've both completely caught up.

"If she's puking, she doesn't have that kind of flu; she has a stomach virus. And yes, she had a flu shot, as did Max. Why don't we both turn in? We may be up a lot tonight." I look at Georgia's gift bags on the dining room table, standing at pink and purple attention, and I'm suddenly glad I didn't cheat on her father. We even made black ones for the boys—a thoughtful touch on her part.

I wake at two a.m. like Regan Teresa MacNeil, bolt upright, and spew my lunch and dinner into the bucket I'd put by the bed for Georgia. They say it's safe to go from clear to dark alcohol. They're wrong. Once I had moved Georgia, moaning and puking one last time, into my bed, taken her temperature—still 101— and washed my face, brushed my teeth, and turned out the light, I lay staring at the ceiling for a good long time, thinking about how I should have been at home tonight instead of out getting high with my ex and stupidly trying to micro-seduce Bjorn. Now it's all I can do to keep my own hair out of the gore—I'm racked with chills and soaking wet. The smell of the fresh hair dye makes me heave again, and it's only after I've returned from cleaning up in the bathroom that I realize Georgia is not in the bed.

I change into a dry T-shirt and sweats, pulling on Thom's flannel robe—which makes me want to cry when I smell it—and stagger out to the living room, where Georgia is sitting on the couch, wearing her purple Aigroeg T-shirt over her nightie. She has QVC on the television, the sound muted. Sheena Easton is selling her own line of porcelain fairy dolls, which seem to be very popular with the wee-hours crowd. Quiet tears roll down Georgia's face, and I sit next to her for a few minutes before breaking her vigil.

"Honey, it's the middle of the night, let's go back to bed." I put my hand on her forehead, but my palm is warmly clammy and she pulls away. She sniffs, tucks her feet up under her.

"Mommy, why am I so sick?" She leans against me and lets me put my arm around her.

"I don't know, baby, but I'm sick too if it makes you feel any better." She tips her head up to look at me, decides I am sick, and shakes her head. She looks down at her shirt.

"Will we still have my party?" Her voice is barely a whisper.

"I don't think so, Georgie, but let's wait until morning."

"Will I get to go to Ella's circus?" Ella's birthday is on Sunday, and it's not looking likely.

"Let's burn that bridge when we get to it, hmm?" I rock her a little, which causes a wave of dizziness. I'm already hungover, my head pounding from the narcotics and the barfing. I'm probably dehydrated too. I hoist myself off the couch to go into the kitchen, and Georgia grabs my arm. I lift her up and feel her bony limbs embrace me in a monkey-hug, her hot head heavy on my shoulder. I'm currently too weak for this but find enough mothering in me to get her to the kitchen counter, where she sits on the cool marble while I mix an Alka-Seltzer–Pedialyte cocktail for myself, straight Pedialyte for her. It's when I throw the empty bottle in the recycling that it hits me—Vera has poisoned us.

Earlier today Vera took Max to the park while Georgia and I stuffed bags together.

"Do Daddy love his job more than us?" Georgia had asked, carefully cutting an *E* out of pink construction paper.

"Of course not, Georgie. He's just got to work really hard right now, but he'll be home soon." I sorted the boy gifts from the girl ones—Georgia decided to go with more humble fare than her classmates, but we found a really cool four-view plastic camera for cheap in Chinatown.

"Do he love Max more than me?" She pretended not to care,

acted like she was just asking random questions, even as she looked at me sidelong, waiting for the answers to be rhetorical.

"Nope. He loves you both the same."

"I hope he don't come home." She stopped cutting, put down the shears. "I don't want to go to the party." I slid her chair next to mine.

"Doesn't come home." I agreed with her, in my own way. "Okay, baby, I know you're mad at Daddy, I get mad at him too sometimes. But we've been so excited about your party for so long, haven't we?"

"I guess so."

"And you know Daddy would be here if he could, right?"

"Yeah."

"Then let's make lemonade, okay?"

"Mommy, we can't have lemonade, it's the *winter*."

"Okay, then let's make snow cones out of the blizzard."

"But it isn't *snowing*."

"Then let's make a silk purse from a sow's ear."

"Mommy, Max is a *dog*, not a pig." She finally let out her trademark giggle and went back to cutting the initials of the kids' names and gluing them onto the gift bags.

Vera swanned in from the park with Max, brandishing a pastry box and setting down the spare keys.

"Where's Granna's Giggles? I've got éclairs!" Georgia, who can smell custard from across town, leapt off her chair, all thoughts of hating her father erased for the moment by his mother, lucky girl. "Jennifer, I know how you feel about sugar, but the kids have been so good, let's spoil them a little, shall we?" She held the box out to me as Max and Georgia nipped at her heels.

"Yes to Georgia, no to Max. He can have some graham crackers," I said. Better to piss off the smaller kid, I always find. Their memories are shorter and they're less likely to sulk.

"*Yay!*" Georgia yelled.

"I really don't see why you won't let Max have any sugar. It's ridiculous. Besides, those crackers have sugar in them too, you know." She put the box on the counter and cut the red-and-white string, giving it to Max to play with—though if I had done the same she would have cautioned me against his hanging himself with it.

"Because he doesn't need sugar and doesn't yet know the difference," I said, handing Max his biscuit, which made him shout, "Gookie!"

"Mommy, *I* like sugar," Georgia said, sticking her finger in the hole where they shot the dough full of custard.

"Yes, honey, I know you do. You're made of sugar, in fact. We can't let you out in the rain, you might melt." I kissed her head. "Thank you, Vera, for getting Georgia a pastry. She's worked up quite an appetite."

"I got one for you, too, dear. You've been looking a little too thin lately. Here." She handed me a plate. I looked thin? Now I had to eat it in celebration of the first indirect compliment she'd paid me since I had Max. "You really know how to make a beautiful Bradley," I believe were her exact words.

Of course, Vera didn't join us. "My diabetes, dear." A faux condition that allows her to remain schoolgirl-thin while she fattens up the rest of us. I took one bite of the pastry and thought it tasted a little funny, but put the thought out of my mind and took a few more bites out of politeness.

Just thinking of it now makes me retch into the sink, causing

Georgia to lean over and do the same. Not one to miss a good puke, Peeve jumps up on the counter and tries to get into the mess; I throw her to the floor. I run the water and force Georgia to drink some more Pedialyte, which she does only because I do it too.

Once back in bed we snuggle down together, and I promise her that we will have the party on another day, that we will go to the circus, that we will take the gift bags to school on Monday, that we will spend the whole weekend together in bed, just like the good old days when I was pregnant with Max.

The next morning finds us weak and disabled, and Georgia starts to whimper even before she wakes. I turn over to find her pillow soaked, her sunken eyes looking up at me.

"Mommy, I think I can go to the party, okay?" She tries to sit up, can't, rolls onto her side, pushes herself up, falls back against me.

"I'm so, so sorry, baby, but I don't think either of us is going anywhere." I lay her down on her pillow, and she stoically receives the truth. "Remember, we'll reschedule the party, I promise. Now, let's try to get some more sleep."

I roll over, hungover, depressed, and still sick to my stomach. My eyes burn from all the crying I've done the past week, and still I manage to squeeze out a couple more tears. Has Thom really run off? And what exactly does that mean nowadays? No, he loves these kids too much, he'd never risk losing their love, even if he's lost his for me. Sniff.

Just as I'm drifting back into sleep, Vera blows into the room, opens the curtains, and cracks a window. She's already showered and buffed to a shine. I don't know what time it is, but no light comes in off the street, so it has to be before seven. Whoever heard of waking a sick person before seven? My rage is so close to the surface I can almost taste it, as irrational as it is pungent. I can suppress this. I can.

"My, it smells a little upsy in here, doesn't it?" She sprays some Lysol into the air in short bursts, creating a cloud of antiseptic before she'll approach the bed. "How is my little patient this morning?" She goes over and lays her hand on Georgia's head. "Well, that feels better." She looks at me. "Goodness, dear, you don't look so good." I would yell at her, but it would only make my hair hurt, and I also realize I need Vera to help me cancel the party.

"I know, I've got it too. Is Max still asleep?"

"Yes, he passed a restful evening with his Granna and is denned down like a little brown bear, thank Jesus. If I've told you once, Jennifer, I've told you a million times, you can't drag these children around this filthy city, picking up God knows what on the subway, the street, *delis*."

"A lot of children live in the city, Vera. And a lot of children who don't live in the city get sick. It's the winter. Kids get sick."

"I don't remember Thom or Theta ever missing a day of school." She picks up my jewelry box and sweeps a hand under it before setting it back down. "Skip's on his way in, he's going to take Max before he catches whatever it is that you've exposed my grandchil—"

"Éclairs."

"Excuse me?"

"I've exposed them to *your* éclairs. I'd go and get Georgia's stomach pumped if she hadn't already done such a good job of it herself. Happily, since I stopped my son from eating one, he should be spared." My voice is a low, pot-scorched rumble.

"Let's take this in the other room, shall we?" I think I still have a fever; my face is on fire. I shut the door behind us, keep my voice quiet.

"Vera, I am more than sorry that I have failed you as a mother to your grandchildren, but I do the very best I can under the circumstances." We stand on opposite sides of the room.

"Why, Jennifer, you haven't *failed* me. Of course you do what you can. I know it is not your fault the way you were raised." She looks around the room, studiously avoiding eye contact with me. This is what she does when she's judging me—she doesn't look down on me so much as not look at me at all.

"Thank you for your help last night." I clench my jaw. "I would now appreciate it if you would pack your toiletries and wait downstairs in the lobby until Skip gets here. I will not have you insult me and my family in my own home, in front of my daughter. Is that clear?"

"I did not mean to insult you. Is it my fault if you feel the need to blame your shoddy mothering on an innocent pastry?"

We both stand in the middle of the room, awash in anger. She wouldn't have chosen me for Thom and I never would have chosen her for me. I'm about to fish the other half of my éclair out of the trash and shove it down her throat when the door opens, and in walks the man who forced us into this relationship in the first place. Vera and I simultaneously glare at Thom.

"Hey! How are two of my favorite girls? And where's the birthday girl?" Thom asks, oblivious to the crackle in the air, dropping his bags at his feet. He is immaculately dressed in a three-piece suit; I cannot imagine where he must have been for the past twenty-four hours to look this sharp—surely not on a plane. I want to hit him and hug him, but more than anything I want him to at least have the decency to look as bad as I do right now.

The dehydration has officially gotten the better of me— probably a good thing, since it means I don't contain enough water to make tears—and I sink to the couch rather than run to my unexpected, possibly piece-of-shit husband. Vera has a split-second decision to make, one that just might be her last.

"Thomas. Good. Well, I'll just get my things and be going." She Wasps-up, smart move. Happily, her belongings are already packed into a wheelie-bag, and she pulls on her fur as she's talking. "Max is sleeping, Georgia and Jennifer are ill, and there's to be no party. The numbers to call are on the counter. I've stayed the night, but—" The intercom buzzes. "And that will be your father. Let's have dinner next week? I'd love to hear all about your trip." She never once looks at me during this speech, and only pats her son on the cheek as she floats through the still-open door, slamming it just enough behind her to signal to me that this is far from over.

"Whoa, what was that all about?" Thom searches my face for clues.

"So what brings you here? Shouldn't you be running off with your partner's wife?" I turn all of my sullen weak-kneed anger on him.

"What?" He snorts. He snorts! "Jen, I know I've been a little mysterious lately," he says, sitting down too close for a sick cuckold's comfort. He smells like airplane. My stomach flips.

"A little mysterious? That's all you've got? How about, sorry for cheating on you, Jen, I didn't mean for you to find out," I say, the words tumbling out of my mouth.

"What are you talking about?" he asks, putting his arm around me. I shrug it off with the last ounce of energy I have. I grab my copy of *Wifey* and slide the photos out of it, thrusting them in his face.

"I *know*, Thom." I watch him closely as he examines the photos, turning them around and over in his hand, no doubt trying to come up with a fresh excuse. I silently pray that he has an airtight one. "I know all about it, so don't even try to lie your way out of this." He hunches over the photos and his shoulders start to shake. So he's going to try and cry his way out of it. He and Bjorn are more alike than I thought. Time to go to Plan B. "What we need to focus on now is what's best for the children. I won't stand by you and be a long-suffering wife, and I'm not going to give you another chance, so don't bother begging." He's practically convulsing, he's crying so hard. Maybe we can find a way to fix this after all.

"Okay, look," I say, after letting him cry a little longer, his face buried in his hands. "Look me in the eye and tell me the truth, tell me all of it so we can move forward."

"Jen." He gasps for air around the word, facing me with tears watering his entire face. "Jen, honey, I don't know how to tell you this," he snorts again, and suddenly I realize: he's not crying, he's laughing.

"You're *laughing*? At a time like *this*?" I stand up; he pulls me back down. My head spins in one direction, then the other.

"Jennifer Bradley, love of my life, mother of my children, star of my universe," he says, wrapping me in a hug. I stay stiff. He pulls away and hands me back the pictures. "These pictures are of *you*."

I stand up rather quickly at this news and find the floor rushing up to meet me on the way back down.

. . .

I feel something a bit too wet on my forehead, and when I open my eyes I'm in bed. The curtains are drawn, but Georgia is no longer in my room. Did I just dream this whole morning? Am I completely losing all sense of reality? And if so, how did this washcloth get on my face? I sit up and instantly must lie back down, due to the acute pain radiating from my forehead down to the base of my spine. On the night table is a sweating pitcher of water and a note. I snap on the light and see the photos next to Thom's scrawl.

"Hey, Angel," it reads, "Georgia was feeling a little better so we've all gone to see *Peter Pan* to make up for the party. We should be home around six. There's soup on the stove. We'll talk later? I adore you, T."

I look at the clock, it's almost six p.m. It's dark in here because the sun has already set. The photos are proof that this all happened, and when I inspect them through my gauze of migraine, the woman instantly becomes me—Bjorn didn't even bother to Photoshop different clothes on my body, he was so certain I would see only the hair, see only what I wanted to see. He probably didn't even mean it to be Stephanie at first, just had to throw that in to convince me. But why?

I've just finished peeing and have washed my face when I hear my small family come storming in the door, preempting a much-desired shower. I'm more than a little surprised to see Vera bringing up the rear.

"Mommy, Mommy, Mommy!" Georgia throws herself at me, slamming a huge red shopping bag into my shin. "Nevernever-land is so beautiful!"

"So I hear," I say, looking over her head at Thom, barely focusing on the small smile in his eyes, but there's still something else there, and maybe I've been double-fooled. Max is slumped in his stroller, his head practically at his elbow. I'll never get used to that rubber-neck baby thing.

"GG, why don't you help Granna heat up the soup, okay?" Thom says, wheeling Max into his room.

"Yes, Daddy, can we first take Amanda out, please?" She follows him, dropping scarf, hat, mittens, and coat as she goes.

"I'm sorry," Vera says, picking up the clothes. "I was out of line."

"Oh," I say, one word short of speechless. "Well. I guess I shouldn't have yelled."

"You were sick, it's understandable."

"Okay," I say, and I go to the kitchen in search of Advil.

"Okay." She follows me, picks up a sponge, and wets it. "You know, we almost lost Thom. When he was little," she confides, swiping at the counter.

"Um, no, I didn't know. How terrible for you. He never mentioned. What happened?" I sit on one of the stools. She looks right at me for the first time in two days.

"Thom doesn't know. He had a very high fever for a very long time and was even packed in ice at one point. They told me that even if he pulled out of it, he'd most likely be retarded." She looks off toward the kids' room. "He's our blessing. Never take a fever lightly, Jennifer. Never."

"Granna, look, Amanda's even more beautiful than I thought!" Georgia runs to us, carrying a large doll that's dressed exactly like her.

"Oh, goodness, isn't she just!" Vera exclaims back, happy to have a distraction from her sadness. "I've got this, Jen—why don't you go help Thom?"

When I enter the nursery, Thom's got Max undressed and re-diapered, quite a feat considering the baby is still asleep. I sit down in the rocker and marvel at Thom's ability to do everything twice as fast and three times as well as I do.

"Did Bjorn give you those?" he asks as he airlifts Max into his crib, covering him with a blanket. The mirth is entirely gone from his voice.

"He said they were Stephanie. That you'd run off together." The rocker creaks beneath me.

"Stephanie." He laughs. "That's a good one. She did run off, with her podiatrist. What else did he say?"

"That you're in trouble. That you faked a vase."

"Pablo filled a hole," he says, using lingo for covering up a failed date-test. The vase wasn't as old as they pretended. He should have shown it to me. "But they're trying to pin it on me. The feds have been tearing up the office in Singapore the past few weeks. I was dying to tell you, but couldn't trust the phones."

"Fish sauce?" I ask. He sits down at my feet, leans back against my legs.

"Yeah, fish sauce. The investigator was there when you called and was trying to track you down. I didn't want her to know it was you."

"The breaking glass?"

"Bjorn sent some clean-up men over to hide evidence, but it was already too late. I'd been cooperating for the past month and had switched out the bad vase. Bjorn doesn't know."

"I'm not going to have to wear a wire and seduce him into telling the truth, am I?" We laugh together at the thought of this, melting more of the ice between us.

"You'd like that, I bet," he says, laying his head on the chair and looking up at me. "Thanks again," he says, more tender.

"For what?"

"For choosing me."

It would figure that Bjorn would tell him about Tunis, bragging that he'd had his shot at me first and rejected me, and it would also make sense that Thom would never mention he knew. I blink hard and change the subject.

"It was only a matter of time," I say. "Pablo's a known cheater. But why you?"

"It's the vase I picked up in Greece and took to Singapore." He slings an arm over my knee. "The original test showed it to be a good three hundred years younger than what the client was expecting, so Pablo plastered the hole and had a 'specialist' redate."

"Okay, so he's wanted in probably five countries—isn't that good enough?" I ask. Thom picks up my foot, plays a silent game of This Little Piggy. "Can't you just say you picked it up from him and move on?"

"They currently have me on trafficking in fraudulent merchandise or something like that."

"Or *something* like that?" I lower my voice, even though lately nothing can wake Max once he's down. "And Bjorn?"

"They want me to give them information on him. Keep my record clean if I tell them everything I know."

"Good. Nail the bastard."

"Indeed."

I rest my chin on his head. I can smell the soup heating up in the kitchen, and I'm suddenly starving.

"They're not going to get much from me. Bjorn's kept me out of the acquisition transactions. I've just been his gofer." He turns around and looks up at me, his hands on my ankles. "This is going to take a while, and I'm officially unemployed, so I want you to take the job with Christy."

"How do you know?" I ask. He shakes his head.

"That's enough questions for now—we're both too wiped out for this, okay? Just go ahead and plan to start on Tuesday." He gets up and helps me out of the chair.

"But what about Bjorn? We can't let him get away with this," I say, my anger coming back to a boil as I realize the extent to which Bjorn's double-crossed all of us.

"You let me worry about him, you worry about us," Thom says, brushing the hair off my forehead. "Feeling better?"

"I guess," I say. "I'm not dizzy or puking, so that's a start."

"You make up with Mom?"

"I think so."

"Good. Thanks. She's been upset about it all day."

"Really?" I ask, remembering how she almost lost this boy. "I mean, really *upset*?"

"Yeah, you totally scared the shit out of her. Wish I could have seen it." We stand over Max's crib, Thom's arm around my shoulder. "She made the soup and drove it back in just for you. You don't know how much power you have over her."

"I guess not."

"Don't let it go to your head."

"I'll try. But I can't promise. Your mother should poison me more often."

"Hey, your tiara's showing." Max stirs, and we tiptoe out of the room in search of my new slave.

Thirty-Four

I KEEP THINKING ABOUT THAT old cliché, "The more things change, the more they stay the same." I even think about it in French, since it was one of the few full sentences I managed to remember. After all this insanity, I'm right back to where I was a couple of weeks ago: Thom is a saint again, Bjorn is a demon, and the only major difference is I'm not as trusting as I once was. My beatified husband is still not all he seems, now that I've been challenged to view him from a jilted perspective. The falsehood of his cheating has hit me as hard as if it were real, carving new pathways in the way I see the world. If I could be so easily swayed to believe something from a man I've never trusted about a man I've always trusted, does that mean that I was secretly hoping for this to happen? Or worse, does it mean that I actually believe that Thom is capable of misdeeds? Even if he wasn't the one to fill the hole, he and I both know that he can detect a polished tamper and must have chosen to look the other way. He has the potential in him to be the criminal, the cheater, the fake. We *all* do.

I'd like to say that I've never committed a crime, but I've

driven drunk, bought dope, held a stash of coke for Penny, and taken money for sex. Once. From a boyfriend. Okay, he gave me twenty dollars per blow job, but it was a little joke between us and hardly a felony. I've gone faster than many, if not most, speed limits and parked in handicapped parking. I've never been given a ticket for anything, never appeared before a judge, never been caught in flagrante delicto.

Pot was not part of my high school experience, but alcohol certainly was. Portia and I would buy a six of Lite from Johnny Clark, a kid in our class who was held back long enough to be legal. We'd stash four in a ditch to keep them cold, and then drive around polishing off two at a time before heading home. This activity escaped the attention of our fathers, who just happened to be at the Improvement Bar and Tavern around the same time of evening. One time Portia actually scored some hard liquor from her dad's wet bar, putting it in an empty shampoo bottle. A not-very-well-cleaned bottle. We mixed it into orange soda and drank the soapy elixir anyway.

When I think of how many times I drove my car into the ditch back in those days, how many times I came close to rolling on icy back roads, it causes in me the sensation that I must have died one of those times and what I'm doing now is the afterlife. It's one thing to think you're immortal, quite another to think you're immolation-proof. It was a thrill to know that I was living *la vida papi*, imitating with my behavior what I found so reprehensible about his. Good for the gander, good for the gosling.

Measure my experience up against almost anyone, though, and you'd see I was a teetotaler. I liked to think I was a loner, Dotty, a rebel, but I was just an average teen in rural America.

At least I can tell Max and Georgia when I find their stashes that I didn't smoke pot until I was twenty. That'll really slow them down. Though God knows there will be some truly lethal drug on the market, or one that they can make in chemistry class, by then. Something that makes them appear completely normal on the outside, that has no traceable aroma, but that totally fucks them up on the inside. I've been warned by parents of older kids that New York City is a teenager's paradise. I've watched the movie *Kids*, lived through my own slice of *Party Monster*—seen my share of fucked-up teens real close. In fact, Penny was under-age when I first met her—and when I held her hand through more than one stomach-pumping. I've given homeschooling very, very careful consideration, and I am preparing to use the idea as a threat. Of course, I would never do it, since I expect both kids to be smarter than their parents—so smart that they won't get caught doing the kind of thing that ends up getting you homeschooled.

And still, I feel infected by Thom's transgression, no matter how small he wants to make it seem. I hope it's easy to explain to the kids why Daddy is suddenly home instead of Mommy, that the role-reversal is a normal evolutionary step in a family. What's harder to explain to them, and maybe I never will, is that I need this job, this new reality, in order to protect myself and them against the day when our world shifts harder than this near miss. When the warmongers let the bombs fall, when the sociopaths come back to howl against the door. How do you teach a child the world is safe when you don't even know which world you're in?

Thirty-Five

I'M WATCHING A TUGBOAT pull a load of garbage down the Hudson River outside of Christy's two-story plate-glass window. We've just finished lunch, and she's on the phone scheduling her driver to come in thirty minutes to whisk her back to the office. I'll be staying here for a couple of hours, formatting the new database. Our temporary office is a straight shot from my apartment on the 1/9 subway line, a couple blocks off Franklin along the river in Tribeca. We've already dubbed the train "the Bloomington Bradley express." Not that Christy will ever ride it—she's got our image to protect, after all. I watch her spotless reflection as she paces across the kilim rug—icy-blond bob cupping her scalpel-sharpened cheekbones, she's awash in Jil Sander neutrals, perfectly camouflaged amid the low-slung furnishings of her enormous apartment.

I've been waiting for the right time to tell Christy all of Thom's news, but I really haven't processed it myself yet, and though he says he's innocent, I still feel a twinge of guilt. Is there something he isn't telling me?

Christy finishes with the driver and clicks to another line.

"Hello, Peter! It's been too long. Yes, Marc did tell me you'd be calling. I think Jennifer and I will be able to help you. Of course. Yes. We understand. It is a very sensitive issue. Not a soul outside these walls. We'll structure a plan over the next few weeks and put it into effect in midspring, okay? Jennifer will contact you by the end of the month, as I really can't have a visible role until May, but please know I'll be here every step of the way." She crosses her arm over her waist, tips back on the heel of one of her spectator pumps. "Yes, resigning was one of the hardest things ever. Thirty years. Mm-hmm. Not until after we sell the Urpigi Fawn; they really want my face in the catalog. Totally amicable. Okay, terrific. You have my word. Ciao." She bounces me a smile. "Our first client. Peter Jacobs. Short-run Impressionists, about six of the twenty in his collection. He's in a spot, needs to raise cash. No museums for at least ten years. By then he hopes to be able to buy them back and donate them himself. I need you to put together a list of prospective buyers."

"I'm not really familiar with the Impressionist collectors," I say, which causes her smile to twinkle.

"Good God, Jennifer, if we knew them, what fun would that be? Don't fear, they'll emerge out of the pointillist woodwork before you know it." She does jazz hands to punctuate how much fun it's going to be. "We just have to put the word out that we're dealing, and the buyers will come to us."

"But how can we put the word out, if you're still under contract?"

"Oh, darling, welcome to the other side of the street. We don't have to put the word out, that's just an expression. Everyone already knows, they just have to pretend that they don't know until I say so. You're a bright girl, you'll figure it out. Now I must get back to my desk. See what you can scare up this afternoon. And don't worry so much about Thom; he'll land on his feet."

She's gone in a blur of beige, and I'm frozen in place. She knows about Thom. And everyone else knows about Blooming-ton Bradley. Which is how Thom knew about me.

I pull my Aeron chair up to my new desk and start to sift through the file Christy has left me, hoping to find an Impres-sionist clue. There are half-written profiles of potential clients, and I flip through until I find Peter Jacobs. He's quite handsome, in an investment banker sort of way: short salty hair, etched-in crow's-feet, fair eyes. Says here date of birth is 3/4/45. Made his money in the family fur business but lately has lost most of it in a failed telecom venture. Wife Hillary, daughter Chloë. Wife Hillary, daughter Chloë. I'll be damned. There are gaps in the in-formation, so I Google him and fill in as much as I can track down. Within minutes I'm at a dead end. I sharpen my pencil. Take a sip of water. Feel like crying. I realize what I'm going to need to really do this job right. Penny. She once cyberstalked her ex's ex-girlfriend's new boyfriend just because she could.

I pull out my cell phone to call Penny and see that I have a message. I had put it on vibrate but never felt it go off. It's Thom.

"Hey, Jen, it's me, I've got GG and everything's fine, so don't panic. Call me." Georgia's supposed to be at school. I'm sup-posed to not panic. I take some deep breaths as I dial. He's been home with them for exactly two days.

"What happened?" I pace over to the window, trying to mimic Christy's nonchalant gait, catch my heel in the carpet, almost twist my ankle.

"You won't believe it," he says. I can't tell if he's amused or throttling some kind of rage.

"Okay, skip the foreplay, spit it out."

"Miss Cartwright lost it."

"What do you mean, *lost it*?" My heart hammers in my chest as I do a mental checklist: she's not the type to carry a gun, I've never seen her mix Kool-Aid. . . .

"Everything was normal this morning, then after lunch she had the kids sit in a circle, then tied them together with jump ropes, and taped their mouths shut. How she got them to sit still long enough is beyond me—I can barely get Max's shoes on."

"She did what!?" My vision blurs, dims, sharpens. Vera's face flashes in front of me, telling me what a good school, what a perfect teacher—the daughter of her friend's new husband. "I'm going to kill her."

"Calm down, it's fine. Bjorn's kid broke free after Cartwright passed out in the coatroom. Rumor is she mixed her Xanax with her Ambien. Or she had a psychotic break of some kind."

"It's not fine. It's far from fine. How's Georgie?" There's no telling how this could set her back.

"She's great. I picked her up after the police questioned us, and brought Ella home too, so Angie could stay at Park Street and sort things out. They're having ice cream and watching TV. Listen." He holds the phone away so I can hear them singing along to *The Little Mermaid*.

"Ice cream *and* TV?" Don't spare the husband, spoil the child.

"Hon, it's been kind of a bad day for them, don't you think?" He's right, of course, but still.

"And Max?" I picture his face smeared in chocolate syrup.

"Asleep. He crashed out on the way back downtown. What a sense of humor that kid's got. He's really a lot of fun now, isn't he?" Yes, he is. Perfect timing. The very day I go back to work, Max turns into Jon Stewart.

"Okay, look, I'm going to run up to the school and keep Angie from strafing the place." I turn off the computer and grab my keys. "I'll be home by dinner. Can you order something in?"

"Got it. You go."

It takes me forever to get uptown, and when I pull up to Park Street, Angie is standing by the curb, Miles strapped to her, face-out, his small feet swinging listlessly in sleep.

"Don't get out, slide over," she says. "Ninetieth and First, please," she tells the driver as she secures her lap belt. "Put your belt on, these things aren't safe. Good thing you came along when you did—five cabs went right past me."

"Where are we going?" I try to buckle my seatbelt as told but can't find the latch, and there's no way I'm putting my hand down the seat crack of a cab. I hold it in place.

"PS 18, Progressive Science Kindergarten. I called ahead and made an appointment. If we're first, they'll have to take us."

"But what about—"

"There is no way in hell my daughter is setting foot back inside that building. If they won't refund our money, I'll go public and sue. I've already called our lawyer."

"Isn't Ty your lawyer?"

"Okay, I called my husband. Same thing." It's the first time she smiles, and I relax a little. "But I'm not overreacting, whether he thinks I am or not. We get one shot in this world. Many chances, but only one clean shot through all the crap. Ella and Miles are not going to get tied to their desks by some crazy fool. I won't stand it." Miles stirs and looks up at his mother, tilting his head back against her breastbone.

"Um, I don't know how to tell you this, Angie, but you seem to be wearing your baby." We're stuck in a gridlock that shows no sign of moving. I'd suggest walking, but I stupidly wore the kind of shoes that Christy wears—don't-fuck-me pumps—and I've already created two blisters and am starting a bunion. You'll know I've arrived when I have my little toe removed.

"I know, isn't he cute? Have you heard that if you feed some babies breast milk exclusively they only poop a couple times a week? Miles hasn't since Friday. He's amazing." She strokes his head with her fingertip.

"Did you just say poop?"

"Mom won't let me swear around the baby. Now that she's helping me out in the afternoons, I have to let her tell me what to do. Since I'm not working, she won't take my money, so the least I can do is respect her."

"And breast milk?"

"Yeah, I got my production back up to full, now that I'm home days. It's cool." Miles starts to squawk, and Angie slips her pinky into his mouth. She's practically the Black Madonna. "This whole stay-at-home thing isn't nearly as bad as I thought. I've got freelance work coming out my, um, ears, and I can feed on demand."

"So you're not going back to work?" This is new news to me. I was counting on Angie supporting my choice, rallying my cause, power-lunching with me at the Four Seasons.

"And miss Miles's first word, his first rollover? I'm just beginning to realize how much I lost out on with Ella—I don't know how I'll ever forgive myself." Miles purrs. "Oh, here we are—right up here on the left, sir," she tells the driver.

Once we find the principal's office we are invited to wait on a bench in the hall. School is out for the day, and the building is quietly settling. The floors are spotless Italianate tile, the walls covered in art and activities. One bulletin board displays duplicate rectangles of Venus on the half shell collages, another has photos from a recent production of *West Side Story*—little boys with slicked-back hair and letter jackets bent over, snapping fingers at their ankles, little girls in poodle skirts dancing on a cardboard cut-out rooftop.

"This place is killer," Angie whispers, unhooking Miles and snuggling him up under her shirt. I look away. "One of the five best public schools in Manhattan. You really have to pull some strings to get in, but we're both in-district and it's an emergency situation, which helps."

"Better than PS 33," I say, referring to our neighborhood's grade school, a shambles of a building cradled in the shadow of an electrical switching station. The humming from the turbines—or whatever is inside the massive brick edifice—is enough to shake a milk carton off a kid's desk. "When we went to check it out—before Vera unveiled her 'gift'—they told us the school is scheduled to be demolished in the next five years, and they won't budget any new materials in the meantime. One of the security doors was held together by gaffing tape. Not an option."

"Ty went to school with the district president. If we want in, we'll get in." She lifts Miles, who is in a milky comatose state, to her shoulder, effortlessly relatching her bra at the same time. "Okay, enough stalling. What gives with the husband?"

"Thom?" I try to play dumb, not ready to admit to my gullibility and my husband's work ethics. "What about him?"

"Why's he home all of a sudden and you're at work? What happened?" She locks me in a gaze, and I'm about to spill every sordid detail when the office door opens, and a very young black woman, dressed in a wave of green-and-blue kente cloth, emerges and wraps my friend in a hug, kissing both cheeks in the process.

"Angie! Come right in, it's been too long." As she leads us through the door, I see that her carefully tailored skirt sweeps up into a small bustle, accentuating what is already a perfect posterior and tiny waist. Her hair is wrapped up in a swath of rough blue silk, and her Pepsodent-white ballet-neck T-shirt exposes the smallest hint of a turtle tattoo that is one shade darker than her jet-black skin. I will my hand from tapping the turtle lightly in appreciation.

"Nichelle, this is Jennifer. Her daughter Georgia is the one I was telling you about." Nichelle gestures to two brightly painted wooden chairs as she takes her place behind a low metal desk.

"I am stunned by what has happened," she says, meeting my eyes and holding my gaze. "Though it is not our way here at Science to question the methods of other schools, I have to admit I am not entirely surprised by this development. We interviewed Miss Cartwright for a position a few years ago and I remember her seeming slightly unstable even then. I had hoped I was wrong." She sits back without blinking. I have the feeling that Nichelle is rarely wrong.

"She never really inspired confidence in me either," I try to explain. "But my mother-in-law thought Park Street was the best for Georgia." Angie lets go with a little snort. "So, tell me about Science," I say, changing the subject.

"Here at Science we practice the three R's—Respect, Routine, and Restraint—but we don't use jump ropes to get our message across. Our feeling is that children thrive in controlled environments. When they know where to sit, how to raise their hands to be heard, how to wait their turn, and what to expect from their teachers, they are then free to find self-expression. We use a blend of many different philosophies and teach through play in the younger grades. For instance, this week our kindergarten is focusing on cleanliness. We have songs and games designed to instill in the children a keen sense of personal responsibility, but none of this is done in a negative environment. We have two teachers per fifteen children in the kindergarten rooms, and four pods, for a total of sixty children. The rooms are assigned by lottery each year, so that the children have a full mix of friends." She sits back, blinks.

"Where do we sign?" I try not to look too excited, act like this isn't the most perfect school I've ever heard of. Angie turns to me and places a hand on my arm and looks back at Nichelle.

"What Jennifer means to say is, would it be at all possible for you to work Ella and Georgia into Science? I know how in demand the school is." Her hand stays on my arm, and if it were anyone else silencing me, I'd slap it off, but I trust Angie, will follow her anywhere.

"Well, I know you don't believe in luck, Angie, but it just so happens that the Michaelson twins are moving to France and Ms. Daily's Green Room will have an opening starting next Monday. We do consider emergency applications more seriously than the usual waiting lists, but Ella and Georgia will be on probation until spring break, at which time we'll get you the applications for first grade in the fall." Her smile has been friendly up until now, when it breaks into a ray of blinding sunshine. "We'd be honored to have you here." I look at Angie, who doesn't reveal a thing. Honored? Who exactly is Angela Little that a principal in a public grade school would be honored to have her daughter enrolled?

"Oh, don't be silly," she says, gives my arm a little squeeze of 'I'll tell you later,' and releases me. "Thank you so much. Would it be possible to get the lesson plans from Ms. Daily so we can bring the girls up to speed while they're home this week?"

"I have them right here." Nichelle pushes two green plastic binders across the desk. "How's the locking going?" she asks Angie.

"Just another inch to go before we twist," she says, touching the black scarf wrapped around her head. "I am getting all kinds of older men hitting on me, thinking I'm holy." They both laugh at this. I shoot Angie a questioning look.

"I'm starting dreadlocks," she tells me. "I've always wanted to, but it's just too hard when you work for corporate America. Getting fired turns out to be the best thing that ever happened to me. Check out my abs." She hands me Miles and lifts her shirt to reveal a washboard. I feel my tummy roll over my waistband; I suck it back up a half inch, shift Miles in front of me.

"Girl, you look fine," Nichelle says. "If I weren't already married . . ." They giggle together at what is clearly a very old joke between them and I finally see the resemblance—if they aren't actual sisters, then they must be cousins. Nichelle walks us out the front door, catching up on various relatives with Angie. This is textbook Angie, claiming that Ty has the connections when it's really her own mastery of the universe that opens doors for our girls. And she's my friend. My friend. Even though I've done nothing to deserve her, there is no question that she has gone out of her way to help me and my kid. As I watch her laugh and shake her head at something Nichelle has said, it occurs to me it's not because I'm special, but because Angie is. I walk a little ways apart from them and carry Miles, snuggling him up to my nose, and as I breathe in baby, I decide that I do believe in luck, even if Angie doesn't.

. . .

The taxi lets me off at the corner, and as I walk up my block I see a woman leave my building. She is about my height and has long black hair held back in a double braid. I run up the block after her, shocked that she would have the nerve to go to my home, see my husband in front of my children. She picks up her pace at the sound of my heels and rushes down the subway stairs. By the time I catch up with her, she's already through the turnstile and boarding a waiting train. I slam my thigh into the metal rod as it stops me from following her.

"Wait—hey, you!" I yell at her back. She turns around to reveal a full beard. Oh. My. What an idiot.

When I get back upstairs, Ty has already picked up Ella, and Thom has bathed and fed our kids, who are propped up in front of yet another video. I'm too tired to argue, and besides, I need to talk to him alone.

"Thom, we need to talk," I say, sitting down at the kitchen counter. He already seems completely readjusted to the time zone and much fresher than I do.

"How did you know about the job?"

"I recommended you." I could swear he said that he recommended me.

"Come again?" I reach over to the sink and run some water over my wrist to cool myself off, and also to focus my mind, chase out some of the demons that have me still seeing phantoms where there are none.

"Christy called me a couple of months ago and asked if I knew anyone great. I said, yeah, Jennifer Bradley." He takes my other hand. "You are the best, Jennifer, you just need to get out there and prove it. You're ready."

"I'm not so sure," I say, a slightly sour taste rising in my throat. I chew a pretzel, fill a glass with water, knock it back.

"I am. And look. I have to tell you something." He turns my palm up, traces the lines. "This thing is going to take a while. There's going to be a grand jury, and once they indict, if they indict, Bjorn will be arrested. Until then, I think I should stay put." I want nothing more than to have my hand back. Being touched is unbearable.

"I hope they nail the bastard. He set you up, you know." The water rises back up my throat, floating a piece of pretzel into my mouth.

"So it seems. I just can't figure out why, though. Not yet, anyway. I know you don't like him, but he's been really good to us— he's one of my best friends. I'm not convinced that Pablo doctored the vase, even. He might have bought it that way."

"Don't be so naive, Thom. Bjorn's ruthless and dishonest. He cut you out of that Egyptian deal years ago and has been holding you down ever since while he makes money off your ambition. Oh, and he tried to convince your wife that you were having an affair."

"Hey, keep it down. Georgia might hear you."

"He's a fraud, Thom," I say above a whisper. "A fraud who will do anything to get what he wants, including selling out his best friend."

"I talked to him today," he says, his voice both tender and mournful, a jilted lover's tone. "He told me you tried to seduce him last week, that you threw yourself at him when he told you about me. Said he was testing you on my behalf with those photos, that he's the one who really loves me, not you."

"That little . . ." I start to answer, but feel caught in a web that I had a hand in spinning. The only way out of this is the truth. "Okay, I did try to seduce him—*sort* of. But you have to understand the circumstances. I was under incredible duress and he had gotten me drunk."

"He told me you'd say that." He pulls his mouth tight, wrestles with the information, then changes the subject.

"Things are going to be hard over the next few months, and we need to get our cash flow up. We're really strapped, Jen, and I don't want to ask Skip for money. How much is Christy going to pay you?"

"I'm not sure," I say, not wanting to leave my tiny infidelity unexplained, yet needing to let Thom take the lead for now. "I mean, I don't know. We haven't worked out the terms of the partnership yet."

"Then we'd better get them worked out. Call her, I'll listen on the extension."

"I can't call her tonight, she's hosting a party for some ambassador. I'll talk to her in the morning."

"Fine," he says. We let the silence drop between us as "Circle of Life" plays in the background.

"I'm going to go take a bath," I say, breaking the standoff. I pat his hand—he doesn't pull it away or flinch—and make my way to the bathroom, brushing the kids on the tops of their heads as I pass by the couch. When I lean into the tub to put the stopper in, I projectile-vomit all over the porcelain. I guess I haven't kicked the bug yet after all. I decide to skip the bath and lie down for a moment. The bed under me feels cold and empty, and I wonder what it will take to bring us back together, and how long it will take, and whether that's really what I want.

Thirty-Six

SOMETHING ELSE YOU SHOULD know about me: I flunked out of college the first time around. I didn't apply myself. I underachieved. I ran out of money and moved to the city, convinced that I was too stupid to do anything but take tickets at the door of a nightclub. Apparently I was wrong about that, since I was fired from my first job for miscounting the nightly receipts. Until today, I had no sense of what a gifted life I was living before Singapore, how easily things can be snatched away. Miss Cartwright probably didn't even see her breakdown coming; she isn't the type who just snaps, no matter how tightly wound I think she is.

A good education is overrated, or so I used to believe. My sixth-grade teacher once gave us an oral spelling test, which included the sentence "The Indian rode up on his Palomino." Only she said, "The Injun rode up on his Palomino." At the word "Injun," all pencils stopped scratching, and heads popped up like prairie dogs. We made her repeat the sentence five times. We all went with "Injun" and were severely reprimanded for being so thick. And no, she wasn't British, didn't also say "juice" for "deuce." Toward the end of that year, she too had a nervous breakdown, but it was many years in the making and happened during midwinter break, when kids were home from school. We didn't even know it had happened until we came back to a permanent substitute, who found neatly arranged stacks of student pictures collected in Miss Mongen's top desk drawer. And in the side drawers was a collection of every piece of candy, every toy, and every homemade slingshot she had confiscated from a child in her ten years of teaching.

There was no Park Street for me to be moved to, no Catholic education to salvage my intelligence. In fact, my education was so paltry that I didn't even know I was smart until a few years ago when late one night I was talking to Cheryl on the phone and randomly asked her if I was a smart kid back in the day. She told me she didn't remember my accomplishments exactly, but that I was indeed the smartest of all her children, always was. Always was? So how come I never heard a whisper of this until my thirties? Would I be more successful if someone had noticed my abilities and demanded more from me, pushed me toward some lofty goal? I do remember that in my junior year, after the state tests were administered and the results known, my guidance counselor sat me down in his office and told me that I wasn't living up to my potential. But people had been telling me that since second grade, and it never meant anything, was never translated into hard facts. Until I met Christy, I didn't even know what the word *mentor* could mean. Rather than tell me I had potential, she kicked my ass harder than the other interns, made me stay later, promoted me sooner.

Georgia's smart, really smart. She learned her alphabet ahead of the crowd, without having it drilled in by me. I try to encourage her and keep a journal on all her accomplishments, so that one day she'll be able to see for herself just how advanced she was and how much I cared. She's adapting to the real world so quickly since I let her out—I'm both proud of her and scared of losing her. Who am I kidding? She's already gone. Only when she's sick do I feel like she even remembers the before time. It's pretty easy to see how women become Munchausen by Proxy addicts. The way kids love you and need you when they're low is like mainlining heroin. Maybe it's the same way with husbands and wives. We say we love each other in the worst of times, taking for granted the good times, never really seeing how both pass so quickly that we shouldn't waste so much of it trying to make sense of the bad instead of celebrating the good. What I do know is that I'm smart enough to put all of this in perspective and find a way to click my heels back home.

Thirty-Seven

WE'RE KID-SWAPPING TODAY, and for the morning I get Georgia while Thom and Max are at the Museum of Natural History. Max is still too young for dinosaurs, but it appears that Thom is not. We are officially Not Talking About It, hoping that in silence this mess will clean itself up. I've just finished my first full week of work, and Georgia is officially Not Talking to Me. In order to win her love back, I've agreed to have a tea party, my least favorite childhood activity. It's bad enough that we have to go to a real tea party for Chloë's birthday in a couple of weeks, but to sit at a play table with Georgia, Amanda, Mr. Bear, and Barbie and pretend to sip tea out of empty tiny cups is the kind of thing that makes me want to set my hair on fire.

"Barbie, would you care for some tea?" Georgia asks the little blonde.

"Why, yes, thank you. That would be nice," Georgia answers on her behalf.

"Amanda, would you mind pouring for Jenfur?" Georgia picks up the tiny teapot in Amanda's hands and pours me some tea. The doll bears an uncanny resemblance to my daughter. I never see her without it anymore.

"Jenfur, do you take milk or lemon?" Georgia asks me in the guise of Amanda.

"Milk, please," I reply directly to Amanda, who then serves Mr. Bear.

"Georgia, may I pour your tea?" I ask my daughter.

"Amanda, will you please tell Jenfur that I already have my tea?" Georgia won't even glance my way. Wonder where she learned that trick.

"Jenfur, Georgia already has her tea," Amanda says.

"Barbie," Mr. Bear says, "can you believe this weather?"

"Well, Mr. Bear, it is frightful cold, but the tea is warm." Barbie turns to Amanda. "And how are you liking your new home, Amanda?"

"It's very nice and I love Georgia very much," Amanda says.

"And I love you too." Georgia kisses the doll. "I think I love you most of all. First you, then Daddy, then Barbie and Mr. Bear. And then the baby." I'm feeling very unloved, with no way of entering into a conversation with all these cold bitches. Okay, so one of them has fur. But since I'm the adult apparent, it's my responsibility to find a way in.

"So, Georgia, how's your new school?" I pretend to nibble on a plastic tea cake.

"Mr. Bear, would you please tell Jenfur that school is fine?" She cocks her head in an amazingly patronizing way. My eyes spike with tears.

"Jenfur," Mr. Bear says in his gruff voice, "school is just fine."

"Would you like a tea cake, Amanda?" my daughter asks her doll. I grab a Pottery Barn catalog off the coffee table. Good time to catch up on my reading.

"Why, yes, Georgia, did you make them yourself?" Amanda says.

"Yes, I'm afraid so." Georgia exhales. "My mommy used to make them for me, but she has to work." Now we're getting somewhere. I don't look up from the picture frames.

"Oh, how sad," Amanda says. "Does that make you very sad?"

"Yes, thank you for asking." Georgia puts a hand to her forehead. "So very, very sad. Barbie, does your mommy work?"

"Yes, Barbie," I say. "Tell us what your mommy does. She designs dolls and runs a multimillion-dollar company, am I right?" Georgia's eyes lock on mine and just as quickly flick back to Barbie.

"But she cooks you dinner, dosen't she?" Georgia fake-pours more tea to cover her putting words in the doll's mouth.

"Why, yes, she do, and she made me this dress too, just like Caran's mommy," Barbie says, even though she isn't wearing a dress, she has on her doctor's coat. Because she is Dr. Barbie, part of Barbie's positive-role-model act to make up for back when she uttered, "Math is hard, let's go shopping."

"So, Mr. Bear," I try to change the subject, "how about those Knicks?"

"GG had fun at the game with Good Mommy," Mr. Bear answers, using Georgia's latest nickname for her father. "Good Mommy is the best mommy ever ever ever."

"Good Mommy's new to the whole mommy game, Geege, and if you think back a week, you'll recall that Good Mommy wasn't even in the country for three months." I slap the catalog down on the tea table, rattling the cups, saucers, and spoons. "I had to go back to work. End of story. You go to school, I go to work, why does it matter so much to you where I am all day? You're rarely home when I get here anyway, with all your playdates and your gymnastics and your Suzuki classes." I'm not shouting, but from the look on Georgia's face I might as well be. She calmly places her hands on the table, pushes out of her chair, and picks up the three dolls.

"I *hate* you," she says, her voice quavering. Without another word she retreats to her room. I stick my tongue out at the back of her head. Good. Now I can read my catalogs in peace. Okay, maybe I overreacted, but I worked hard for the Mommy moniker and I'm not giving it up so easily. I gather the whole stack and cozy up on the couch. It's been a long time since I had quality commercial time. I won't let her serve me up this helping of double standard. I don't think I ordered a single thing during the holidays. I will not let this little bout of temper ruin my day off. I can hear Georgia talking to Amanda, but I refuse to eavesdrop on my daughter. She's speaking in a normal tone of voice. Oh God, don't tell me I'm the one who threw the temper tantrum. The one who feels left behind.

I happen to be picking up a stray Duplo block just outside her door when I hear her singing, "Ella's mommy stays home, Daisy's mommy stays home, Dalton's mommy stays home . . ." and on and on in her tuneless way. A whole litany of good mommies. It's almost as though I never blew up. Does she really care so little about me that she can just go to her room and make up a song as though I don't exist?

I pick up Peeve—the only one who truly loves me—retreat to the couch, and craft a little tune of my own. "Ella's mommy used to work, Daisy's mommy used to work, Dalton's mommy used to work, but then they all got fired." Silence from the other room. She's working on what "fired" means, asking Amanda if the mommies played with matches. Hah. She does hear me, I knew it. Okay, I've let this game go far enough and rather than start to feel

ashamed of myself—which I have every right to do—I go to the
pantry and pull a box of brownie mix off the shelf. Open the
fridge, get the butter and eggs, put the cake pan on the counter
just hard enough to make it sound like I'm baking. I catch a
flicker of color in my periphery, but if I acknowledge her first, I
lose. I nuke the butter. Georgia slides along the couch. I turn on
the oven. She puts Amanda down on the play table. I pour the
powdered mix and oil into the bowl and reach for an egg.

"Mommy, I crack the eggs, remember?" She looks up at me
with those enormous hazel eyes.

"Sure you want to?"

"Yes, please."

"Okay, bring your steps over." She slides her stepladder next
to me and cracks the eggs one at a time, fishing the bits of
eggshell out of the batter.

"I miss you too, you know," I say to her. She nods her head
once.

"I don't hate you," she whispers. I kiss the top of her sweet-
smelling head. We each take a spoon and stir together in silence,
then transfer the batter to the pan. She dips her finger in the middle of the gooey brown lake and sticks it in her mouth, then does
it again and sticks it in my mouth. I smile around her finger and
she smiles back. She giggles. I giggle. She smears batter on my
nose, I smear batter on hers. I put the pan in the oven and we
wind up on the couch together, licking the mixing bowl.

By the time Thom and Max return, we've eaten nearly all the
brownies. They find us laid out on the couch, chocolaty-milk-
mustachioed and belly-bloated. If we were sheep, they'd have to
kill us, puncturing our stomachs to let out the methane gases collecting there.

"Whoa, what the heck happened here?" Thom greets us. Max barrels across the room yelling *dada*—at me—and throws his entire thirty pounds across my stomach. I can't help it, I fart. Well, what would you do? These people are the very definition of family. Max waves his hand in front of his face and says, "Ooo, stinky," just like I taught him. My pride, my joy.

"Daddy Daddy Daddy, where have you been so long?" Georgia rabbits out. "We had a tea party with Mr. Bear and Amanda and Barbie and tea cakes and then I got mad and Mommy got mad and then I went to my room and sang some songs and then we baked brownies and then we sat on the couch and then you came home and then I told you a story." She practically ignites from all the beaming she's doing at her father.

"So what did you put in the brownies?" Thom asks me.

"Sugar, pure white refined no organic nothing but sugar, Duncan Hines, yeah baby." I roll Max off me onto the floor. "She's all yours. I recommend you take her somewhere you can plug her in and power up the lower half of Manhattan. How's my boy, ready for our nap?"

"We had real food for lunch. Remember real food, Jen?" He tries to be mad at me, but he's been suffering through Georgia's cold front by having to tell me things she wants me to know. This is a welcome change for all of us, our first whiff of normal since Thom came home. "He should be ready for his nap any time now."

"Is that so, big boy? Are you a beefaroni? Are you my beefy boy?" Max climbs back on me and tries to bite my arm, administering fresh bruises in the process.

Once Thom has agreed to take Georgia to *Peter Pan* for the fifth time, Max and I are left in the quiet backwash of her incessant chatter. I'm on the couch, watching him from the horizontal. He brings me toys and books; we look at pictures and words. Every few minutes or so I say, "Night, night?" waiting for him to go down for his nap so I can sleep off my sugar crash.

"So, Max, now what do we do?" Thom's only had him for a week, and I've completely forgotten how to entertain him. But entertain him I must: every minute I'm with him now must be *quality*. Maybe if I sit up, that will be quality. "Night, night?" He looks at me and laughs. I pick up a pen and notepad and begin making my lists for the coming week. Thom's nowhere near the organizational whiz I am, and if I don't write every last thing down for him he forgets to buy even diapers until we're scrounging the diaper bag for one last one. "Night, night, Maxie?" Why won't he go to sleep already? He's a good napper. He's full, he's had his milk, and now he should want to sleep. I want to sleep. I could sing to him, but the only song that has ever put him to sleep is "White Christmas," and I would feel stupid singing that in the middle of January in the middle of the day. He brings me a large, plastic purple caterpillar with letters painted on its many feet. God, how I hate this toy. It has different settings—letters, phonics, music—and if you pull its cord it sings the alphabet song. God, I hate the alphabet song. If I had a nickel for every time I've sung the fucking alphabet.

"A B C D E F G, H I J K, LMNOP. Q R S, T U V. W X, Y and Z. Now I know my ABCs, next time won't you sing with me? Yay, Max, yay, good guy!" There's a version of this song that ends "Tell me what you think of me." What kind of masochist came up with that one? He pulls the cord again. We sing again. He doesn't quite have the hang of it yet, but does manage *t u v* pretty well. His curls have just started to grow back, and I have to admit he looks even more handsome with his hair short. He pulls the cord again.

"Night, night?" This time he takes the bait and runs off to his room. I haul my Betty Crocker off the couch and follow him. I lift him into the crib, he grabs his blankie and pacifier and lies down. I leave, pull the door closed. He screams. And screams. Like he's being murdered. I go back in; he stops screaming, gives me an Oscar-winning smile, and says, "Up, pease?" I turn to leave; he throws his pacifier at me and starts screaming again. I match him decibel for decibel. He stops, bewildered. He starts again, I start again, but this time I turn the scream into a laugh, attempting to get him to mimic me into a happier place. He doesn't fall for it, so I take him back out to the living room.

A grueling hour of baby sing-along later, Max is finally asleep and all I want to do is wake him up and apologize for not wanting to be with him, for not rising to the challenge and enjoying his company while I had it. Now I'm wide awake and looking for a diversion, as I've finished all five lists, four for Thom and one for me:

1. What to do with Max on what day
2. When to pick up Georgia and where to take her next
3. What to buy and when and where to buy it
4. Where to go when you feel like your head is going to blow off
5. To Do

While checking over my To Do list one last time, I realize I need someone even more organized to help me at the office. I call Kate, she might know of someone.

"Hello?" she answers, sounding a little brownie-baked herself.

"Hey, Kate, it's Jennifer." She doesn't respond. "Jennifer Bradley?"

"Oh, hi! I know like twenty Jennifers, I'm so so sorry!" Maybe I shouldn't have called her. I didn't know I had so much competition. I mean, how many of *them* did she tell her real birth story to?

"It's okay, I get that all the time. So how are you?" I pick up Max's clippers and trim my nails while I talk. He could dig to China with his if he had to.

"Really terrific. Kyle's taken Jax to his mother's, and I'm having some quiet time, pampering myself. I have a beauty mask on right now—I love the way they peel off."

"That sounds like a great idea." I finish my fingers and start on my toes. "I was thinking about going out and getting a pedicure and then I remembered that I'm the only one here with the baby."

"Oh, gosh, I did that once when Jax was teeny. I ran out to get some coffee and a bagel and I was so sleep-deprived that I completely forgot that he was in the house until I got back. Can you imagine?" Not really, but I don't tell her that.

"Wow that must have been scary."

"Yeah, it was pretty scary. . . ." She drifts off, no doubt replaying that day. We succeed millions of times and never remember, but fail once and there's no forgetting it. "Hey, Jen? I'm glad you called. I've been thinking about taking you up on your offer."

"My offer?"

"You know, the C-section offer. But I was thinking that maybe I could do some babysitting for you now and earn the money in advance. You said you were using a babysitter so you can work part-time, right?" I don't remember telling her that, but then I do talk a lot.

"Yeah, I did, and I was, but now Thom's home and, well, he's taking a little time off from work to, you know, spend with Max. He's very modern that way."

"Sheesh, you're lucky, Kyle would never take time off during the week. That's great for Max." She goes quiet again, I don't know how to fill the gap. "Well, that's okay then, forget I asked."

"You know what, though," I say before I think, "I am hiring someone at my new office—"

"I'll do anything, anything at all."

"You'd be working with Penny—"

"I love Penny!"

"And doing some pretty basic clerical stuff—"

"I'm an excellent typist, and I know the alphabet really well."

"Don't we all?" We laugh together, and this seems like the right phone call to have made. "Can you start on Monday? Just part-time, and you can leave Jax with Thom."

"Yes, yes, please. I mean, I have to ask Kyle, but I don't think he'll mind as long as I'm home in time to make dinner. We really could use some extra money." I hear her sniffle.

"Aw, come on, don't cry. We're beyond that, aren't we?"

"I'm just so happy, is all, I haven't been happy in a long time, I think. Not really happy. I'd better go and peel this thing off my face. I'll call you tomorrow for all the details after I talk to Kyle and hopefully see you on Monday?"

"You got it. Have a good weekend." I made her happy. I made Georgia happy. When Max wakes up I'll make him happy too. And maybe I'll even find a way to begin to make Thom happy again. I'd like to see all those other Jennifers spread this kind of joy without ever leaving home.

Thirty-Eight

THEY SAY THAT ONCE you have children you forget what life was like before them, that you cannot imagine the world without them in it. I find instead that I obsess about all the things I used to do, the way my body used to look, all the traveling Thom and I were able to do at the drop of a hat. We once went to Venice for a long weekend. Last November was the first time we left the children overnight. And not because we don't trust other people, but because we are insane.

I was also told repeatedly before I had Georgia that my life was "going to change." "No, really, it's going to change." Thom heard it at least twice as much as I did. But isn't change the whole point of having kids? I was ready for a new challenge, for a different perspective. Cynicism had threatened to overtake my brain, and I needed a way out of the hypernarcissistic culture surrounding me. Having kids slows down the brain, reteaches it what it thinks it already knows so well.

Then they told me that I would never sleep through the night ever again. They were pretty much right on that one, though there were a couple of years between Georgia and Max that I got caught up. And now that Thom is at home he lets me sleep until eight every morning. Maybe so we can continue not talking, maybe because he really does love me. Though I may have my problems with Vera, one look at Skip many years ago told me everything I needed to know: the Bradley men mate for life. Even when Vera is haranguing Skip for something he did or didn't do, he has a look of pure adoration in his eyes. He just says, "Yes, dear," and fixes the problem.

I found some old wedding pictures packed into a cigar box. They were taken by a friend that I haven't spoken to in years. I was stunned by how young Thom and I were, even though it wasn't that long ago, and how happy we were before the babies came. There is no denying that they have changed our lives, and entirely absolutely one hundred percent for the better. But I still know exactly what it was like to feel that carefree and to have life be that uncomplicated. If anything, it's a sharper feeling in reflection than it ever was at the time. I'm beginning to realize that I don't have to romanticize the past or try to recapture my glory days by having a midlife pseudo-seduction of a man I despise. What I need to do is kick my wounded pride to the curb and, along with it, my shame.

Thirty-Nine

DESPITE HER CLAIMS to the contrary, Georgia is happily ensconced in Science, and I have been able to dedicate my extra energy to Bloomington Bradley instead of ventriloquist tea parties. We've moved our headquarters to an office in a converted fur factory in Chelsea, giving me a five-minute commute to work and the luxury of going home for lunch with the boys. I've brought Penny in and put her in charge of client profiling, and happily Kyle has agreed with Kate that doing some random clerical work in the afternoons would be good for them both—her intensive mothering really comes in handy when organizing an office.

"Hey, you guys think I should have my hair thermally straightened?" Penny asks without looking up from her computer.

"I hear it's pretty hard on your hair," Kate says, though her own is as stick-straight as mine.

"All the five-year-olds are doing it these days," I tell her, marveling at how little my days have really changed. I look at the many pictures of Max and Georgia on my desk, gauge how much I miss them, decide it's just enough, and go back to layering information into PowerPoint.

Ever since my run-in with the éclair, I've been feeling out of sorts: nausea, mainly, but bone-gripping fatigue as well. When I woke up this morning my breasts were killing me, so maybe I'm just getting my period again. It's probably just a fibroid and PMS and oh, I don't know, a little bit of stress perhaps, but I've made an appointment with Dr. Sarah just in case it's something bad. It would be just my luck to have everything fall apart just as it's all finally coming back together.

"Hey, J, did I tell you that Mikhail said 'pirouette' the other day?" Penny asks around a mouthful of scone. "It was fantastic. And then he almost completed one. I was telling Madeline that I think he's going to be perfect for Joffrey." Not that any of us lives through our kids.

"How is Madeline, and why is it that I've never met her?" I ask.

"You guys just wouldn't get along at all," she says, clicking away. "She's pro circumcision *and* cosleeping."

"Isn't that like being a member of the NRA *and* PETA?" Kate says. I'm so proud of her.

"No, because that actually makes sense," Penny says. Kate and I stop what we're doing and look at her. "What? What did I say?"

"You think that people should have guns so they can shoot other people?" I ask.

"Not me, but some people do, and if you think about it, it can make sense." We let this lie and go back to our respective desks. I look over at Christy's cube, which is indistinguishable from the rest of the office—we're all on the same tasteful playing field. Her sense of fairness is remarkable.

When I asked Christy about the partnership terms, she handed me an envelope, saying, "I think you're going to like it here." I was so nervous to look at her offer that I waited until I got home that night and Thom and I opened it together. She nearly doubled my previous salary, paid me a small signing bonus, and offered a standard but generous commission on any art I personally place with a buyer. It's great working for an independently wealthy woman who appreciates you and knows that you don't have a trust fund for her to take advantage of. Thom was even more impressed than I was. If we get enough clients before the end of the year, I should be able to keep the household together without taking out a loan. At least this part of my life seems to be back on track.

Penny breaks my reverie with a shouted "Aha! Check this out, Jen." She hits a button on her computer and paper starts shooting out of the printer. She gathers the information and brings it over to me. "Here, read this. No, don't read it, let me tell you what it says. I hacked into the grand jury computer—says here that Mr. Peter Jacobs, CEO of Wide World Telecommunications, is being investigated for skimming. How cliché." It's almost as bad as an art dealer being investigated for fraud, but I don't tell her that, of course. "And this page says that his wife, Hillary Jacobs, helped him remove important documents from his office, in her pocketbook. She's suspected of shredding and dumping them."

"Wow," I say. Kate looks up from affixing colored labels to manila files. Her stomach has really popped, and she's a cute and perky pregnant, wearing a tight-fitting baby-blue Polo dress—I can tell she's more comfortable now that she looks sexy again. That four-month point is a chunky-looking bitch, no matter who you are.

"Wow is right." Penny waves Kate over. "And get this—a year ago their membership to the Park Isle Country Club was revoked after Peter tried to bribe a comember. His kid was rejected from the member's kid's kindergarten, and he was trying to buy her a place."

"Chloë?"

"The one and only. Seems she failed the admissions test. Something about a speech impediment."

"Does it say how old she is?"

Penny shuffles a couple of pages.

"Six this weekend."

"Let me see that." I take the paper from her hand. It's Chloë's birth record. Damn, Penny's good. "I knew it! What else you got?" I can't wait to tell Angie.

"Um, guys, aren't we supposed to be finding someone to buy his art?" Kate asks. "Do you think it's right to go digging into his family problems?"

"Shut up," Penny and I say together. I tag on a smile.

"Go on," I tell her.

"Okay, he's originally from Montville, New Jersey. Went to public school but graduated top of his class and took his B.A. and M.B.A. at Harvard. Last year they moved from Weehawken into a town house over by Gracie Mansion. Talk about a burn rate— they've got a horse farm out in the Hamptons, a helicopter he flies himself, and a yacht. I didn't know people still had yachts." She goes back to her computer, having spent all the information she's gathered. "Hey, did I tell you that I think Mikhail is actually starting to think for himself? I hate it that he might have an original thought."

"Great work, Pen, keep digging. And then start filling in some of these blanks." I hand her a disk with Thom's electronic Rolodex. "Do a search for Impressionist collectors, but cross-reference it with new money. New money never keeps the same art for more than a few years. That will give Peter time enough to buy them back, if he can, but also might provide us with a resell client. I'll be right back." I go down the hall to the floor bathroom and shut myself in a stall. I bend over at the waist and let the nausea pass as I slip a piece of antacid gum into my mouth. The outer door opens, and I quickly turn around and sit fully clothed.

"Jennifer, are you in here?" It's Kate.

"Yep—everything okay?" I pull some toilet paper off the roll, drop it, and flush it while zipping and unzipping the Prada pants I bought back in November. They only just finally fit. I bite down hard on the gum, leave the stall.

"Yeah, are *you* okay?" She looks at me like something might be seriously wrong with me, and like she might not have this job for long. Or maybe I'm just projecting my own hypochondria.

"I think I'm still feeling the aftershocks of Georgie's flu," I tell her, but we both know it's been about a month already and I should be over it by now.

"Oh, 'cause you look a little pale. Er than usual. I guess. But then I don't know you that well yet, maybe you're always pale? Er than most?" She has to stop doing that thing where she breaks a word between sentences; the motion of it makes me sweat.

"I'm pretty pale, it's true." I try to laugh it off, splash some water on my face. "Look, you can see my veins right through my skin." I pull up my sleeve to reveal my ivory wrist, then move to pass her. She stops me at the door.

"Sure, just one thing, though. Thanks." Her gaze is so intense I have to look away. We both know what she means. I give her hair a stroke.

"It's nothing, really."

"It's everything, *really*."

By the time I leave work the three of us have finished a twenty-page presentation for Peter Jacobs, complete with recent comparative auction prices for the artists he wants to sell and thorough background checks on the five potential buyers. It makes me wonder what we'll find to do tomorrow.

When I get home and unlock the door, I'm greeted by the strong smell of curry: normally something that would bring me to my knees in a good way, it sends me straight into the bathroom. As I pass through the silent apartment I see that it is a complete disaster zone. There are vegetable peelings all over the counter, a spilled juice box on the floor, dirty dishes everywhere, and that's just the kitchen. I flick the light on in the living room and turn it back off just as quickly. I can't stand to make a mental list of all the things out of place. You could never accuse me of being a meticulous cleaner, but after the day I've had this level of chaos could put me right over the edge, if I had any energy left to get me to the edge in the first place. I decide to take a shower, where I find Peeve curled up next to a small but disgusting hairball. Just as I'm stepping out of the steam, the door flies open and in rush Max and Georgia, nearly knocking me over.

"Mommy, Mommy, Daddy and Swen took us to Kiehl's!" Georgia shouts over Max's "Mamamamamamamama!"

I barely get a robe around me before Thom and Sven follow close behind, Sven stopping at the threshold with Lily in his arms.

"Anyone else in Manhattan want to see me naked? Get out, get out!" I shoo them all out, except for Max, whom I fold into a million tiny kisses once the door is closed.

"Did Daddy take Maxie shopping?" I sit down on the floor with Max in my lap.

"Dada, MaxMax, Mama," he says, pointing to his chest at the appropriate name.

"Don't forget GG," I tell him.

"GG soocay!" His new favorite word is *suitcase*. He has a tiny green one that holds an entire family of rubber ducks.

"Hey, let me see those teeth." Max tips his head back and opens wide. "One, two, three, four, five, six, seven, eight, nine, and almost ten!" When did that happen? Last time I counted, he had six. I hold him closer as he tries to open my robe and get at my boobs.

There's a knock at the door and Sven pokes his head in.

"Mind if I join you guys?" Max reaches his arms out to Sven, says "Hi," blows him a kiss.

"What, you want a cheap feel, too?"

"Nope, just want to tell you how much I miss you. Thom's great, but he's no Jen."

"You're just saying that so I don't hate you. You hate it when I hate you." I pout.

"You're right. Thom's a blast. Where have you been hiding him?" He tweaks my nose. "Hey, we gotta run, I haven't seen my Tom since we got back from Athens. Call me?" I nod; he kisses my forehead and is gone.

When Max and I finally emerge from the bathroom—I decided to give him a bath while we were in there to avoid the overpowering curry smell as long as possible—I find the living room still a complete mess. The kitchen, however, is greatly improved, almost clean.

"Hey, your friend Sven is great," Thom says, dishing up curried something. "I got this recipe in Singapore, I hope you're hungry."

"Mommy, I made you this today at school." Georgia points to

the fridge, where there is a very rough drawing. She is holding
Amanda, naturally. "Can you see what it is?"

"Um, a family?" I take a stab, since it's always been one of her
favorite drawing topics.

"It's a daddy and kids." We're back to punish-Mommy mode.
"Why do all the brown mommies pick their kids up at school, but
not the white ones?" she asks rhetorically and stomps off to her
room before I can form a reply.

"She's quite the inquisitioner, isn't she? And wow, what a
temper—wonder where she gets that from," Thom says, laying
the food out on the counter. He takes Max from me and puts him
in the high chair attached on the end. "So, what did you do all
day?" He kisses me on the forehead, takes off his frilly apron.
Why does everyone keep kissing me on the forehead?

"It could not have gone better. We assembled an irresistible
collection of buyers for the Jacobs collection. Thanks in no small
part to you." I muster the last of my energy to show how good I
am at my new job, even though I'm still in my robe and may stay
this way the rest of my life.

"Thanks, ma'am, just doing my job." We sit at the counter. He
yells for Georgia, but she doesn't appear. Max is already shoving
curried rice into his mouth faster than Thom can cool it off. I
keep trying not to smell through my nose or breathe through my
mouth. I segregate the untouched white rice and the gloopy-
looking sauce, still waiting for the antacid to work long enough to
get a forkful of food into the air.

"Did you know that Sven was in the Olympics?" Thom has already finished the food on his plate. I scrape some of mine onto
his. "Hey, you okay?"

"Yeah, I'm just not really in the mood for spice. But it smells really delicious, and Max seems to love it. Thanks so much for making it. I'll take some leftovers to work tomorrow." Georgia emerges from her room, enters the kitchen, and gets a package of instant macaroni and cheese out of the pantry. "I'm hungry," she says to her father, dangling the envelope from her fingers. She sets Amanda on the counter. The doll's synthetic hair has been braided since last we saw her.

"Why don't you try some of Daddy's food, GG? I made it for you special—here's your plate. You wanna try it?" He's going to lose this one, but you really can't teach them anything they don't want to know, so I hold my tongue.

"I guess," she says, shrugging her shoulders up to her ears. This translates to: no, but I will if it gets me what I want quicker than throwing myself on the floor. She climbs onto her stool—which action is made more difficult by the grip she now has on her dinner of choice—picks up her fork, and takes the smallest amount of food, possibly a single rice grain. It's barely made it past her lips when the fork goes back down to the plate, where it will surely stay. She leans her forehead into her hand, sighs deeply, and gingerly places the packet on Amanda's lap. The doll looks right at Thom.

"So what do you think—good, right?" Love is blind after all.

"I guess," she whispers, and a tiny tear slips down her face and lands on the blue lettering of her beloved.

"You want something else to eat?" he asks.

I eat a forkful of white rice, swallow, and feel every grain as it sticks going down. The mac and cheese is starting to look good to me too.

"I don't know," she mouths. She's in her final lap, drawing her last breath.

"Oh, for God's sake, Thom, just make her the damn pasta."
Georgia flinches; she knows how much I hate her rendition of
Camille. "Do you think between shopping for overpriced beauty
products with my friends and whipping up gourmet dinners, you
could maybe pick Max's diaper up off the couch? It smells like a
fucking zoo in here." I push away from the counter and retrieve a
yogurt from the fridge. "I'm going to go watch TV."

The minute my butt hits the couch I feel the silence from the
other room catch up to me; you can smell the fear in the air. The
only one of them who doesn't know better yells, "Dada, don."
Max toddles into the living room naked from the waist down, his
face smeared with curry. He leans against the coffee table and
pees on the floor. I lift him onto my lap with his bottle of milk
and he says, "Nemomamapeas?" The microwave timer beeps in
the kitchen and I'm starting to feel like a total shit, so Nemomamapeas for the nine hundredth time it is.

A mere hour later Thom and I are in a bed standoff. I've tucked
the sheet down my left side in order to avoid any accidental contact. I'm still pinched-lip mad, and he's countering with the silent
treatment, his lanky tan leg thrown over the comforter for effect.
We're both "reading"—me, chapter 2 of *Wifey*, him, *Maxim*.
This is clearly a habit he's picked up outside the house, as this is
the first copy to grace our bedside.

"Honey, can I ask you a question?" he asks out of the blue. I try
to register a tone, any tone, in his voice, but there doesn't seem to
be anything there. Is it possible that I'm in this standoff alone?

"Um, yeah?" I rest my never-to-be-read book on my chest.

"I'm just reading this article—well, letter, I guess, it's not really an article—but it's all about how this guy is dating three

women at the same time and having sex with all of them at different times of the day. You know, breakfast, lunch, and dinner sort of thing." He clears his throat, lowers his voice to a whisper. "He says that they all like to, you know, take it, um, well, up the you-know."

"The 'you-know'?" This is not at all the conversation I expected to be having after the scene I made earlier. I quickly contemplate what his question could possibly be, come up with nothing except maybe a request for something that I'll never in a million years do. "So what's your question?"

"Do you think we're getting old?" He puts the magazine down, rolls onto his side, and props his head up on his hand. I appraise my spouse with a clear eye, try to gauge whether his nose has grown, count the hairs emerging from his ear, poke his non-existent love handle. I flush with the thought that we're about to have sex for the first time since he came home, that we might actually be ready to put January behind us.

"What makes you say that?"

"I didn't know that women were so forthcoming about, well, *that,* is all. It's like there's a whole new generation of kids out there with a whole new set of standards. Does that make me a prude?"

I roll over to face him, touch his cheek.

"It's just experimenting, honey, just like we did when we were young. Haven't you ever done anything that seemed crazy, sexually speaking?"

"No, not really, unless you count getting a blow job from a hooker." The shock of this confession makes me sit up, knocking the book to the floor.

"You did what? When?"

"Oh, God, Jen, sorry, sorry, it was years ago, just before I met you in Cairo, with Bjorn." He gives me a sheepish look at the mention of that name as he pulls me back down on the bed. You can live with a man for years and still not know everything about him. "Ever since you, I've never needed anything like that—you're far better than a blow job from a cheap hooker." Now, where have I heard that one before? Huh. I must be really, really good.

"From what I understand, all the young ladies are doing it these days," I tell him, my expertise in this area bolstered by his compliment. "Seems they like the taboo aspect of it, though I think it's entirely antifeminist. Just when you think we've stopped having to give men whatever they want, we turn our tails in the air and say, here, have at it. It also supports my theory that straight men are always looking for a gay experience without having to cross the line."

"Aw, come on. Now who's the prude?" he teases me. "I mean, Bjorn's been into it for a long time—he's always telling me how hot it is to do it that way first with a new woman."

"Like I said. Gay." To my surprise, Thom laughs at this. I match his tone, conspiring against his banished friend.

"Bjorn is the least gay man I know," he says, mocking Bjorn along with me. I don't know how we got there, but we're back on the same side.

"Gay, gay, gay." I scoop my book off the floor, pretend to read.

"Look, even you have to admit, he likes women, not a gay bone in his body."

"Except one, clearly." I turn a page. "I think I need reading glasses, is that possible?"

"It is not gay to have sex with a woman up the you-know," he says, mildly defensive. "It is gay to have sex with a man."

"Oh, really? So if I were to do you up the you-know, then you'd be gay?" He blows out all his air and flops onto his back.

"You don't argue fair," he says, pretending to be shot in the chest. "It's just all pleasure, Jen, why do you have to give it 'gay' and 'straight' labels? Can't it just be good, clean fun between consenting adults?"

"Thomas." I roll over, stroke his chest, and clear the sheet between us. "When I say 'gay' I don't mean it in a derogatory way. Good Lord, no. I simply mean 'not straight.' Honestly, I don't know what the big deal is. All men would like to have something stuck up them—it's a pleasure principle, you're right—from what I hear, there's nothing like having your prostate directly tickled. But women don't have prostates, so there's really no point to a woman having that particular part of her anatomy toyed with—unless she likes the taboo, which is another conversation entirely. So for a man to want to do a woman up the you-know, as you so tactfully call it, I have to think that it's a male fantasy of power and the titillation of getting to do ass without having to do a man and, ergo, maintain a ridiculous veneer of heterosexuality. I rest my case." He's gone all hard now, so he knows not to argue this point any further or risk losing my interest. I switch gears. "Auda will not come to Aquaba. Not for money . . ."

"No." He moans as my hand slips under the sheet.

". . . for Feisal . . ."

"No!" He switches off the light.

". . . nor to drive away the Turks. He will come . . . because it is his pleasure."

"Thy mother mated with a scorpion." He rolls me onto my back, and we start our foreplay giggling.

"Hey, Thom, I have to tell you something." I suddenly feel serious.

"What's that," he murmurs into my hair.

"I'm sorry for earlier. It was wrong of me to yell." A tear slips down my temple. "You're an amazing father. I'm just jealous, I guess." He looks me in the eye. "And I'm sorry about Bjorn—" He silences me with a hand over my mouth.

"It was a bad time for both of us. He used us against each other, and we both made mistakes for him. Let's just let it go, okay?"

I give him a small nod as he lowers back down over me into a kiss that makes me forget all of it—Bjorn, the job, the kids, the health cloud. I toss them all off as I put my trust back in the one thing I know for certain: I love this man.

Forty

BREADWINNER.

    My new favorite word. If it weren't for Bloomington Bradley, we'd be in serious trouble. I'm going over all the finances, and even with my signing bonus we will have to borrow against Thom's retirement money to make ends meet until Christy and I close some deals. I had no idea just how high our burn rate has been. I always left everything to Thom, direct-deposited my checks into a joint account and let him pay the bills and manage our debt. Once I was home, he gave me a house allowance. I never even knew exactly how much he brought in.

    I am now taking on the responsibility of balancing our entire budget. If I had known how close we were to asking Vera and Skip for help, I would have found another way. I want to be mad at Thom, but he was doing his best, and at least he has invested wisely and opened retirement accounts and college accounts and made sure that his insurance policy will cover the mortgage on this place if anything happens to him—say, for instance, if he makes me ask his mother for help. I could have him snuffed and bail us out, maybe even buy a new identity so I would never have to see her again. Thom has pleaded with me to be easier on Vera, but since the éclair affair, and even our uneasy truce, I'm more resistant and have set some ground rules between us. She can see her grandchildren only with one of us present, and she's not to set foot in our house uninvited. I know it seems harsh, but she's bullied me since we first met, and sometimes you just have to stand up for yourself.

My father's mother was a loathsome bitch. She tortured Cheryl endlessly when we were little. She lived a few blocks away from the trailer park in a big house with four bedrooms all by herself. I remember her coming over to our trailer after Cheryl had cleaned and making snide comments about what a bad housekeeper her daughter-in-law was, how her stepgrandchildren were amuck-runners, how their father was a *homosexual*. What could anyone ever expect from them? Meanwhile, she showered Andy and me with new clothes, toys, loose change. We'd play at her house while Cheryl worked and then Grandma would send us home for dinner with cookies in our hands. And when Dad would come home off the road, he'd make matters worse by stopping at her house first for a plateful of oven-fried chicken and mashed potatoes.

If I'm alive to see Max get married, you know I'll be the perfect mother-in-law. I'll stay out of his choices and never make his wife measure herself against my son's love for me, and I'll take care of her babies if she wants me to so she can know the power of bringing home her own bacon too.

Best news is that Thom and I are arguing again, in that playful, artful way that I so love. I'm finally starting to see myself through his eyes, trusting him to be right about how equal I am in this relationship. I'm also starting to see his side of things, how hard the pressure to be the one who keeps the lights on can be on a person, how he must have been going nuts hiding so much of the burden from me so I could focus on the kids. They say that the grass is always greener, and I'm thinking that they're pretty much right. Thom has fallen into staying at home with such relish that it makes me wonder if I ever enjoyed it that much, or if maybe I've needed this perspective to throw myself back into parenting and make it meaningful again, even if I have to do more with less time.

Forty-One

THE VERY LAST THING I want to be doing on my day off is
going to a five-year-old birthday party for a six-year-old, in
a doll store filled with small children and their mommies. As we
push through the revolving door, it is clear to me that Georgia
doesn't really want to be here either. She clutches my wrist in her
right hand, Amanda in her left, ready for her return to the
Mother ship. Georgia and Amanda are wearing matching pink
dresses with white faux-shearling coats and red mittens. It is
Valentine's Day, and the store is also decked out in red and white
and pink. So am I, for the record. Georgia thought it would be
nice for all three of us to dress the same—Hillary Jacobs had
nearly insisted on it in the invitation. Georgia's right, it *is* nice.
Soon enough the day will come that she doesn't even want to be
seen in the same state with me, much less the same dress, so I've
donned the outfit as requested. I'm feeling a little crampy this
morning and have thrown in a tampon and taken some Excedrin
just in case.

In the cab uptown Georgia had asked me once again when we
were going to reschedule her party. I tried to explain that I've

been a little busy lately and we're going to just have to wait until the spring.

I'm seeing triplicate as three generations of women, girls, and dolls swarm around us, dressed identically. This would be a good time to drop acid, or so I imagine. As I maneuver Georgia out of coat check, I spot Angie and Ella next to a display of twenty-odd dolls standing like a choir encased in Plexiglas.

"Mommy, Ella's friend's name is Cathy," Georgia says, tugging me down to whisper in my ear.

"Her doll?" I whisper back.

"No, her *friend*. They're not dolls, they're *friends*." Is it me, or is it creepy in here? I was against Georgia getting one of these Stepford dolls, but as Vera managed to get one in the house when I was in a coma, I've relented, but ever since then, the matching outfits have been arriving on a weekly basis. I swear to God she must have stock in the company. This is my first time in the store, and I'm trying to keep an open mind.

"Hello, Ella, and you must be Cathy," I say to Ella and her doll—friend.

"Hello, Ms. Bradley. She doesn't say much," Ella tells me. "She's new to this country. Her mommy adopted her from China. Her name was Chin-Yee, but it's a little hard to say, so they Americanized it."

"Is that so?" I look at Angie, who shrugs and rolls her eyes.

"This is Amanda." Georgia holds her up for Angie's inspection.

"Hello, Amanda," Angie says, taking the doll's hand. "It's a pleasure to meet you. I love what you've done with your hair. Ella, why don't you and Georgia take a look around?" The girls run over to the book display and start picking through the titles. It's still such a relief to see Georgia actually engage other children without needing my approval. She's really come out of her shell.

"Kill me," Angie says. "Kill me now. No, better yet, let's go find Hillary 'You need that shredded?' Jacobs and kill her instead."

"Oh, come on, it's not that bad here. It's wholesome. Middle American."

"Let me show you something." She plucks three playing-card-looking pieces of paper from the display and fans them out in front of me. "These are the black girl choices—Oprah, Whoopi, or Whitney. Not a Halle or Iman or Beyoncé in sight. See here on the card where it says 'textured black hair'? You don't see any of the white dolls with 'textured Jewish hair' or 'textured Irish red kinks,' now do you? Chin-Yee was my idea. I have enough trouble keeping Ella's hair untangled, I need another nappy head in my house?" Angie twists one of her own dreads. "Just look at that doll's silky tresses. If that doll hair salon over there really wants authenticity, then they better be adding some wigs and weaves."

I turn to look into the case of dolls, and as I look from one to the next I notice that most of them have the exact same face with tiny upper teeth showing in a sweet smile. Only the black dolls have larger noses and fuller lips. And the Asian doll has a slight slant to her eyes. Otherwise, it's only the eye, hair, and skin colors that are different. No breaking the mold here. I do like their little-girl-body shapes, and how they all have the same starter-uniform. In fact, the more I look from face to face, the more I like them, and I consider asking Georgia if Amanda would like to take a friend home for herself.

"Jen, you in there?" Angie snaps her fingers in front of my

face, which is not an easy task, seeing as how my nose has left a spot on the glass. I wipe it off with my sleeve.

"Yeah, just kind of mesmerized, you know what I mean?" As I tune back in to the world around me, I catch a snippet of my daughter's voice from the other side of the display.

"When I get big you know what I wanna be?" she asks. I catch her reflected in a mirror on the wall; she and Ella are talking to Emma Jones, an opalescent-skinned blonde with white hair.

"I wanna be a vet and work with dogs, like my mom," Emma says.

"I'm going to be a doctor," Ella says. "And Cathy will live with me at the hospital."

"I wanna be a mommy and have lots of kids and I'll stay home with them until they're all growed up." Georgia catches my eye in the mirror. Okay, so maybe she was better shy and retiring. It's not enough that I'm wearing pink? "I'd never go to work when they need me the mostest."

"Jennifer! Angela! I'm so glad you could make it! Here's our birthday girl!" Hillary Jacobs must need a hearing aid, she's always shouting. Chloë is dressed in a red beaded flapper's dress, a feathered headband pinned to her wispy hair. She may be six posing as five, but today she looks post-op fifty, starved down to fit into the shapeless shift just in time for benefit season to kick into full gear. Her doll is one of the original American Girls—Kit, a spunky, pre-Depression-era doll who has bobbed hair and a thirst for life. Of all the trios in the room, the resemblance among these three is the most frightening. Ella, Emma, and Georgia scramble around to hold court, and to make their dolls feel inferior over Kit's red sequined dress.

"Jennifer, a moment?" Hillary takes me by the arm and leads

me to the window. "Thank you so much for your discretion in the matter with our art. I just really want the paintings to have a good home, and I hope that they'll all get to stay together. It's funny, I imagined we'd be working with Thom on this. But life's just like that sometimes, isn't it?"

"You needn't worry about a thing, Hill—may I call you Hill?" I can see Angie past Hillary's quick nod, pretend-shredding a program into her pocketbook. "Christy and I are the *souls* of discretion." I lean in to whisper for effect. "We've put together a list of collectors that will make you and your art *very* happy." And here I am, talking business at a kid's party. Georgia's right, I should be ashamed of myself.

"Great. We really should do that dinner, okay? I've got to attend to the other guests—enjoy the festivities! Come, Chloë!" She claps twice, and the little red lapdog yelps into her wake as we're all pulled upstairs to the tearoom.

There are no specific seating assignments, so Angie and I quickly grab the table closest to the door, hoping that no one will want to sit with us, and that at the very least we'll have a quick getaway if needed. Georgia seems relieved by our choice: the farther away from the white-hot center of activity, the happier she is. The tables are decorated in a Roaring Twenties theme—there are strings of fake pearls for everyone to adorn themselves with, including the dolls, and flapper-esque feather tiaras. Angie helps Ella put the elastic on over her thickly intricate twisted cords of braids, and Georgia and I get the dolls seated in tiny chairs that are artfully attached to the table next to the girl's chairs. The dolls even have their own place settings, with tiny tea cups and plates. Georgia gives Amanda her napkin.

Just as we get settled, two women descend upon us with their girls and dolls.

"Hello, I'm Bunny, and this is my daughter Evangeline, and my granddaughters Tatiana and Ariel—and their friends Tammy and Wanda." Bunny's a stately sixtysomething, with a light-peach-tinted pageboy and a butter-soft handshake. We introduce ourselves as they all get situated. "It is a pleasure to meet you all," Bunny continues in a pitch-perfect Southern drawl. "And how do you all know Chloë?"

"Our daughters went to school with her at Park Street," I respond for both of us. Angie's hackles went up the moment this foursome approached, her arms crossing automatically in front of her. Tatiana and Ariel, who are clearly nonidentical, as Tatiana is skinny, tall, and freckled, while Ariel is short, plump around the middle, and, well, swarthy. Even at her age she could do with a full face wax. "And you?"

"We live next door to them in the Hamptons," Evangeline says through clenched teeth, her mouth a tangle of wires. "Sorry about this, but I've had my jaw wired shut recently; it's a little hard to talk."

"Oh, my. Sorry, what happened?" I ask.

"Nothing happened," Bunny answers for her, pressing her daughter's arm gently to indicate her taking of control. "She's just had a terrible time losing the baby weight from the twins and nothing was working. It was either this or gastric bypass." As she's explaining, Bunny removes a slimming shake and a straw from her pocketbook. "Baby doll, you just let Momma know when you're ready to eat, okay?"

I feel a sharp kick under the table, but know better than to look at Angie. I do steal a glance at Georgia and Ella, who seem to be missing the best part of the conversation. It's just as well, I don't have the capacity to explain this one.

Waiters and waitresses dressed in cutaway tuxes, cloche hats, beaded dresses, and other roaring attire swarm the room with three-tiered trays, depositing them in front of the guests with pinpoint accuracy. Bunny intercepts the one destined for Evangeline with a sharp shake of her head. This woman could stop a glacier.

"Mommy, look how pretty," Georgia says as she greets her plate. "Which one do I want first?"

"I think we start at the bottom and work our way up to the top, sweetie." I point to the delicate crust-free sandwiches on the lowest plate. "See—the sandwiches, then the scones, then dessert." Her eyes follow my finger and get wider until they can take in everything at once.

"I'm saving that one for very last!" She lightly strokes a petit four in the shape of a tiny pink present, done up with a polka-dot bow.

"Sounds like a plan, Stan."

"Would you look at this death trap," Bunny says from her side of the table. "Waiter, waiter. Come here." Two Gatsbys pass her unheeding. "How very uncivilized. I cannot in my right mind eat this." She turns to Angie. "Dear, would you mind fetching me a waiter?"

"Why would I mind?" Angie scrapes her chair back and crosses the entire room in order to find a waiter. I sit in the silence of her vacuum. Ella and Georgia chat about their new school, feed their dolls, swing their legs.

"So, Bunny, are you from around here originally?" I try to rise above my desire to follow Angie in her pursuit of time away from this table.

"Good heavens, no, I'm from Savannah. I've just come up to help Evangeline with her diet. And Ariel, too." It's then that I notice that Bunny has taken apart Ariel's sandwiches and left her only the insides—removing the white bread to her own plate. Ariel pokes at salmon and cucumbers, a small stack of ham and cheese. She's really no more plump than her doll Tammy, but without the pressed-on smile she looks utterly desolate. "Tatiana, do Grandma a favor and take Ariel's scone, you could use a little extra."

"Mommy," Georgia says, tugging my sleeve. "Can we go after lunch? I don't like it here." Great, now Bunnicula has ruined my daughter's fun. Just as I'm about to change the subject to the weather, Angie reappears with a waiter.

"Oh good, dear, thank you. Now, pardon me, waiter, but my granddaughter cannot eat any of these sweets, would you be a dear and find us some fruit? And you may as well take away my plate too, this food will surely kill you as let you eat it." She turns to our girls and smiles. "Now, Ella, is it?"

"Yes, ma'am," Ella says with a brief nod.

"And Georgia. Now, there's an honorable name." G looks down at her plate, not sure if honorable is a good thing.

"Ella, you should ask your momma if you can come out to our house for a week or two this summer. The girls would love to have a little friend to play with, wouldn't you, girls?"

"Yes, ma'am," they respond in unison.

"We have a swimming pool, and real air-conditioning—"

"Mother," Evangeline tries to interrupt, throwing Angie a 'forgive me' look.

"And we can have a barbecue with chicken and ribs—"

"*Mother*," she tries again, clamping her hand down on Bunny's forearm.

"And even watermelon, if you'd like. I bet you'd like that, wouldn't you? You could even invite your friend Georgia, if you'd like. Do say you'll let her come out, it would be a nice break from the city. A girl needs to see the country in the summer." Bunny folds up her napkin and lays it beside her unused plate. I slip a little bit down in my chair, not knowing which direction Angie's wind is about to blow.

"My, that is the most gracious offer, and I'm sure that Ella would very much enjoy visiting with you this summer." Not the gale-force I was expecting, but she could be just winding up. "And then perhaps you wouldn't mind if Tatiana and Ariel came over to our house in Sagaponack. We're right on the beach, and we have a couple of ponies they could ride. We could make them some grilled salmon over a bed of greens. Would you like that, girls?"

"Yes, *ma'am!*" they shout. Bunny turns a paler shade of peach.

"Oh, well, um, my, that would be ever-so-kind of you, to be sure," she stammers. "We really must trade numbers before you leave. You will excuse me for a minute?" She pushes away from the table and in her wake the girls start giggling and Evangeline lets out a large gurgle, practically choking on her liquid lunch.

"You," she points at Angie. "You, I like. As soon as she goes back south, I will have you over. Sorry about the Fresh Air Fund treatment, no one can stop her. And I've given up trying."

"No worries," Angie says. "It's not my first encounter with the Old South."

"Mine either, sorry to say. That's why I left. Here, sweetie, have some of Tatiana's scone." She sneaks a bit of clotted cream and jam-encrusted scone to Ariel. Tatiana gives her a withering gaze. They're nice enough, but altogether too damaged to ever try and see again. A wave of exhaustion comes over me, and I lean over to Georgia.

"You still wanna get out of here?" I whisper in her ear. "We could take the cakes to go?"

"Yeah!" she yells in a whisper back.

"Sorry, Ange, we have to get going, Thom has a pickup basketball game this afternoon—I promised him I wouldn't let him miss it." She gives my hand a squeeze of thanks.

"I think we should be going too, right, Ella, Cathy? Nice meeting you all, do give my regards to your mother," she says to Evangeline as she pushes away from the table.

"I don't know if I could have shown such cool," I say to Angie while we wait for our coats. The girls poke through their gift bags. "What a witch."

"Look, Mommy! A mini-iPod! In pink!" Georgia jumps in place, her eyes shiny. "What color you get, Ella?"

"She doesn't know any better, it's just how she was raised," Angie tells me. "And besides, to her, she was doing something nice for all the nasty things her people have done over the years."

"Mine's purple, my favorite," Ella says, holding it up for Angie's inspection and approval.

"Wow, baby, that's a very generous gift. We should make a special thank-you card when we get home, okay?" She helps Ella into her coat, then turns back to me. "It's actually harder for her than it is for me, if you think about it. I wasn't raised to hate white people, but she was raised to fear us. And then she meets nice 'black folks' and it gets all screwy in her head. Best thing always is to just play it even—as long as you know who you are, they can't touch you."

"I'll try to remember that." As I help Georgia on with her white fluffy coat, I suddenly realize that I haven't felt sick all day and maybe feel even a little bit more crampy.

"And look, Mommy! Coconut! My very own dog at long last!" Georgia collapses to the floor, clutching a stuffed white-confection Westie to her chest, lost in a lover's swoon. She's never been this dog-crazy, but if that need is satisfied by one that doesn't chew my shoes and shit on the furniture, then so be it.

"*Me too!*" Ella yells as she plops down on the floor next to Georgia. "Isn't she beautiful? Look, Cathy, we have a puppy!" Angie and I exchange glances.

"You know," I say to her as we watch our girls page through the Coconut companion book with what looks like rapture, "if a store can make them this happy, it can't be all bad, right?"

"Yeah," she says, putting her arm around me. "I gotta admit, I've got my eye on that historical Addie doll. She scared me at first, but her story's well-meaning, and it would be good for Ella to learn about freed slaves and how hard the women in her family tree worked so she could have a pony on the beach."

"Hey, how come you've never invited *me* out to your fancy house in the Hamptons?" I ask as we bundle the girls toward the door.

"What makes you think I actually have one?" She looks at me in her you-people-believe-what-you-want way before giving me a light, loving slap on the back of the head.

Forty-Two

M Y NECK IS GETTING OLD. I haven't minded the small lines etching my face, or the lumps on my thighs, or even the slight genetic sag at my jawline. But my neck? I was putting lipstick on in the car the other day when I first saw how the skin pulls together and up right above my throat. I started to tell Thom, but thought better of it. Why point out such an odious flaw? I just need to buy a few more turtleneck sweaters and go to Elizabeth Arden for an anti-aging facial. I can feel the skin pulling even as I sit here. I've spent the past five years pointing my chin up to stretch out the wattle only to have damaged the delicate skin that supports it. I'm reduced to a one-inch jaw angle. With every moment that passes, my neck gets that much older.

I'm going to be sixty when Max graduates from college. I guess I should have thought of that before I went on birth control in my twenties. I've found myself staring at him and Georgia more and more lately. I don't know if it's because I see them less, or if I'm turning into Cheryl. Whenever I see her, she just sits and stares at me. If we're at a play or a movie, she's constantly looking at me to gauge my reaction against her own. I see her in my peripheral vision but never return the gaze. I'm starting to understand it now. I would drink my kids in with my eyes if I could. I hear people say "It goes so fast" and "They're little for such a short time," and I know that I can't understand this from this end of it, but if I as much as blink, they will be taller than me, walking out the door to return only for holidays, and they'll grudgingly negotiate less and less time spent with me as the years go by and I want them more and more.

Yesterday I went to St. Patrick's Cathedral and bought a cross with a tiny Jesus nailed to it. I also went up the street and found a simple Jewish star for Georgia in the Diamond District. It's not that I've gotten religion, but that I'm starting—after the whole neck thing—to appreciate how much effort it takes to carry a cross without complaining, and I like the symbolic metaphor of these slight charms. Whenever I'm tempted to bitch about work or the kids or Thom, I tap mine lightly through my clothes and am comforted by its slight weight. I don't know where I'll go when I die, but I hope that it's somewhere with a good view of Georgia and Max. When I fall asleep every night now, I hold my breath for a moment and pray for one more good day with these small people.

Forty-Three

I'M FINALLY AT THE GYNECOLOGIST. When I got here, Dr.
Sarah asked me how I was feeling and what I'm here for, seeing
as I'd just had a pap smear six months ago. I told her about the irregular bleeding, the nausea, the cramping. That I was concerned
I was developing another fibroid, as my abdomen was slightly
distended, even though I've lost nearly ten pounds in the last
month.

"Great," she said. "Let's go take a look around."

As I lie on my back waiting for her assistant to get the sonogram machine going, I start to panic, finally stripping away the
denial I've held myself in for the past weeks. What if it's cancer?
Cheryl and Nancy's mother died of lymphoma when I was a kid.
She had some excellent wigs and blew smoke out the side of her
mouth. Other than that, I have zero memories of her. Maybe I remember it wrong and it wasn't lymphoma, maybe it was cervical
or ovarian. Just as I'm breaking into a clammy sweat, Sarah enters, wearing a lab coat with Chanel buttons sewn onto it.

"Let's get this party started, shall we?" She goops up my stomach and turns the screen to face away from me. That's it, she

knows something. She doesn't want me to freak out when I see the tumor that's going to rob me of my reconstructed life. I knew that the job happening the way it did was too good to be true. I tap Jesus and pray that Max remembers something about me other than what the pictures and videos tell him years from now. Sarah clicks away, humming a little to herself. Her eyes get a tiny bit wider, she catches herself, suppresses the emotion that's jumped into her face. She moves the device more quickly, starts clicking with the mouse in her left hand. Thom should definitely remarry. Someone pretty, younger than him. Who can give him more children. It was never fair of me to ask him to marry older. He has so much life in him. Sarah lets out an "um-hm," and I can't bear it any longer.

"What, what is it? Tell me, I can take it." A tear slips down my face. "Is it hot in here, or is it me?"

"Just one more minute, hang in there." She clicks some more, jabs my tummy with the wand.

"No, really, I think I'm going to pass out." A wave of dizziness swarms me.

"Here, lie on your right side, that should help. Let me show you what's going on in there." A slight smile pushes at her lips. I turn on my side as she turns the monitor.

"What the fuck!" I yell, seeing on the monitor the last thing I could have expected—not just a fetus, but one with arms and legs and, yes, a penis. "How the hell did that happen?" I nearly fall off the table.

"Steady on, Mommy," Sarah says, handing me a cup of water. "Take a sip, calm yourself. Looks like you do have a fibroid—just a little one—but because it's so close to the cervix, it's been caus-ing the irregular bleeding, making you think that you were having periods. By my calculations, you're about fourteen weeks pregnant."

"Fourteen *what?*"

"Weeks. Three and a half months. Congratulations, you've made it through the first trimester without a snag."

"Unless you would consider being pregnant in the first place the snag, that is." I really am going to pass out. I do a rapid inventory of my night out with Heath and the possible brain damage I've already done this child. Not to mention the two bottles of champagne back in November. Oh yeah. Right. November.

"Okay, Jen, I'm going to get you a scrip for prenatal vitamins. I want you to take two a day for the next two weeks, that should help with the fatigue. Otherwise you seem healthy and full speed ahead. Do you want to know the sex?"

"If that's not a penis, then we'd better have a little talk." Shit, shit, shit, it wasn't the fucking éclairs, it was the fucking baby. Georgia was just doing what kids do: bring home disease and puke it all over you. "So when am I due, prom night?"

"By my calculation, you're due August 23," she says, spinning the plastic due-date slide rule.

"Oh, no, that can't be. I've got to launch the new company in September."

"Well, since this will be your third C-section, we'll want to get you in a little before your due date. You'll have plenty of time to recover and do the launch." This from a woman who delivered Georgia a week after having twins of her own. I don't think I should argue with her. And besides, why can't Thom be the one to suffer through the utter banality of the first two months of life?

"Great, yeah, sounds good. Can I get dressed now?" The walls of this sterile room are closing in; I need to get up and out of here. So it's not cancer. I guess I can look on the bright side.

"Yes, but make an appointment with Carley for a full sonogram at the hospital next week, okay? We need to check the little guy's heart. And your amnio?" She wipes the gel off my tummy and gives it a little pat. "You're going to do great, I just know it. I'll see you in three weeks?"

Once she's out of the room, I check myself into a daze. I get dressed, make my appointments, hail a taxi for the parking garage, call Penny and tell her I'm not feeling well, and pick up the car. Before I've even thought about where I'm going, I'm headed north on the Thruway. Home.

When I pull into the yard two and a half hours later, there's a strange car in the lot. It didn't even occur to me to call first, that Cheryl might have clients in session. Or that she might be booked up the whole day. I look over to the garage and see a light on in Dad's kitchen. I go knock on the door.

"Daddy? It's me, Jenny." I push the door open. "Daddy, are you in here?"

"Hey, kitten, happy almost birthday! What brings you way up here?" He's wearing one of his trademark blue denim shirts, and as he envelops me in a bear hug I burst into tears against the worn-smooth fabric. "There, there." He pats my head, strokes my hair. "What's all this?" He holds me out at arm's length, I let go with a sob, and he pulls me back to him. "Not such a happy birthday? Let's go sit down in the kitchen, you wanna cup of coffee?" I sniffle down a notch, nod my head. As I dry my tears on my sleeve, he puts a cup of cold coffee in the microwave. He's always done this, made a full pot in the morning only to reheat it cup by cup the rest of the day. I hear CNN on in the living room, something about the war on terrorism, something about the president getting on a plane for somewhere. When the coffee's hot, Dad stirs in a generous amount of cream and sugar, just how I like it but never take it.

"So now," he says, pulling up a chair at the table across from me. "You want to tell me about it? Or do you want to wait for your mother?"

"I'm pregnant." Just like that. I can say it just like that. I restart crying.

"And that doesn't make you happy?" I can tell he's holding back his own joy at the news. Everyone thought we were done.

"I've got a new company to run, and Thom can't work until God knows when, and we're on a really tight budget, and I'm only just now losing my Max weight, and oh, I just can't be pregnant. It's just not convenient right now." I look up at him and see he's smiling.

"If you ask me, it's never convenient." He's got a point. "That's what makes it so mysterious."

"But I'm going to be forty in two days. I haven't even had time to adjust to that. I had planned on wallowing around for a little while and now I just won't have the time." I'm really reaching for things to complain about. Women over forty have babies all the time. I'm not even special in this one small thing.

"Speaking of that, I want to tell you a little story, okay? I was going to wait until Sunday, but now seems as good a time as any." I lean into the table, camouflaging my rapidly growing tummy. He glances at me, looks away. "A long time ago a boy and girl fell in love. He was a football player, she was a cheerleader. It was the fifties, so this was a common thing. They got married right out of high school, moved to another county, and he started selling insurance and set her up in a nice little trailer house." I'm suddenly uncomfortable sitting forward, and I lean back. "This girl was real trouble—drank too much, smoked like a chimney, swore like a sailor, flirted with married men, drove too fast, complained about every little thing—but he loved her the way he did, the only way he could. It wasn't enough, though, and one day she went out and drove herself into an early grave."

"I have to pee." I jump up from the table and move through a fog to the bathroom. I keep thinking this day is going to get better, but it's turning out to be far worse than I would ever have imagined. When I sit down to pee, only a tiny amount comes out. I stand up and instantly need to pee again. I decide to sit for a few minutes. I'm not sure I like where the story is going, I've heard this part before, but there's usually a baby—me—in the picture, and a lot less fast living. The TV clicks off. Dad never turns off any of his three televisions. I finally ease myself out of the bathroom, hoping to snap out of this scene. No such luck, I'm still above the garage. Dad's moved to his beat-up old La-Z-Boy—the reason he was exiled here in the first place, if you ask me—so I sit down on the edge of the couch, slamming my knee against the coffee table in the process.

"Now, where was I?" He cracks open a beer. My untouched coffee mug has moved itself to a side table.

"Um, early grave?"

"Oh, yeah, right. Thanks." He lights a cigarette, takes a deep inhale, then realizes he can't exhale in my direction and ends up coughing the smoke toward the window while putting the cigarette out. "Sorry, kitten, I wasn't thinking. Anyway, around the same time, the dead wife's older sister shows up on his doorstep, two kids by her side and another in the oven. He offers her the spare bedroom, which she shares with her kids. Once the baby is born, they decide to marry and move back to their hometown. They tell people that the new baby's mother died in an accident, that the new wife's ex-husband had run off and left her, and how lucky they were to find each other."

"Can I ask you a question?"

"Anything."

"Why didn't the new wife want people to know the baby was hers?" I can't help talking in his language. There are tears in his eyes and a white line where his top lip should be.

"I'm glad you asked that. Well, because the father skipped out, and she didn't want her daughter growing up thinking he'd left because of her. She thought it better for the baby to think that love could overcome circumstance. I guess it just wasn't *convenient*." He looks me in the eye and picks up another cigarette, rolling it between his fingers.

"Okay. Here's another. Why did the football player wait until the baby turned forty to tell her the truth?" I'm getting a little mad now. I didn't come here for more information, I came here to escape information. I'm up to here with people informing me of things I'd rather not know. They've lied effectively to me for this long, why stop now?

"He promised her mother." He looks into his bottle of beer. "And because he is her real father, as far as he's concerned. She was the best gift anyone ever could have given him." He's got me there—even though this is a bit of a shock, it doesn't change at all the way I feel about them.

"And where is this 'new wife' now? Does she know that you were going to tell me this story today?"

"No, I can't say that she did. She thought it was going to be Sunday. Go easy on her, will you?"

. . .

I sit in the terra-cotta waiting room, listening to the muffled voices behind the door. A woman is sobbing and her partner is mumbling, "There, there." Cheryl really should get a noise machine. Eventually I hear the outer door open, then snug closed. I could lie down right here and sleep for another forty years, given the chance. But something tells me this day is far from over, and sleep will just have to wait. I gave Dad enough time to call Cheryl and prepare her for me sitting out here. When the door opens, her eyes are glistening. She holds her arms out to me, I sink into them.

"Happy birthday, my darling," she says into my ear. "It's so good to have you back. Come inside, lie down." She leads me by the shoulders and settles me onto the reclining couch, taking my hand and stroking my brow. "It must be quite a shock, yes?"

"You could say that." I will not cry. I will not cry. I will not . . .

"I was going to abort you, you know." That knocks the tears right out of me. So much for the sentimental reunion with my long-lost birth mother.

"But I thought you were pro-life?"

"I was and I am, but that doesn't mean I'm not pro-choice. I knew of three different doctors who could do it illegally, but I didn't have the money. Charlie emptied the bank account before he left. Took everything worth anything. Left only a short note." Oh God, of course, I also have a birth father. And from what I remember, he's gay. It's all starting to make sense in a crazy kind of way. "I was working as a waitress and couldn't scrape the tips together to even buy milk for the other kids. How was I supposed to have another baby? Will took me in, never asked any questions, did what I asked. He was so happy to call you his own, to take real ownership of you. It was a clumsy story we cooked up, but in small towns they'll believe anything as long as it makes good gossip. Then we had Andy and were a real family. Birth control never once worked for me, you know that?"

"Hello, tree, I'm apple." Hysterical laughter bubbles up from deep inside me. I go a little dark in the head from my inability to laugh and breathe at the same time. When I can finally get a word out, I gurgle, "I'm pregnant, Cheryl . . . or should I call you Mom?"

"Let's not rush things, shall we?" She helps me sit up to gain control of my hyperventilation. "With Judy, I had a daughter. With you, I've always had a best friend." I wait for my news to hit. "You're what? How did that happen?"

"Oh, I think you know better than most how that happens." We fall into a girlfriend giggle, and I realize she's right: I don't have a mother, I have a best friend.

"Oh, stop. Of course I know. I guess it doesn't matter, in any case. Another grandchild, how wonderful!" Or another friend, it depends on how you look at it—she's never been much of a grandmother either.

"Yeah, it's just fucking awesome," I say, my humor turning black. "Yippee. Can't wait to ruin my life for the third time."

"How could it possibly ruin your life? You have beautiful children. If it's your job you're worried about, don't. Stop living in your head and engage your wonderful, surprising life, Jennifer. If you had a little more faith and a little less fear you would be able to see just how charmed your life really is." The enormity of this concept stops my spiral. She sees my puzzlement. "You're destined to have it all, you know that, don't you? You always have been. You're the brightest star in my galaxy, and if you ever tell any of your siblings, I will have you killed."

"I'm destined to have most of it. If only I could figure out what to do with some of it. Doing the impossible gets a little old after a while." She said I'm her brightest—that alone is worth the forty-year lie.

"But what else is there to do? Doing the possible gets even older a lot quicker. If I had it to do all over again, I wouldn't have changed a thing. Without the lows being so low, I wouldn't know how high the highs can be. Now get up off this couch and dive back in. There's a difference between having a great life and creating a great life. Few people get the opportunity to do the latter. Don't squander it on misplaced self-pity." I stand up, if only to get her to stop speaking in platitudes. She's a nice best friend, but an annoying one too.

"Okay, okay. Will you ride back to town with me? I'm too tired to drive myself, and I have a lot more questions to ask you. And Daddy too."

"Of course, and then we'll babysit, and you and Thom can have a night out on the town to celebrate all your good fortune. We were thinking about coming into town for a surprise visit anyway, just let me go grab my bag. Oh, and Service Master is coming to clean out the oil your father spilled in the garage last week, don't let me forget to leave them a note."

"I'm sorry, who did you say is coming?" I can't believe her sometimes. I swear she's gaslighting me.

"Service Master." She waves me away with her hand as she walks away.

"Yeah, right. Thought you never heard of them—" I yell after her.

While she's upstairs I take a minute to look at all the pictures on her desk and try to piece together the mystery that is my childhood. Cheryl and Nancy looked nothing alike, and I look exactly like Cheryl, in particular the way I start a smile on one side of my mouth and let it spread across. As Cheryl likes to say, if it had been a snake, it would have bit me.

By the time the three of us get back to the city, there's a light dusting of snow on the streets and it's almost seven o'clock. I'm wrung out but rested, having slept the two hours down. So much for the questions. I've waited this long to know about my parallel life, I guess I can wait a little longer. We ride up the elevator in silence, but I notice that Dad is wearing a go-to-church-on-Easter shirt. I've called ahead so Thom will be ready to leave when I get here, after I make a quick costume change and maybe take a shower. My stomach's still sticky from the gel. I'm starting to like the little pulse I feel as the fetus is already gerbilling around down there. When I push against the door and walk into the apartment, it's completely dark.

"What the hell?" Panic starts to rise as I grope for the light switch. Which kid is in the hospital and why?

"*Surprise!*" The lights come on full-blare, and I'm thrown back against the wall. My apartment is stuffed with people from every corner of my life—Portia, Sven, Christy, Penny, Tricia, Kate, Georgia, Max, Lily, Jax, Vera, Skip, Francesca, and on and on. In the middle of all stands Thom, beaming and holding his arms out, repeating "Surprise" again, as though I didn't hear it enough the first time. A large banner runs across the room proclaiming "HAPPY TENTH BIRTHDAY JENNIFER!" Very funny. I turn on my heel and walk out the door, shutting it behind me. This is not funny. It's not even close to funny. Even if I were wearing a clownfish suit, this still would not be funny. I hear the door open behind me as I stab the elevator button repeatedly, watching the light climb from one, two . . .

"Jen, wait . . ." It's Thom, that fucking traitor.

Three, four, bingo. I get on the elevator and hit the DOOR CLOSED button as hard as I can. He grabs the door just in the nick of time.

"How could you!" I yell. "You know the policy. *It is never my fucking birthday.*"

"But, Jen, just listen."

"Shut the fuck up. You listen. *It is never my fucking birthday.*" The elevator stops on two. The Mercers get on with their son and German shepherd. "Sorry, didn't mean to swear in front of the dog." They greet us with stony silence. Thom puts his hand on my shoulder. I shrug it off. He moves a step closer, I move a step away.

When we get to the lobby, I just keep walking. It's snowing hard now, and I'm blinded by the wind driving icy flakes into my eyes. Thom takes my elbow as I run across the street.

"Come back upstairs, will you? It's only people who love you, Georgia and I have spent a lot of time planning this. How about you forget you don't like surprises just this once? For me?"

"How about this for surprises, Thom." I stop and spin against him, fists to chest. "How about this morning I found out that I'm currently carrying a practically full-term baby, then this afternoon I'm told that my mother isn't my mother, my best friend is, and finally, the rat-fink father of my born and unborn children has mounted a surprise attack birthday party on me two full days before I turn fucking forty on fucking leap day—a day that doesn't exist seventy-five percent of the time. *I don't like surprises, okay?*"

"We're pregnant?" He takes a step back.

"So it would seem."

"How?"

"No fucking rubbers for fucking sound familiar?" I make a circle out of my thumb and finger, jab the index finger of the other hand repeatedly in the center. He grabs my hands, pins them by my side, and gets as close to my face as he can without actually kissing me.

"Lawrence, I can't make out if you're a bloody madman or just half-witted."

"I have the same problem, sir." I fall against him, my anger spent, my mind slowing to a crawl. Cheryl's right, really—I have a charmed life, and if I weren't so damned afraid of losing any part of it I could spend more time enjoying it.

"What is it?" he asks.

"A boy."

"Can we name this one Lawrence?"

"We named the last one Lawrence."

"Then why do you call him Max?"

"I don't know, it just suited him." He leans us against a parked car. We look up at the apartment and see all my friends looking out the windows at our scene, the snow obscuring the details of their faces, but not the warm glow of the room.

"Jen, you know you don't have to do it all, right? You can let me do some of it. Just name it, and I'll do it." I shiver at the thought; he pulls me closer.

"Will you breast-feed Larry until your nipples are raw?"

"Except that."

"And you call this love?"

"Look, we don't have to go back upstairs, we can do whatever you want." He slips his hand into my coat and lays his palm against my belly. "Or I can clear the apartment and we can get into bed and then you can try and explain to me all the other things you were babbling about a minute ago."

"Oh, I think I'd rather go upstairs and have people yell surprise at me a few more times. You know how happy that makes me." We wait for a taxi to throw new slush onto our shoes before dashing across the street. When we get to the shelter of the entryway, Thom stops me and hands me a flat package wrapped in newspaper.

"What's this?"

"Just open it, will you?"

I tear the paper off with my numbing fingers to find a four-by-six-inch framed photo. It's the picture of us at River Café, without the Photoshopped wig.

"Oh, and I got you something else: Bjorn's been indicted. I'm off the hook."

I burst into tears as he produces a candle, holds it out to me, and lights it.

"Now, make a wish."

I close my eyes and try to think of something to wish for, but after a quick inventory I realize that, in my own way, I really do have it all.

Epilogue

W E'RE GOING TO NEED new shirts. Pink and purple are too January."

"But they've never been worn, sweetie, and things are a little tight right now."

"Mommy, *please?*"

"What colors?"

"Orange and red. Those are my new favorite colors."

"Orange and red, check."

"And I want to have Mr. Gregory and Ms. Daily."

"Your teachers?"

"My *life-guides.*"

"Okay, that sounds nice."

"Mommy?"

"Yes, Geege?"

"Where do babies come from?"

"Funny you should ask."

"Why funny?"

"Well, I need to tell you something."

Eyes narrow.

"Mommy and Daddy love each other very much, and that's why we had you, and then we had Max."

Eyes wide.

"And now because we love you guys so much, we're going to have another baby."

Eyes pinched shut.

"Geege?"

"No. You're. Not."

"Um, yes, we are."

"No. You *promised*. No more *babies*."

"I don't remember making a promise like that."

"When you brought Max home you said no more babies never."

"Okay, maybe I did. But I guess we're all a little surprised."

"It better not have a penis."

"It might."

"Can it be a girl baby this time?"

"We could always go to the store and buy you a girl baby. How about that?"

"You can have a baby on one contrition."

"Okay, which condition?"

"That I don't have to take baths with it or Max. I'm almost *six*."

"Deal."

Eye roll, hug.

Acknowledgments

Much thanks:

To Amanda Weinstock, without whose spark I would have never had the idea to write this book; Susan Douglas and Meredith Michaels for begging me, with their book *The Mommy Myth*, to write something both entertaining and meaningful for all mothers; and the many mommies who have shared their stories with me.

To my graces: Jenny McPhee for fairy-godmothering both my son and my book; Haven Kimmel for lighting the way; Portia Racasi for her twenty years of service; Sloane Tanen for her slaying ability to tell it like it is; Lauri del Commune for her kindred spirit; Deborah Cowell for her pinpoint brilliance; Madeline McIntosh for being my champion; Kendra Harpster for her boundless belief in me; and Mindy Marin for shaking the pom-poms.

To Bo Flynn, Tommaso McPhee, Obadiah Kimmel, and Gideon Burnes Heath for being such unusual and funny fellows.

To Bill Goldman, Peter Gethers, and David Rakoff for constantly inspiring me and setting the bar ever higher with their writing, mentoring, and friendship.

To Cathy Scheibe and Kathleen Flynn—as much as my mother may be like Cheryl, my mother-in-law is the exact opposite of Vera. Thank God!

To my family at Free Press for their unwavering support, and to the many wonderful writers I've worked with over the years for showing me how this is done.

To Michael Connor, George Witte, Sally Richardson, John Murphy, Courtney Fischer, Kevin Sweeney, and everyone at St. Martin's Press who have worked so hard on my behalf. To Benjamin Dreyer for his eagle eye and Maris Kreizman for her heart of gold. Not to mention Maury Rubin and his unbelievable pretzel croissants—fuel for more than a few chapters.

To Sarah Burnes for her insight, incomparable loyalty, sense of humor, and impeccable timing.

And Elizabeth Beier, without whom I am an unvarnished, unpublished nothing.

But mostly to my husband, Brian Flynn, who is never even *occasionally* boring.

Amy Scheibe

Interviewer: *What was your inspiration for writing* What Do You Do All Day?

Amy Scheibe: A few things. One was a dear friend of mine who was in the thick of staying at home with two kids. She was both loving and feeling trapped by the particulars—the playdates with nannies, the desire for time of her own without feeling guilty, wanting to get back to her writing. She told me a funny story about a woman canceling a playdate at the last minute, but sending her nanny in her place and asking, "You do speak Spanish, don't you?" and that started the idea.

What drove it from the first sentence, though, was a keen desire after having my first child to present an entertaining, yet issue-driven, novel about mothering. Much is written about mommy wars and the fork-in-the-road—that is, returning to the workplace or staying home—but so little of the nuance of the outcome of this decision is ever teased out and articulated. I wanted to try and show as many types of moms as I could, and to show that the dirty little secret about going back or staying home is that they both ultimately leave you, to some degree, yearning to do the other.

I: *Is this book, then, about your own experience as a stay-at-home mom?*

A. S.: If you consider maternity leave staying at home! No, the stay-at-home parts are really a homage to the women I know who do it day in and day out, because I don't think I could do it—certainly not as well as they do. The media-driven "myth of the mommy war" gives little space to the idea that people are different and bring many kinds of talents to the parenting table. Mine happen to be with older children, and I may find that when my kids are a little older, I'll want to be home for them. But I'm sure I'll still be working the hours when they are at school.

I: People often say that most first fiction is based on the writer's life. How much of What Do You Do All Day? *is about you?*

A. S.: I'd say about fifty percent, but exaggerated to make my life seem interesting enough to read about. For instance, I did date a man who acted when he was a child, but he's gone on to do other things and he was always very nice and fun to be around. Heath is much more sexy and dangerous than that. Like Jennifer, I also grew up in a trailer house and at the poverty level, and, though I've lived in New York City for more than twenty years, I still am that girl at heart and can be easily shocked when I hear that someone's kid has a pony! Not that there's anything wrong with that, but where I grew up, having a horse was something only the wealthy farmers could afford. I wanted to create that conflict inside of Jennifer—she's very aware that her problems are often luxury problems, but that doesn't mean they don't exist.

I: Where does the title come from?

A. S.: I originally wrote the book with the working title "Playdate," as I wanted to have every other chapter be about Jennifer going on playdates and meeting other mommies and nannies and daddies, but as time wore on, my agent felt less and less like tying the title to such an artificial conceit and tried to get me to rethink the title. At some point, another book came out called *Playdate* and she seized the moment to kill "Playdate." I was brainstorming with a friend and he asked, What is the one thing that Jennifer hates to hear? and the title just came out. I realized that this is the plight of the woman who stays at home—she is endlessly doing things that keep the household and the children and the marriage glued together and even so, at the end of the day, a man walks in, sees the place in chaos, and in a querulous tone says, "What do you do all day?" and all the wonderful and beautiful and joyous things that mom has accomplished fly out the window. But the irony is that even those of us who work outside the home get asked that question. It's a human question, a conversation starter like, "How are you?" but it carries such a weight of duty and obligation when applied at the wrong moment.

I: *How long did it take you to write the book?*

A. S.: About nine months for the first finished draft, and then another three months of working with my editor.

I: *So it was like having a baby?*

A. S.: Exactly. In fact, it was after I had my first baby that I felt this surge of creativity that needed an outlet, and once I struck on the idea, the passion I had for mothers and babies just sort of flowed out of me in unexpected and surprising ways.

I: *Jennifer at one point admits to being depressed. Do you think that depression occurs more in mothers?*

A. S.: Actually, I think it may happen equally to mothers and nonmothers. It's not so much Jennifer spending all her time with children that makes her depressed, but she does have a tendency toward depression and buries her feelings in the quotidian duties of motherhood until they flow back up and overwhelm her when Thom leaves the country. It's so easy to fall into a pattern of extreme mothering where you get a little addicted to doing for your children first and more and more until one day you realize you've put the oxygen mask on them and not on yourself—exactly the opposite of what they tell you to do.

I: *Why did you choose to have Jennifer conflicted about religion?*

A. S.: I wanted her to find a way to deal with her problems without falling back on a construct that would ease her burden without her having to work them out for herself. And I wanted her to find a way to impart morals to her children by using different religions. Living in New York City requires a huge amount of compassion and tolerance on a daily basis, and it's crucial that Jennifer be able to teach her kids how to navigate even if she can't connect to her own religious upbringing.

I: Why did you send Thom to Singapore?

A. S.: I needed to create a vacuum in Jennifer's life by tipping the responsibility balance out of her favor. Here she is, adjusting to the fact that she may have caused a nervous breakdown in her daughter simply by protecting her too much, then coming to terms with letting Georgia go when she's left completely responsible for the welfare of both children. This is enormous, and it gave me a way to surface Jennifer's resentment toward Thom simply for his ability to *leave*—whether it's every morning or for three months. This is not something she ever gets to do.

I: Though Jennifer has lived in New York for twenty years, she claims to never have had a friend who is black. How is that possible?

A. S.: For as much as America—and New York City, in particular—is a melting pot, the irony is that it is sometimes incredibly hard to cross the color line into true friendship. And Jennifer comes from a place that is pretty white, so her upbringing hasn't given her the cultural sensitivity required for her to make a true bond. I created Angie for a few reasons: to show that motherhood is the kind of bond that can transcend cultural differences; to portray as honestly as I could Jennifer's disappointment in herself that she is "tone deaf" in this way; and, ultimately, to give voice to a black character who goes against stereotypes.

I: Jennifer uses a lot of colorful language. Was that a conscious choice on your part?

A. S.: Jennifer is a colorful person, one who spends a lot of time with small children and is not able to use all the words at her disposal. But she also spends a lot of time in her own head, where she's able to let off the steam of controlling her language by letting loose a little. I also think that curse words can serve as punctuation; where an exclamation point may not be strong enough to evoke just how frustrated one may feel in the moment, a quick four-letter word can sum it up pretty succinctly.

I: Your other career is editing books for a publishing house. How does it feel to be on the other side of the process?

A. S.: For the most part, it feels great. I have an advantage that most writers don't—I know the way things work, so nothing about being published is shrouded in mystery, and I can hear the bad news along with the good and anticipate things like deadlines (for instance, I've completely missed the deadline for this interview, but because I'm editing an author who has missed her deadline for a book coming out the same month, I'm well aware of the flexibility of said deadline. I also know that I better get this to my editor ASAP!). Basically, I just feel soooo lucky to be published at all because I know better than anyone just how hard it is for a novel to find a good editor.

I: Do you think being an editor gives you a competitive advantage for getting published?

A. S.: Absolutely, if you mean was it easy for me to find an agent, because my first job in publishing was at Knopf where my agent was then an editorial assistant. We've grown up in the business together. But that doesn't mean the material doesn't have to be good—I was held to the same standard as everyone else when it came to the novel being acquired.

I: Will there be a sequel?

A. S.: You never can tell.